# ACCLAIM FOR CO

"Once again Colleen Coble has delivered a page-turning, can't-put-down suspense thriller with *Secrets at Cedar Cabin*! I vowed I'd read it slowly over several nights before going to bed. The story wouldn't wait—I HAD to finish it!"

—CARRIE STUART PARKS, AUTHOR OF *FORMULA OF DECEPTION*

"*Secrets at Cedar Cabin* is filled with twists and turns that will keep readers turning the pages as they plunge into the horrific world of sex trafficking where they come face to face with evil. Colleen Coble delivers a fast-paced story with a strong, lovable ensemble cast and a sweet heaping helping of romance."

—KELLY IRVIN, AUTHOR OF *TELL HER NO LIES*

"This is an engrossing historical story with plenty of romance and danger for readers to get hooked by."

—*THE PARKERSBURG NEWS AND SENTINEL* ON *FREEDOM'S LIGHT*

"Coble... weaves a suspense-filled romance set during the Revolutionary War. Coble's fine historical novel introduces a strong heroine—both in faith and character—that will appeal deeply to readers."

—*PUBLISHERS WEEKLY* ON *FREEDOM'S LIGHT*

"This follow-up to *The View from Rainshadow Bay* features delightful characters and an evocative, atmospheric setting. Ideal for fans of romantic suspense and authors Dani Pettrey, Dee Henderson, and Brandilyn Collins."

—*LIBRARY JOURNAL* FOR *THE HOUSE AT SALTWATER POINT*

"*The View from Rainshadow Bay* opens with a heart-pounding, run-for-your-life chase. This book will stay with you for a long time, long after you flip to the last page."

—*RT BOOK REVIEWS*, 4 STARS

"Set on Washington State's Olympic Peninsula, this first volume of Coble's new suspense series is a tensely plotted and harrowing tale of murder, corporate greed, and family secrets. Devotees of Dani Pettrey, Brenda Novak, and Allison Brennan will find a new favorite here."

—*Library Journal* on *The View from Rainshadow Bay*

"Coble (*Twilight at Blueberry Barrens*) keeps the tension tight and the action moving in this gripping tale, the first in her Lavender Tides series set in the Pacific Northwest."

—*Publishers Weekly* on *The View from Rainshadow Bay*

"Filled with the suspense for which Coble is known, the novel is rich in detail with a healthy dose of romance, allowing readers to bask in the beauty of Washington State's lavender fields, lush forests and jagged coastline."

—*BookPage* on *The View from Rainshadow Bay*

"Prepare to stay up all night with Colleen Coble. Coble's beautiful, emotional prose coupled with her keen sense of pacing, escalating danger, and very real characters place her firmly at the top of the suspense genre. I could not put this book down."

—Allison Brennan, *New York Times* bestselling author of *Shattered*, on *The View from Rainshadow Bay*

"I loved returning to Rock Harbor and you will too. *Beneath Copper Falls* is Colleen at her best!"

—Dani Pettrey, bestselling author of the Alaskan Courage and Chesapeake Valor series

"Return to Rock Harbor for Colleen Coble's best story to date. *Beneath Copper Falls* is a twisting, turning thrill ride from page one that drops you headfirst into danger that will leave you breathless, sleep deprived, and eager for more! I couldn't turn the pages fast enough!"

—Lynette Eason, award-winning, bestselling author of the Elite Guardians series

"The tension, both suspenseful and romantic, is gripping, reflecting Coble's prowess with the genre."

—*PUBLISHERS WEEKLY*, STARRED REVIEW FOR *TWILIGHT AT BLUEBERRY BARRENS*

"Incredible storytelling and intricately drawn characters. You won't want to miss *Twilight at Blueberry Barrens*!"

—BRENDA NOVAK, *NEW YORK TIMES* AND *USA TODAY* BESTSELLING AUTHOR

"Coble has a gift for making a setting come to life. After reading *Twilight at Blueberry Barrens*, I feel like I've lived in Maine all my life. This plot kept me guessing until the end, and her characters seem like my friends. I don't want to let them go!"

—TERRI BLACKSTOCK, *USA TODAY* BESTSELLING AUTHOR OF *IF I RUN*

"I'm a longtime fan of Colleen Coble, and *Twilight at Blueberry Barrens* is the perfect example of why. Coble delivers riveting suspense, delicious romance, and carefully crafted characters, all with the deft hand of a veteran writer. If you love romantic suspense, pick this one up. You won't be disappointed!"

—DENISE HUNTER, AUTHOR OF *THE GOODBYE BRIDE*

"Colleen Coble, the queen of Christian romantic mysteries, is back with her best book yet. Filled with familiar characters, plot twists, and a confusion of antagonists, I couldn't keep the pages of this novel set in Maine turning fast enough. I reconnected with characters I love while taking a journey filled with murder, suspense, and the prospect of love. This truly is her best book to date, and perfect for readers who adore a page-turner laced with romance."

—CARA PUTMAN, AWARD-WINNING AUTHOR OF *SHADOWED BY GRACE* AND *WHERE TREETOPS GLISTEN*, ON *TWILIGHT AT BLUEBERRY BARRENS*

"Gripping! Colleen Coble has again written a page-turning romantic suspense with *Twilight at Blueberry Barrens*! Not only did she keep me up nights racing through the pages to see what would happen next, I genuinely cared for her characters. Colleen sets the bar high for romantic suspense!"

—Carrie Stuart Parks, author of *A Cry from the Dust* and *When Death Draws Near*

"Colleen Coble thrills readers again with her newest novel, an addictive suspense trenched in family, betrayal, and . . . murder."

—DiAnn Mills, author of *Deadly Encounter*, on *Twilight at Blueberry Barrens*

"Coble's latest, *Twilight at Blueberry Barrens*, is one of her best yet! With characters you want to know in person, a perfect setting, and a plot that had me holding my breath, laughing, and crying, this story will stay with the reader long after the book is closed. My highest recommendation."

—Robin Caroll, bestselling novelist

"Colleen's *Twilight at Blueberry Barrens* is filled with a bevy of twists and surprises, a wonderful romance, and the warmth of family love. I couldn't have asked for more. This author has always been a five-star novelist, but I think it's time to up the ante with this book. It's on my keeping shelf!"

—Hannah Alexander, author of the Hallowed Halls series

"Second chances, old flames, and startling new revelations combine to form a story filled with faith, trial, forgiveness, and redemption. Crack the cover and step in, but beware—*Mermaid Moon* is harboring secrets that will keep you guessing."

—Lisa Wingate, *New York Times* bestselling author of *Before We Were Yours*

"I burned through *The Inn at Ocean's Edge* in one sitting. An intricate plot by a master storyteller. Colleen Coble has done it again with this gripping opening to a new series. I can't wait to spend more time at Sunset Cove."

—HEATHER BURCH, BESTSELLING AUTHOR OF *ONE LAVENDER RIBBON*

"Coble doesn't disappoint with her custom blend of suspense and romance."

—*PUBLISHERS WEEKLY* ON *THE INN AT OCEAN'S EDGE*

"Veteran author Coble has penned another winner. Filled with mystery and romance that are unpredictable until the last page, this novel will grip readers long past when they should put their books down. Recommended to readers of contemporary mysteries."

—*CBA RETAILERS + RESOURCES* REVIEW OF *THE INN AT OCEAN'S EDGE*

"Coble truly shines when she's penning a mystery, and this tale will really keep the reader guessing . . . Mystery lovers will definitely want to put this book on their purchase list."

—*RT BOOK REVIEWS* ON *THE INN AT OCEAN'S EDGE*

"Master storyteller Colleen Coble has done it again. *The Inn at Ocean's Edge* is an intricately woven, well-crafted story of romance, suspense, family secrets, and a decades-old mystery. Needless to say, it had me hooked from page one. I simply couldn't stop turning the pages. This one's going on my keeper shelf."

—LYNETTE EASON, AWARD-WINNING, BESTSELLING AUTHOR OF THE HIDDEN IDENTITY SERIES

"Evocative and gripping, *The Inn at Ocean's Edge* will keep you flipping pages long into the night."

—DANI PETTREY, BESTSELLING AUTHOR OF THE ALASKAN COURAGE SERIES

"Coble's atmospheric and suspenseful series launch should appeal to fans of Tracie Peterson and other authors of Christian romantic suspense."

—*Library Journal* review of *Tidewater Inn*

"Romantically tense, but with just the right touch of danger, this cowboy love story is surprisingly clever—and pleasingly sweet."

—USAToday.com review of *Blue Moon Promise*

"[An] outstanding, completely engaging tale that will have you on the edge of your seat . . . A must-have for all fans of romantic suspense!"

—TheRomanceReadersConnection.com review of *Anathema*

"Colleen Coble lays an intricate trail in *Without a Trace* and draws the reader on like a hound with a scent."

—*Romantic Times*, 4 1/2 stars

"Coble's historical series just keeps getting better with each entry."

—*Library Journal* starred review of *The Lightkeeper's Ball*

"Don't ever mistake [Coble's] for the fluffy romances with a little bit of suspense. She writes solid suspense, and she ties it all together beautifully with a wonderful message."

—LifeinReviewBlog.com review of *Lonestar Angel*

"Colleen is a master storyteller."

—Karen Kingsbury, bestselling author of *Unlocked* and *Learning*

# SECRETS AT CEDAR CABIN

# Also by Colleen Coble

Lavender Tides Novels
*The View from Rainshadow Bay*
*Leaving Lavender Tides* Novella
*The House at Saltwater Point*

Rock Harbor Novels
*Without a Trace*
*Beyond a Doubt*
*Into the Deep*
*Cry in the Night*
*Silent Night: A Rock Harbor Christmas Novella* (e-book only)
*Beneath Copper Falls*
*Haven of Swans* (formerly titled *Abomination*)

YA/Middle Grade Rock Harbor Books
*Rock Harbor Search and Rescue*
*Rock Harbor Lost and Found*

Children's Rock Harbor Book
*The Blessings Jar*

Sunset Cove Novels
*The Inn at Ocean's Edge*
*Mermaid Moon*
*Twilight at Blueberry Barrens*

Hope Beach Novels
*Tidewater Inn*
*Rosemary Cottage*
*Seagrass Pier*
*All Is Bright: A Hope Beach Christmas Novella* (e-book only)

Under Texas Stars Novels
*Blue Moon Promise*
*Safe in His Arms*
*Bluebonnet Bride* Novella (e-book only)

The Aloha Reef Novels
*Distant Echoes*
*Black Sands*
*Dangerous Depths*
*Midnight Sea*
*Holy Night: An Aloha Reef Christmas Novella* (e-book only)

The Mercy Falls Series
*The Lightkeeper's Daughter*
*The Lightkeeper's Bride*
*The Lightkeeper's Ball*

Journey of the Heart Series
*A Heart's Disguise*
*A Heart's Obsession*
*A Heart's Danger*
*A Heart's Betrayal*
*A Heart's Promise*
*A Heart's Home*

Lonestar Novels
*Lonestar Sanctuary*
*Lonestar Secrets*
*Lonestar Homecoming*
*Lonestar Angel*
*All Is Calm: A Lonestar Christmas Novella* (e-book only)

*Alaska Twilight*
*Fire Dancer*
*Where Shadows Meet* (formerly titled *Anathema*)
*Butterfly Palace*
*Freedom's Light*

# SECRETS *at* CEDAR CABIN

A Lavender Tides Novel

COLLEEN COBLE

Thomas Nelson
Since 1798

*Secrets at Cedar Cabin*



Published in Nashville, Tennessee, by Thomas Nelson. Thomas Nelson is a registered trademark of HarperCollins Christian Publishing, Inc.

Thomas Nelson titles may be purchased in bulk for educational, business, fund-raising, or sales promotional use. For information, please e-mail SpecialMarkets@ThomasNelson.com.



Publisher's Note: This novel is a work of fiction. Names, characters, places, and incidents are either products of the author's imagination or used fictitiously. All characters are fictional, and any similarity to people living or dead is purely coincidental.

ISBN: 978-0-7180-8586-5 (library edition)

**Library of Congress Cataloging-in-Publication Data**

Names: Coble, Colleen, author.
Title: Secrets at Cedar cabin / Colleen Coble.
Description: Nashville, Tennessee : Thomas Nelson, [2019] | Series: A Lavender Tides novel ; 3
Identifiers: LCCN 2018032841 | ISBN 9780718085841 (paperback)
Subjects: | GSAFD: Romance fiction. | Suspense fiction.
Classification: LCC PS3553.O2285 S45 2019 | DDC 813/.54--dc23 LC record available at https://lccn.loc.gov/2018032841

*Printed in the United States of America*

19 20 21 22 23 LSC 5 4 3 2 1

*For my sister-in-law Mary Rhoads*
*Sister of my heart!*

## *Chapter 1*

Bailey Fleming glanced out her patient's window into the parking lot, but the swirling snow obscured all but the dim glow of the streetlamp. She smoothed Thomas Dutt's sheets. "Even though it's early November, the Snow Queen has officially claimed the Keweenaw." With the sheets changed a fresh, lemony scent replaced the stink of urine.

Thomas fixed a blank stare at the sea of white and didn't reply, but she knew he was in there somewhere. Every now and then he'd surprise her with sudden bits of information about his forty-year history as a physician or he'd quote a poetry couplet to her. She'd already combed his remaining wisps of white hair over his bald spot, brushed his perfect teeth, and gotten him dressed for the day, but he'd be unlikely to move much from his chair by the window.

Being with the elderly was her happy place. She felt connected and needed here with them.

She spared another glance out the window. Six inches of snow swirled around from the overnight storm and another twelve inches were predicted by evening along with sixty-mile-an-hour winds. Rock Harbor, Michigan, already lay sluggish under the heavy blanket, and getting around would be difficult. Bailey's workload was going to be crushing today. Some nurses and aides living in the county probably wouldn't make it in with this blizzard.

She thrived on the challenge though. These elderly folks were the family of her heart.

Ruby, one of the other aides, poked her head in. "Kyle is here to see you. I put him in the conference room."

Bailey curled her fingers into her palms. What was he doing here? She'd said all she intended last week. "Thanks, Ruby. I'll run over there now." She gave Thomas's pillow a final pat, then squatted beside him. "I left you some fresh water, Thomas. I'll come back and read some Robert Frost to you later, okay?"

Sudden clarity surged into his eyes. "'In leaves no step had trodden black.'"

This sweet man's flashes of wisdom made her love him all the more. She patted his liver-spotted hand. "That's right."

Squaring her shoulders, she moved past Ruby and hurried down the hall. She stood outside the conference room, staring at Kyle through the open door for a long moment. It had been a fairy-tale dream that Kyle Bearcroft, lead singer of the rock sensation Bearcroft, would see her at a concert and marry her after a whirlwind courtship of two months. Kyle was not much taller than her own five feet eight inches, but he came across as larger than life. In constant motion, he was as mercurial as the Upper Peninsula weather, and it was one of his many charms. Even now he paced the floor with quick, energetic movements before he stopped to gaze out the window at the swirling snow.

Everyone thought he was rock royalty, but this prince had

quickly shown his toad-like qualities and exposed every hidden wart. Seeing him reminded her of all he'd stolen from her. What man would want her now, even if she dared to dip her toe back into the dating pond? She'd allowed herself to dream of a real home and family. How ridiculous.

Lifting her chin, she stepped into the room and drew the door shut behind her. "What are you doing here, Kyle?"

Did he know how he looked all romantic and forlorn there by the window? His blond hair perfectly styled. Probably. The woody fragrance of his Dior Intense wafted to her, and she wanted to stop breathing, to exhale every part of him trying to persuade her to overlook his lies.

She crossed her arms over her chest. "I want you to leave."

He turned to face her. His blue eyes the color of Lake Superior caressed her, and the resistance-melting smile emerged. It used to set loose butterflies in her stomach, but now she recognized it for the weapon it was. A sword that had separated her from the purity she'd intended to save for her husband. Her *real* husband.

"You didn't use to be so cold."

"That was before I knew you were a bigamist, Kyle, and that all your charm was because you'd practiced it so often."

He flinched at the word *bigamist*. "What are you going to do?"

That's what this was all about? He wanted to make sure his crime didn't get out. "I'm going to take care of my patients and try to forget you ever existed."

The furrows between his brows eased. "Who have you told?"

"My mom. That's it. She's the only person who knew we were married." He'd said he wanted to keep their relationship quiet to protect her. What a liar.

He fumbled a folded paper out of his pocket. "My attorney wants you to sign a nondisclosure agreement. I've put a house in your name, too, and I'll give you a hundred thousand dollars."

Fury washed up her neck, and she batted the paper away. "I'm not a whore you can pay off, Kyle. I was your *wife*, or so I thought. The media would have a field day with this, wouldn't they? But don't worry. I'm not about to let the world know what an absolute fool I was. Please, just leave me alone."

Her heart had been ripped out of her chest when she overheard him speaking to his real wife. She lived on a ranch in Idaho with no internet and little contact with the media. He'd actually thought he could get away with it, and he probably would have if she hadn't forgotten her phone. She went back to get it, and he hadn't seen her come in. She heard everything, all the sickeningly sweet talk. When Bailey confronted him, he hadn't even tried to weasel out of it.

When she asked him why, he'd held her angry gaze and shrugged. "You wouldn't sleep with me otherwise."

Her cheeks heated, and she gulped at the bare truth. She didn't know if she'd ever be clean again.

The paper landed on the pointed toe of his black boot. He stared at it, then stooped to pick it up. "Look, can you just sign the thing so I can reassure my lawyer?" He pressed the envelope in his other hand into her palm. "Here's the deed. See, I've already made it out in your name. It's all legal." He set a key down on the table.

Tearing up the deed would be a grand gesture, but all the fight drained out of her. With the envelope in hand, Bailey stalked to the door and jerked it open. "Get out. I never want to see or hear from you again or I *will* contact the media. Leave me alone, and your secret is safe."

Her face burned as he passed her. She shut the door behind him and propped her back against it until she stopped shaking. She stuffed the envelope in her pocket where she could deal with it later.

Her stomach churned, but she still had a lot of the workday left. Bailey strode to the bathroom attached to the conference room, went to the sink, and splashed cold water on her hot cheeks. She gazed in the mirror. *I'll pass muster.* Her long black hair was wound up in a bun, and her green eyes looked calm. Bailey Fleming, super aide to the geriatric. She tried on a smile, but tears flooded her eyes instead. She wiped them away, then scooped up the key on the table on her way to the door.

When she stepped into the hall, she saw the sheriff heading her way. Mason Kaleva had been the sheriff for the two years she'd been in Rock Harbor, and most everyone liked the big bear of a man. She hoped he wasn't here to deliver accident news to someone.

His gaze connected with hers, and he stopped a moment, then approached her. His hand settled on her shoulder with a comforting squeeze. "I need to talk to you, Bailey. Is there somewhere we can speak in private?"

She searched his face for clues and saw sympathy. "What's wrong?"

"Look, there's no easy way to deliver this news. It's your mother. She was shot this morning."

Bailey's knees buckled, and she would have fallen if he didn't have hold of her. "She's in the hospital? I'll go there right now."

He eased her onto the floor, then knelt beside her. "I'm sorry, but she's dead."

She closed her eyes and shook her head. Dizziness struck her, and she rested her forehead on her knees where she sat crumpled on the floor. She was going to black out.

❦

His top man, Chey, shut the door behind him and entered the large room paneled in walnut finish. "She's dead, King." His lips pressed into a hard line above his black goatee.

*King.* One of the other men had called him that with a sneer in the early years, but he'd turned the moniker into something real. He'd done what had to be done to acquire this position, and he enjoyed the perks that came with being the absolute ruler of his organization. His word was law, even when he'd had to order the death of someone he loved.

He stood at the window looking out at his beloved garden and closed his eyes. He patted his pocket, then drew out a cigar and inhaled its cherry aroma. Chey could wait.

She'd meant a lot to him once upon a time, but he couldn't afford to let emotion strip him of his business. From the moment she'd called him a month ago, he'd known it would have to end this way. There had been no other choice.

He opened his eyes, lit his cigar, and blew out a curl of smoke. "It was quick and painless as I ordered?"

Chey's dark eyes were expressionless. "Yes, King. Clean shot to the head. We made it look like a mob hit and tied her hands behind her back after it was over."

He tried not to picture it. Her blonde hair spread out on the pillow was the stuff of dreams even twenty-four years since he'd seen her last. And her eyes always seemed to see inside his soul. He hadn't wanted to kill her, but Chey couldn't know of his weakness.

"I appreciate your tight adherence to orders."

The man always did an excellent job. Was he dreaming of seizing this chair someday? If Chey was worth his salt, he was. He was already in his forties—a good age for the responsibility. His dark-brown eyes took in everything, and he never showed emotion. All excellent traits for leadership.

King pulled a paper toward him. "How's the shipment?"

"On target. We have ten women arriving from Cambodia on Saturday, and we'll disperse them as seems appropriate."

His fingers were in many pies, but the trafficking piece had become one of the most lucrative. What should he do about Bailey? He couldn't afford to be soft. Not if he wanted to stay in power. Any one of his men would be happy to supplant him at the slightest sign of weakness.

There was no telling how much Olivia's daughter knew. "Eliminate the girl too."

"Yes, sir." Chey's Italian leather shoes squeaked on the marble floors as he exited the office.

Alone, he could let his emotions show. King sank into the chair and opened his laptop, then navigated to his video file. His subordinates had sent him many videos of Olivia over the years, from the time Bailey was an infant to just a month ago. Small lines around Olivia's eyes didn't mar the perfection of her face. He'd hoped someday she'd come back to him, but even though he'd called her on occasion, she held firm to her determination to abandon their love unless he left his wife.

Impossible. Every bit of his empire would crumble without the authority of his wife's name. He might be able to hold it together a few years, but without warning a shot would inevitably ring out, and he'd be dead on the ground in a puddle of blood.

He hadn't been willing to risk it. Once Bailey was dead, all of his secrets would be behind him. No one would ever know what he had done, how he had achieved this chair. His power would be secure.

Somehow he found himself at the window again staring at the rhododendrons, their roots already resting in their winter blanket. Olivia had loved rhododendrons, and much of the garden had come about because of her. His wife disliked them, probably because she suspected why he collected them. They'd never really talked about his long-ago mistress, but he had no doubt she knew. Her father would have seen to it that she knew everything about him and any of his peccadilloes over the years. Though Olivia was the only one who'd mattered.

Did her father know King had ordered Olivia's death? Probably not. Her father had likely forgotten her name by now.

King had to make sure of that.

He probably should have arranged something that appeared accidental for Olivia, but he hadn't wanted her to suffer.

His phone rang and he glanced at the screen, then sighed as he plastered on a smile before answering the FaceTime call. "Hello, darling."

His wife had lost whatever beauty she'd had. Her jowls made her resemble a hound, and only her brilliant hazel eyes had remained the same. Her main attraction was her name and her connections. She had the power to topple him if she chose.

She wore a gray dress that did nothing to complement her curves or her coloring. "Are you still at the office? We're going to be late for the girls' ballet recital."

"I'm on my way. I'll meet you there." He rose and grabbed his jacket from the back of his leather chair.

She was still shrieking in his face when he ended the call and slipped his phone into his jacket pocket. He went out the side door to the garden and lingered for a long moment. Touching the stiff rhododendron leaves, he let himself remember Olivia. Ballet could wait. His wife could wait, and so could his business.

## *Chapter 2*

Ava had to be inside. Lance Phoenix adjusted his binoculars and focused on the building across the street in the early morning light. His breath fogged in the air as he studied the place. It looked like every other warehouse on this block in south Tacoma, but agents had seen men coming and going at all hours.

It housed more than shelves of automotive parts and other supplies.

He motioned to the FBI senior agent, his partner Daniel Atkinson, to move into place across the street, and he crouched as he ran after him. Other members of the task force couldn't be seen but were in position. A muscle in his jaw jumped, and Lance made an effort to calm his nerves. He couldn't let hope distract him.

At his command the SWAT members charged the side door, and fists pounding on the metal echoed in the cool air. "FBI!"

When no one answered the door, the SWAT team quickly broke through the lock and fanned out inside the building, searching for imprisoned minors and johns.

Search warrant in hand, Lance stepped into a large room with a stage at the far end. The place reeked of pot, booze, and human suffering. A teenage girl standing in the doorway pushed unkempt black hair out of her eyes.

His breath seized in his lungs. Ava?

But this girl had green eyes, not brown. And she was only sixteen or seventeen. Ava would be twenty-one now.

The girl tried to wrap her flimsy robe around her better and hugged herself. "I didn't do anything."

Lance held his hands out, palms forward. "You're not in trouble. We're here to rescue you. Where's Alfie Jackson?"

A flicker of hope lit her face, and she took a step toward him. "He's not here." She looked past his shoulder toward the door. "I-Is my mother with you?"

The despair in the words nearly brought him to his knees. Though this girl wasn't his sister, her rescue was just as important. "We'll get you back to your mom. What's your name, and who else is here?"

"I'm Sarah Hosteler."

He recognized the name. "Your dad has called our office every week. Your parents never gave up hope of finding you."

Her eyes flooded with tears. "Can you call them now?"

"I need to ask a few questions first." He jotted down everything she told him. Three other girls were here, all imprisoned for the past six months, two of them from Vietnam. This ring particularly favored Asian girls.

As the girls scurried into the living room with the agents, he studied their faces. All were teenagers, and none were Ava. The ones who weren't Asian had been forced to dye their hair black.

"What can you tell me about your captors? Did they teach you a Cambodian dance?"

Sarah's eyes widened. "Not me, but there was one here who had been trained in Apsara dance. Alfie took her and another girl away."

His pulse jumped. "Do you know anything about them, their names, ages?"

She shook her head. "We weren't allowed to use our real names. One of the two who'd left was older though, in her early twenties. She had long black hair." Sarah paused. "Well, it *was* long. She got hold of scissors and chopped it off. Alfie was super mad at her. I think that's why he took her away."

"What color were her eyes?"

"Dark brown. She was Asian."

It could be Ava, but the chances were slim. Lance wasn't sure how he'd managed to hold on to hope all this time, but he couldn't let it go. Not when there was even the slimmest chance he'd find his sister alive someday. The FBI knew the traffickers trained the most elite women as Apsara dancers, but he had no idea if Ava was one of them.

Daniel motioned him over. About five ten and stocky, he was a man Lance would trust with his life—and often did. Ten years his senior, Daniel was steady, thoughtful, and experienced. He took off his cap and rubbed his blond hair. "That snake is like smoke. He always seems to slip right out of our fingers."

"Sarah said he took two others away yesterday."

Daniel's gray eyes sharpened. "How old?"

"One was in her early twenties with black hair and brown eyes. Asian." He ignored the sympathy in Daniel's face and rushed on. "Let's call the families. Give them some happy news."

And he'd have to call his own parents and tell them Ava was still missing. He'd been five when she was born. With her thick thatch of black hair, she resembled their Cambodian mother while he looked more like their Scottish father—other than his thick dark hair. The tiny baby had smiled up at him, and he adored her ever since.

He would never give up until he found Ava and she was back home with the family who loved her.

The blizzard shut down Rock Harbor for two days, but Bailey managed to get around with chains on her four-wheel drive. She went through the motions of picking out a casket, buying a cemetery plot, and arranging for her mom's service. Her mother had never attended the little church on the hill, so the funeral would be mostly for Bailey's solace. Her stepbrothers were much older and hadn't seemed interested to hear of Mom's death, so she doubted they would come. Mom had married their dad when they were in their twenties, and upon his death three years after the marriage, they'd quit visiting.

This was all on her shoulders.

She sat at the kitchen table with the contents of her mother's safe-deposit box in front of her. Though it was only three, the heavy clouds made it as dark as twilight. The wind howled around the windows that looked out onto six-foot-high snowdrifts, but the little house was snug and warm.

Sheba, her Savannah cat, wound around her ankles. With her black spots and long legs, she seemed more like a cheetah than a house cat. Sheba had been a gift from Kyle when they married. The cat acted almost like a dog, which was a breed trait, and when Bailey took her on walks with a leash, she barely managed to get two feet before someone stopped to ask her about Sheba. Though she was technically still a kitten, she came to Bailey's knees, and she was the friendliest, most social creature Bailey had ever seen. She especially loved to play catch with a ball and hide-and-seek.

"Hungry, sweetheart?" Bailey got out a raw food patty and broke it into pieces in Sheba's bowl. With a cat this precious, she wanted to do everything she could to ensure Sheba lived a long time.

With the cat taken care of, she stared at the manila envelope, thick with unknown contents. Why had it been so important to her mother?

Mom had been acting odd for several days before her death—staring off into space, bursting into tears for no reason, and talking about her childhood. Mom's final request the morning she'd died was for Bailey to bring this box home with her after work.

Could these contents lead to her mother's killer, or was Bailey reading too much into it?

She opened the manila envelope's flap and dumped out the contents. Stacks of hundred-dollar bills landed on the table and several papers fluttered out. The odor of money wafted to her face when she fanned through the stacks of bills. There had to be at least fifty thousand dollars here, maybe more.

A small white envelope with her name on it was buried at the bottom of the pile. She broke the seal and pulled out the single sheet of paper. Her mother's handwriting scrawled across the page, and her heart gave a squeeze. Mom only wrote so sloppily when she was upset or in a hurry. Was she ready to read it? Bailey had no choice.

Dear Bailey,

There are so many things I wish I'd told you, and I'm hoping I had time to explain what I did and why I did it. If I didn't and I'm already dead, there's no time now. You must leave town immediately. Take the money and disappear before he gets to you. Don't talk to anyone, and don't tell them where you're going. Don't talk to the police. He will hear about it and you'll be a target.

Go somewhere and hide. Don't trust anyone. I've told him you know nothing, but he doesn't believe me. I'm not sure how to get out of this or how to keep you safe, so this note will have to do.

Whatever happens, remember I loved you with everything in me.

Mom

Bailey rubbed her hand over her face. Had Mom been running from the killer all these years? After Eric died when Bailey was five, they'd moved so often that she had gone to seven different schools. How did she make sense of this? If only Mom had been able to tell her everything. What was she going to do? Where could she go if she followed her mother's instructions?

Mom's message was specific, but how could she get away and hide?

The deed Kyle had given her!

She'd stuck that envelope and key somewhere when she'd gotten home, but where? She found it pushed into a desk drawer.

She pulled out the papers and studied the attached home photo. Where on earth was this? It looked remote. The cedar-log home had a steeply pitched roof and floor-to-ceiling windows. Through the thick pines around the house, she caught a glimpse of blue water in the distance. It looked utterly charming, but the paper fluttered from Bailey's numb fingers when she saw the address.

Lavender Tides, Washington—the same town where Mom had grown up.

When Bailey was little, she used to pester her about grandparents and her father, but Mom always said she could never go back. Any questions about her father were met with stony silence. Why would Kyle have a house *there*? And even more puzzling, why would he put the deed in her name?

She thought back to every interaction between Kyle and her mom. Mom had been eager for her to marry Kyle, which was strange now that Bailey thought about it. There had been no counsel to wait until she knew him better—just girlish enthusiasm overlaid with a bit of desperation. At the time Bailey had thought Mom didn't want her to miss the chance for a better life. But maybe she'd been wrong.

A soft sound like something sliding across the icy deck came to her ears. She lifted her head and gazed out the office window. Her snug little house looked out on a wilderness area on the outskirts of town. She'd never had an intruder beyond the occasional deer or raccoon. The noise came again, and a chill darted down her spine when the knob on the back door turned.

She scooped everything on the table back into the manila folder, then grabbed Sheba and bolted for the front door, pausing long enough to snatch her purse and coat off the hook by the door.

She opened the door and stepped into the wind. Her SUV

was down three steps and across a few feet of yard. She leaped from the porch and landed in three feet of snow, then slogged through it to the vehicle.

Her breath frosted the windshield as she jammed the key in the ignition and cranked the engine. It sputtered a moment, then started. She put the gearshift in Drive and pulled away as a figure dressed in ski pants and a ski mask ran her direction.

A sharp report in the cold air made her jump. He was shooting at her! The old Mazda Tribute's tires spun for a heart-stopping second, then grabbed and hurled the vehicle down the street and away from the house. She glanced out the back and saw the figure racing down the street toward a white pickup she didn't recognize.

Even chains didn't keep her vehicle from sliding on the icy streets, but she managed to reach the heart of town. She slowed to pull into an open parking spot in front of the sheriff's office until she looked in the rearview mirror. Would the sheriff even be able to keep her safe? The note said "he" would hear about it if she went to the police.

*Stay or go?*

Her mom had said to flee, but how could she leave before her mother's body was in the ground? She wasn't sure when the coroner would release her mom's remains. It could be a week, and the murderer was already after her. If she waited, the town might have to buy a burial plot beside Mom's.

Bailey glanced at the envelope on the passenger seat. There was a house in her name out in Washington. She couldn't hide like Mom wanted her to. Her mother's death proved hiding didn't work. The killer had eventually caught up with her, and he'd catch Bailey, too, unless she found him first.

She pressed her boot on the accelerator and headed for highway M-28. Somewhere she'd have to change vehicles, but for now she cranked the heat as high as it would go.

She had hoped she'd found a home at last. Her heart squeezed as the lights of Rock Harbor disappeared into a swirl of white.

## *Chapter 3*

The snowstorm had delayed Grayson Bradshaw's visit to the Upper Peninsula town of Rock Harbor, Michigan, but he finally sat across the desk from the sheriff. "You're telling me Bailey has been missing for two days?"

Sheriff Mason Kaleva nodded. "What does the Coast Guard Investigative Services want with this kind of murder?"

Grayson had flashed his badge to get in to see the sheriff. "She's my sister. What can you tell me?"

"Footprints marked all along the back patio, and she left her front door open when she fled. I'm fairly confident the intruder tried to break in, then shot at her as she was making her escape. We retrieved a spent shell casing. The house was tossed and quite a few items taken, including her computer."

"A routine theft?"

The sheriff shook his head. "I think the killer wanted us to think that, but with this coming on the heels of her mother's murder, I don't buy it. There's very little evidence one way or another though."

Grayson hadn't expected anything like this when he arrived. "Any idea where she went?"

"All we know is Bailey retrieved something from her mother's safe-deposit box at the bank an hour or two before neighbors reported the break-in. My deputies arrived on scene almost immediately, but no one has seen her since. We've been dealing with a blizzard, so most residents have been holed up inside, out of the wind. I don't know how she managed to navigate the roads out of here without mishap."

"Could she still be in the area, maybe staying with a friend?"

"We checked with her coworkers and her church. No one has seen or heard from her." The sheriff leaned back in his chair. "I thought her brothers were all quite a bit older."

An explanation was in order. Grayson cleared his throat. "She doesn't know anything about me. I'm not one of her stepbrothers. From what we have been able to dig up, Bailey was actually stolen at birth by Olivia Fleming twenty-four years ago. I was two at the time, and our sister Shauna was eight. We were with our mother at the grocery store when an earthquake struck. Our mother was killed from injuries suffered in the quake after giving birth to Bailey. After rescuers dug us out, Shauna thought we were dead until a few months ago. She immediately started searching for us and found me a month ago.

"My birth name was Connor Duval, but my new parents changed my name. Olivia was a paramedic in the grocery store at the time of the earthquake and helped deliver Bailey, whose real name is Brenna. No one even knew Bailey survived until Shauna started digging. Shauna called Olivia a couple of weeks ago to talk to her about delivering Bailey but got nowhere. In fact, Olivia hung up on her. So I came to talk to them face-to-face."

Sheriff Kaleva rubbed his five-o'clock shadow. "It all makes me wonder if this kidnapping is somehow tied in with Olivia's murder."

"What can you tell me about her murder?"

"Her hands were tied behind her back, and she was shot in the head. It was brutal."

"An execution?"

"Looked like one. She was a nice lady and well liked in town. She'd worked as a paramedic here for a couple of years."

"Have you been able to find out anything about her background?"

The sheriff's broad forehead wrinkled in a frown. "She doesn't really exist. I couldn't find a birth certificate, and we've only been able to track her employment back about ten years. Bailey mentioned to a coworker that they had moved every few years."

"On the run maybe."

The sheriff nodded. "Looks that way now. I'm sorry I can't be more help. If you find Bailey, please let me know. I have plenty of questions for her."

Grayson recognized a dismissal when he heard it. He stood and extended his hand. "I'll do that. Thanks for your help."

He exited the building into a winter wonderland in front of colorful Victorian storefronts. The smell of coffee enticed him to the Suomi Café, and he ordered coffee and a Finnish pancake he couldn't pronounce. He pulled out his phone and called his girlfriend.

Ellie didn't even say hello. "Gray, did you find her?"

"Sorry, hon, it's bad news." He told her what he'd discovered. "So she's on the run, probably from whoever shot her mother. No one knows where she's gone or how to find her."

"That poor girl." Ellie's voice trembled.

"If only I'd gotten here a few days sooner."

"It wasn't your fault. You left as soon as you wrapped things up here."

Ellie was trying to put a good spin on things, but if Bailey was hiding from a killer, she would likely change her name and disappear with no trace.

"I'll keep searching, but she's not going to be easy to find."

"I know." Ellie's voice wobbled again. "You've come this far though. I have to believe she'll turn up."

He just hoped she didn't turn up dead like Olivia. The first thing he planned to do when he got back to Lavender Tides was investigate Olivia Fleming. If he discovered more about her background, it might lead to Bailey. He still had to call Shauna. That wasn't a call he was eager to make. His sister would be extremely upset since it had seemed the three of them would finally be together.

Now it might never happen.

Lavender Tides looked charming with its painted Victorian storefronts. From the street Bailey could see the white boats of the marina in sharp contrast to the gorgeous blue of the water. Every night in the various motels she'd stayed in across the country, she read everything she could about this town. Part of the Olympic Peninsula, it sat in the rain shadow of the Olympic Mountains and had a drier climate. The signature crop in this area was lavender, but the purple flowers were long gone in November, and she had no idea if she'd be here long enough to see them next year.

Why had her mother ever left this idyllic place? Just looking at it, Bailey felt an inexplicable draw.

Her stomach rumbled, and she drove down to the water and parked by the Crabby Pot. Sheba meowed behind her, a plaintive reminder that she was hungry too. Delicious seafood aromas wafted toward her, and her mouth watered. It was already three, and she hadn't eaten since breakfast in the motel.

She harnessed Sheba and walked her across small pebbles to the food truck where she ordered fish tacos for her and plain raw fish for Sheba. The server eyed the cat but said nothing. Bailey took Sheba and the food back to a picnic table where she shooed away several gulls peering at her with hungry black eyes. They squawked in protest at the cat but didn't fly far.

Sheba hunched over her food to eat and kept her eye on the birds.

Bailey couldn't believe her life had changed this much in just a few days. Now that she was here, what was she going to do? First order of business was to find the cabin. Then she'd hunt for work. The money her mother left wouldn't last forever. She planned to hire a private investigator to look into her mother's death. Last night in the motel she'd searched the internet for an investigator and had emailed one but hadn't heard back yet. Once the murderer was behind bars, she could resume her normal life.

Something told her catching the killer wouldn't happen fast or easily. She wouldn't keep running like Mom had done though. This place was where she'd make her stand, get to the bottom of what drove her mother's fear, and uncover the identity of the monster who stalked Bailey now.

Sheba finished her meal and meowed up at her. The cat

needed exercise, so she got out a ball and released Sheba from the harness. They spent several minutes playing fetch.

"Hello," a female behind her said. "You've got a good arm. And what an interesting-looking cat."

Bailey smiled at a young woman holding a tray of food. About her age and on the thin side, she had blue eyes and curly brown hair. "I was a softball all-star."

"Mind if I join you? There's gull poo on the other three tables. I swear, the owner can spray those things off and in five minutes they're dirty again."

"Sure, glad for the company." Friendly conversation would keep Bailey's thoughts from spinning around and around like a gerbil on a wheel.

"What kind of cat is that?" The woman set her tray down on the table as Bailey scooted over.

"She's a Savannah cat, bred from the serval with a domestic animal. She's about six months old."

"She looks like a small cheetah. Really amazing. Is she mean?"

Bailey put her hand on Sheba's head, and the cat purred as she licked her chops. "She doesn't have a mean bone in her body. She's very playful and sweet."

The woman sat across from Bailey. "You just passing through or here for a visit? I'm Mackenzie Blackmore, by the way. Friends and family call me Mac."

"Um, Bailey. Bailey Fleming." Should she have used a fake name? But she had to work, and her ID was in her real name. It was a common enough name, so she should be all right, at least for a while. "I'm actually just moving to town."

"You're kidding! Welcome to Lavender Tides." Mac scooted on the bench and pointed. "See that beauty out there? That's my tall ship, *Lavender Lady*. I teach Asian studies at the college, but sailing is my passion. Once I get my strength back, I'll take her out for her maiden voyage."

"She's beautiful. I've never gone sailing. You've been sick?"

A shadow clouded Mac's eyes. "It's a long story, but I'm doing okay. I need to gain a bit of weight, and I'll be right as rain. I'll have to take you sailing sometime." She waved at a distinguished-looking man in his fifties who smiled and came their way.

A woman about his age accompanied him. She was dressed in slacks and a too-tight sweater she kept tugging down. The wind tossed her salt-and-pepper hair around her genial face.

Mac smiled up at them. "This is Mayor Thomas Weaver and his wife, Melissa. He's been our fearless leader forever. Meet Bailey Fleming, our newest resident."

The mayor smiled and reached out to shake her hand. "Welcome to town, Ms. Fleming."

"Thank you. Call me Bailey." She touched fingers with his wife, and they chatted a few minutes before the two moved off.

"Nice people." How often did one meet the mayor right off the bat? What a sweet, friendly town. She felt safe here—or at least like she might be safe eventually.

Mac took a bite of her food. "Where will you be working?"

"Well, that's the thing. I don't have a job yet. I'm a nurse, so I hope it will be fairly easy to find something."

"A nurse, you say? There's a small hospital with a few beds on the outskirts of town and a doctor's office on Main Street." She fell silent a moment. "Actually, my ex-husband could use a little looking after. He's been blind since an accident. The doctor says he could recover his sight at any time, but it's already been two weeks, and everything is still black."

Bailey heard the concern in her voice. They must have had a friendly divorce, or else it hadn't been Mac's idea. "That's terrible. I've seen a few cases like that, and they usually do recover."

They talked a few minutes about the injury and the things Bailey had seen in her training and her work.

Mac raked her curly brown hair back from her face. "He's impossible to deal with. Black moods, grumpy as all get-out."

"That's pretty normal. Blindness is hard to deal with. I'm sure he's depressed."

"I've been bringing him food, but he hates me checking on him. Would you be interested in paying him a visit every day?" The salary she named seemed generous for the small time investment.

"That's not exactly nursing work, but I'd be glad to do it. I could check his eyes and help clean him up. I've taken care of nearly blind patients with macular degeneration. I could start teaching him how to do things for himself too. Has he had any training like that?"

"Are you kidding? He's sure his sight will return, and he refuses to try to learn anything. His mom, Helen, has been stopping by, too, but she doesn't get anywhere with him either. Maybe a stranger, a health-care professional, could get him to listen. I mean, he might not recover his sight. It's a possibility."

"Yes, it is. Do you want to see my résumé? I have a copy in the car. I've worked at a nursing home for a year. I'm an RN, graduated with top honors."

"Sure, I'll take a copy, but I can see you're a good person, calm and steady, too, which is what Jason needs." She reached for her purse and drew out a small notebook to scribble on. She tore off a paper and handed it to Bailey. "Here's his address.

I'll tell him you'll be stopping by to meet him. He'll probably grouse about it, but I think you'll be good for him."

And just like that she had a job. While it wasn't for a ton of money, it would help preserve her cash, plus she'd have time to investigate her mother's past. Bailey fetched her résumé from the car, finished her lunch, then headed out to find her new home.

## *Chapter 4*

Her supposed haven didn't appear to be much of a sanctuary out here in the middle of nowhere. An engraved wooden sign with the words *Cedar Cabin* swung in the wind from a pole at the road. The home lived up to the picture in Bailey's possession. She steered the white Ford Fiesta she'd bought at a used-car lot in Ironwood into the drive and parked. Wildflowers tangled their way through weeds and grass all the way across the yard to the edge of the forest. The rosebushes in the planting bed could use a trim as they sprawled over the sides of the brick that should have corralled them.

The house appeared in decent shape, though it could use some minor repair. The siding's cedar planks fit tightly together, and the windows turned blank faces to the deserted road fronting the place. Bailey had seen only a couple of other houses as she'd followed her phone's GPS to this spot. A mile back the pavement had given way to macadam and then to dirt. The road seemed to end just past the cabin.

The isolation felt both intriguing and terrifying. She got out, picked up Sheba, then squared her shoulders and marched to the front door. Should she knock to be sure the cabin was vacant? Through the window in the door she saw bulky furniture in the living room. The place seemed unoccupied.

She shifted Sheba to one arm, unlocked the door, and pushed it open before she could chicken out. The scent of dust and emptiness hit her nose, and she stopped at the light switch. When she flipped it, nothing happened. She toggled it again, but no welcome light pushed away the gloominess. Was the bulb burned out? She stepped into the living room to the end table beside the shrouded sofa and switched on a lamp. Nothing.

Sheba began to struggle, so she let her down to explore.

Of course there was no power. No heat, no electricity. What was she going to do? She'd passed a motel on the edge of Lavender Tides, but she didn't want to spend more of her cash if she could help it. The temperature was supposed to fall into the thirties tonight. She needed heat, but it was already past five. The electric company wouldn't be open again until Monday.

Three nights without heat and lights. She'd endured worse.

She thrust back the heavy curtains and sneezed as dust flew up her nose. Dim light from the overcast afternoon filtered into the room. The tiny living room opened into a kitchen on its left side and a bedroom on the right. Ladder stairs near the kitchen led to a loft. More drapes covered the windows at the back, and she opened them to reveal a view of the nearby woods. Blue water peeked between the trees. A lake or the ocean? She didn't have a good sense of the lay of the land here.

The living room held a fireplace, and she'd spied a stack of wood near the back deck. It took some work to get the stuck flue open, but she managed it, then brought in an armload of wood.

A few minutes later she had flames licking at the tinder. The woodsy scent of a fire wafting in the air cheered her immensely.

While the fire spread its warmth into the chilly room, she inspected the house. The bedroom was small, and the fixtures in the bathroom still looked new, though the brass style came straight from the nineties. A sheet covered the king bed in the bedroom, and she pulled it off to feel the mattress, which seemed to be dry. She found sheets in a big dresser by the door and held them to her nose. While they didn't smell fresh, they were clean. She changed the sheets and checked the pillows, which were dry as well.

She could sleep here.

She went outside to get the few things she'd bought on the way. The whine of a chain saw carried through the trees, and she saw a man cutting up a downed tree twenty feet into the woods. An older woman hovered nearby.

The man waved. "Hello there." The roar of the saw cut off, and he set it down, then came toward her with the older woman in tow.

The woman's eyes held a vacant stare. Dementia, poor lady. "Bailey Fleming. I just moved in next door."

The slightly built dark-skinned man seemed fixated on her dark-purple hair. She'd dyed it to confuse her identity a bit. "Nice to meet you, Bailey. I'm Jermaine Diskin. From the next house over. You probably passed my wife's lavender farm on the way out here."

"Nice to meet you." The friendly expression in his pale-green eyes and his easy grin settled her hackles.

"You bought the place?"

She hesitated. "Just renting for now." She held out her hand to the woman. "What's your name?"

The woman's white hair curled limply around her face and the straggly ends just brushed her jaw. It could use a good wash. She wore stained gray slacks and a red top that had been buttoned wrong. She angled a blank stare Bailey's direction and didn't answer. She was likely in her eighties.

Jermaine shifted on his feet and looked down. "This is Lily Norman. She lives on the other side of me, and um, she wandered out to see what I was doing."

"Does anyone live with her?"

He shook his head. "She's lost weight, and I don't think she's eating."

"Family?"

"A daughter who lives somewhere out east. I've tried to find her number at Lily's house, but I haven't been able to locate her."

Bailey warmed to the man. He seemed to care about the woman. "I'm a nurse. She has Alzheimer's?"

"Probably, though she hasn't been diagnosed as far as I know. Hey, I could use some help checking on her for the next few weeks. Michelle and I are going on a trip to Hawaii, and I've been worrying about leaving Lily alone. No one lives on this road except the three of us. I'd pay you if you'd look in on her and text me occasionally with how she's doing."

She couldn't tell him no, not looking into the sweet old lady's face. "You don't need to pay me. I'd be happy to check on her while I'm here, just to be neighborly."

"You rented the place? I've wanted to buy it, but it's in the hands of some kind of holding company, and no one ever answers my emails."

Holding company? The deed was clearly in her name. Her thoughts raced. Jermaine would be gone awhile. That might be enough time to dig out the secrets here at this house. "Um, yes, I rented it for a-a couple of months."

He brightened. "Great. You'll love Lily. She's a sweetheart."

If Bailey wanted to figure out what had happened to her mother, she'd have to meet people eventually. "Okay, I'll need a key."

And just like that she was part of the neighborhood, such as it was.

❦

Downtown Seattle always made King feel a little inconspicuous in a comforting way. No pretense, no pandering staff. Here he was just a businessman striding through the streets with a throng of latte-carrying women and men surging around him. No one knew about the power he wielded. He could order any of them shot and they'd never suspect him of the deed.

King stepped into a coffee shop and ordered his own latte and a cookie, then settled at a table overlooking the bustling street as he waited for Chey to join him with an update on the situation in Michigan. The coffee was good and strong, the way he liked it, and he took off the lid to let it cool a bit.

Chey strode down the sidewalk with determined steps. As usual he was expressionless, but a frisson of alarm went up King's back for some unknown reason. Chey didn't drink coffee, so the man headed straight to the table when he entered.

He pulled out a chair and sat down. "Our mission was unsuccessful," he said quietly.

"What?" King's voice reverberated on the tin ceiling, and

he moderated his tone as the only other patron glanced their way. "How is that possible?"

"She escaped during the attack and managed to get out of town. In Roger's defense, the break-in happened during a blizzard, and she knew her way around. He didn't."

"Where is she now?"

Chey folded his hands in front of him on the table. "That's a good question. We found her SUV in Ironwood, Michigan, but she could have gone anywhere from there. It's along one of the main routes out of the Upper Peninsula. She could have gone to Chicago and east or west."

"What vehicle is she driving now?"

"A white Ford Fiesta."

"Plates?"

"She left the plates on her SUV. We suspect she stole plates along the way."

"If she did that, she must know something. Or who she's up against." While he would never admit to a raised pulse, the sensation in his chest was definitely that of alarm. A feeling he wasn't used to. "What are you doing to find her?"

Chey lifted one brow. "Everything we can, but until we know where she's headed, our hands are tied. It's a common vehicle, and we don't have a plate. We've dispersed her description to our network, but it's going to be difficult to track her down."

Incompetents. King pressed his lips together and tamped down his ire. Bailey was a loose cannon. He should have ordered her death at the same time as Olivia's, but he'd allowed emotion to cloud his judgment. A ludicrous lapse of judgment on his part, but no more.

"I want her dead," he said through clenched teeth. "Make it happen, Chey."

"I'll do my best, sir, but we might want to make . . . contingency plans."

King drew back and looked at his second-in-command. How much did he know? He'd never questioned why Olivia was to be killed, yet he seemed to understand she held some grave importance. He didn't dare question what Chey knew because it would show weakness.

"It is not that important. She will be found, and she will be killed. If not, anything she knows is only an embarrassment, nothing more. And it can't be tied to me anyway."

That sounded much too defensive. He took a gulp of his coffee. "The shipment?"

"We had eight living girls delivered. Two unfortunately did not survive the trip, but they've been temporarily put in storage until we can dispose of the bodies."

"They should have been tipped into the sea."

"There was nothing on hand to weight the bodies. It will be taken care of."

He listened as Chey told him of the last haul from the casinos they managed and the take from the last shipment of drugs. Everything else was going well. This would fall in line too. Bailey couldn't hide forever.

When Chey left, King drummed his fingers on the table and considered what he knew about Olivia and the advice she might have offered Bailey given the chance. She'd moved quite often over the years, though he'd always kept track of her. They had an agreement, one he'd been careful to honor as long as she had. The problem came when her identity had been uncovered.

From there it was a reasonable assumption that everything else would come out too.

She'd lived for a while in Nashville, then in a small town in Indiana. She'd disappeared for a while in Chicago, but he'd found her in Forest Park. From there she'd gone to Austin, then to Phoenix, and finally to Michigan. Would Bailey run to any of those places? Where had they lived the longest?

He ran through the years in his mind. Phoenix. They'd lived there for five years. The longest stretch had been during Bailey's college years. She might have made friends she would run to now.

He phoned Chey and told him to take a hard look at the Phoenix area and to check out the school Bailey had attended. One piece of information up his sleeve was Bailey's phone number. He gave that number to Chey as well and told him to call it. If she was as smart as her mother, she would likely have tossed it, but he might get lucky.

He had another thought and called Chey back. "I've changed my mind. Before you kill her, bring her to me. I want to talk to her first. She's very beautiful—and young. We might want to put her to work instead."

"You sure that's wise?"

He frowned. "You're questioning my order, Chey? That's not a healthy option."

"I'll find her and bring her to you."

Chey's quick backtracking calmed King's anger but only for a moment. This situation had to be dealt with. Fast.

## *Chapter 5*

The afternoon wind off Rainshadow Bay whistled through the trees and snaked down Lance's back. He put down his binoculars long enough to zip up his jacket. "This is the first time we've seen any evidence of the cabin being occupied in three years."

Daniel knelt beside him. "Could be a squatter. The power hasn't been switched back on."

The sun gilded the treetops, and he let his gaze linger on the pretty scene. Once upon a time he'd hoped to have a cabin in the woods with Rachel. She'd thrown his ring back at him the third time he'd had to fly out of town for work. To be fair, he'd had to miss his own engagement party that weekend, but it had clearly shown him that she was only in the relationship when things went her way. She'd never really understood the importance of his calling.

Ava came first and always would.

Baker Holdings had owned this cabin for twenty years, and three years ago Daniel had discovered the property in an investigation. There'd been evidence that someone ran drugs through here as well as human trafficking, though they'd never made an arrest. Used syringes and bags with traces of drugs had been found in the trash can out back as well as used condoms, but Lance's supervisor wasn't convinced the holding company was at fault. According to him, someone could have used an empty house to conduct business, but he'd let Daniel and Lance run with their suspicions.

Baker Holdings had been formed in Panama, which was the most popular country for creating holding companies, and many of those were fronts to launder money. Baker Holdings hid their activities well, but that didn't mean they couldn't make a mistake. A neighbor the next mile over had seen woodsmoke curling from the chimney and had reported it to the sheriff, who had called Lance. Maybe it was nothing, but he needed to check it out.

A white Ford Fiesta sat in the drive, and the cabin's drapes remained open. The wind brought the scent of smoke his way, and he glimpsed a figure inside outlined by the glow of the fire. He tried to focus his binoculars but the person moved away too quickly.

"We could go to the door and talk to the occupant," Daniel said.

"If we identify ourselves as FBI, it might tip our hand. I'd rather keep an eye out and wait for something to go down." Lance stood and dropped his binoculars to let them dangle around his neck. "The last time we were here, I noticed the place could use some upkeep. Rot in the back deck, a hole in the roof, and the back door had been busted in so it didn't fit right. My dad taught me a lot about carpentry. How about I go introduce myself and ask if they're looking for any help with the place? I can say I'm a neighbor."

"If it's a squatter, you'll be able to tell right away."

Lance nodded. "Right. You cover me."

Daniel pulled out his Glock. Lance darted down the street to throw himself belly down on the ground behind a fallen tree. He went to his blue GMC Acadia and slid behind the wheel, then drove it down the road and into the drive. He pasted on a smile as he walked to the door.

A gust of wind sent woodsmoke into his face, and he coughed as he rapped on the door. There was a slight flurry of movement inside, but he couldn't see anything. "Hello?"

The door cracked open, and a young woman stood half revealed in the shadows. Her long purple hair with a striking widow's peak set off her large green eyes. Her strong bone structure and vivid coloring made her quite memorable. His suspicions flared into overdrive at her appearance though. He'd seen plenty of imprisoned girls with dyed hair over the years.

"Can I help you?" Her husky voice held a hint of fear.

Since he was six two, she had to be close to five eight. Even her sloppy sweats didn't hide her curves, but he made sure to keep eye contact. "Good evening, miss. I'm Lance Phoenix and I live a mile that way." He tossed a single nod to the west. "I saw the smoke of your fire. Thought I'd welcome you to the neighborhood."

Color ran up her neck and lodged in her cheeks. "Th-Thank you. News travels fast around here. I just arrived this afternoon. I didn't think to get the power turned on, and I had to start a fire for heat. I'll get the utilities switched on when the office opens."

"Be careful with that. The place has sat empty for years, and there might be damage from critters to the wiring."

Her eyes went wide. "I smelled some mouse droppings. I'm not sure what to do. I need power."

"I'd be happy to take a look at things for you. We like to be neighborly around here."

She smiled. "I met the next-door neighbor already. So much neighborliness is a little overwhelming."

She didn't seem like a squatter but a bonafide occupant. "You own this place?"

The color washed out of her face, and she opened the door a little more. "I'm just staying here for a while."

Which wasn't exactly an answer. Her caginess kept him on high alert, and she still hadn't told him her name. "I'm Lance, like I said. Lance Phoenix. What's your name?"

She bit her lip. "It's Bailey. Bailey Fleming."

The name didn't ring a bell. "It's too dark to see much tonight, so how about I come back tomorrow and check out the wiring before you get the utilities turned on? Is there anything I can do for you tonight?"

She shook her head. "I'm just going to bed early. Thanks for your help. I'm happy to pay you."

"Just being neighborly, like I said. Sleep well. I'll come by around eight in the morning if that's okay."

"I appreciate it. I can't even fix coffee yet."

"I'll bring you some." He gave her a final grin, then headed back to his SUV.

He drove off, then stopped to pick up Daniel at the curve in the road where they couldn't be seen. "I'm not sure what I think about her. She seems innocent enough but didn't really want to tell me her name, and she was cagey about how she happens to be here. I'll come by tomorrow to check out her wiring though. Maybe I'll find out more. She says her name is Bailey Fleming."

Daniel fastened his seat belt. "I'll do some digging into Baker Holdings and see if any Flemings pop up."

❧

Shauna Bannister leaned back against her husband's strong chest as he dropped a kiss on the top of her head. "I wish Grayson would call. Surely he's found Bailey by now. He arrived in Rock Harbor yesterday."

She and Zach had only been married a couple of months, and everything was still new and exciting.

"It all takes time, honey." Zach released her and moved to the coffeepot to pour the brew into two mugs. "Maybe she has a lot of questions and they're talking it all out."

"I can't take it any longer. I'm going to call him. If he's with Bailey, maybe he'll put her on the phone so I can talk to her too." After discovering her brother and sister were still alive, Shauna had them both constantly on her mind. Reuniting with Grayson had been a dream come true, but she longed with everything in her to hold her baby sister again.

"I don't blame you. I know you didn't sleep much last night."

"Like not at all." She called her brother's number.

Grayson answered on the second ring. "I was about to call you, Shauna."

His voice's grim tone caused a hard ball to form in her stomach, and she put the call on speakerphone and moved to Zach's side. "What's wrong?"

"Olivia's been murdered, and the killer broke into Bailey's

home. While she was there. She's on the run, and no one knows where she's gone."

"Oh no! Was she injured?"

"I don't think so. At least no blood was left behind. Unless Bailey surfaces on her own, we'll have a hard time tracking her down."

Shauna wanted to cry. "I should have gone out there right away, the second we discovered her whereabouts."

"None of us had any idea she or her mom were in danger. The sheriff suspects some kind of organized-crime connection because her mother was killed execution style."

Zach set a comforting hand on Shauna's shoulder. "Was there any evidence of a connection between Olivia and organized crime?"

"The sheriff didn't find anything like that. It was the manner of the killing that made him suspicious."

Shauna pushed back her disappointment. "Are you still there or on your way home?"

"My flight doesn't leave until tomorrow. I'd hoped to find her so I gave myself enough time to fill her in and get to know her a bit. I thought I'd poke around here and see if I can uncover a lead on where she might have gone. Maybe a friend would have an idea."

"That's a great idea. Let us know what you hear," Zach said.

"Sure will. Talk to you later."

Shauna was still processing her grief as she laid her phone on the counter. "We might never find her, Zach." The sensation of her baby sister in her arms as a newborn had never left her. "What if the killer gets to her? Why would anyone want to shoot her mom?" She stared at his dear face with its strong jawline, blue eyes, and dark-brown hair.

"There's a lot we don't know about Olivia. Why would she steal Bailey? Maybe that's the first place to start as we try to figure this all out."

She wrapped her arms around his waist and leaned into his strength. "How do we do that?"

"She had to have some friends when she was here. People she worked with, neighbors, that kind of thing. I hadn't pursued any of that since I managed to find her. It's time to do that, I think."

"You're awesome." She nuzzled her nose into his neck and inhaled the aroma of his skin, earthy and warm.

"Gotta keep my bride happy."

Should she tell him? She'd thought to have a romantic seafood dinner and tell him, but the news was about to bust out of her.

She took his hand and tugged. "I have something to show you."

He came willingly enough as she led him through the house to the master bedroom. Her pulse fluttered in her throat as she reached into the nightstand drawer and withdrew the surprise. She opened her palm to show him and smiled up into his face.

A puzzled line crouched between his eyes as he looked at what she held out. His jaw dropped and his eyes went wide. "A pregnancy test? I don't know how to read these things."

"See the two lines? That means we're having a little Zach."

He hooted and grabbed her, then lifted her in his arms. "A baby? We're having a baby?"

She clung to him as her stomach did a slow roll with the twirl. "That's right, Cowboy. As nearly as I can figure, the little man will make his appearance in July."

With her still in his arms, he sat on the side of the bed and cradled her close. "I'm rooting for a girl with your green eyes."

"That would be all right too." She rested her head on his chest. "I have to admit I'm a little scared. We both want this so badly. I'm afraid to hope I'll carry this baby to term."

"You didn't have any problems with Alex, did you?"

"No, but I had a miscarriage when he was a year old. I'm a little spooked."

His dark-blue eyes were tender, and he leaned in close enough that his breath warmed her cheek. "God loves to give us good things. Let's just trust him and try not to worry."

"I'll make an appointment with the midwife right away. I'll feel better once we hear a heartbeat."

"When's that?"

"Eight to ten weeks. I'm going to push for an eight-week appointment." She cradled his face in her hands. "It's going to be pretty exciting around here."

"It already is." His lips came down on hers in a sweet kiss of promise.

## *Chapter 6*

At least he had somewhere new to look. Lance took off his jacket and hung it in the closet, then rolled his neck around to ease its stiffness. He was supposed to go to Daniel's for dinner tonight, but he'd rather sit at his computer and see what he could find out about the intriguing Bailey Fleming. He had just enough time to take a quick shower before heading to Daniel's for little Milo's first birthday party.

His phone rang as he went down the hall to the bathroom. His dad's face filled the screen, and he nearly didn't answer. How did he tell his dad he'd failed again?

He pressed his lips together, then answered the phone. "Hey, Dad."

"I saw the newspaper article about the FBI bust last week. Why didn't you call to tell me about it?"

"There wasn't anything to tell, Pop. We rescued several teenagers, but there was no sign of Ava, and Jackson is still at large."

His dad sighed. "I'd hoped you were just keeping it under wraps until you knew more. No one had seen Ava?"

"No." He didn't dare tell his dad that there'd been a

dark-headed young woman there. Pop would leap to the quick assumption it had to be Ava, and the calls would start coming several times a day.

Lance's old foe helplessness swamped him. His parents had never recovered from Ava's disappearance five years ago, and neither had he. Maybe none of them ever would. The suspense was the worst. Every night when he went to bed, he saw her face, and first thing in the morning he heard her calling his name, begging him to save her.

His parents' guilt pierced even deeper. There had been the typical teenage fights with Ava that transitioned into screaming matches as she approached her sixteenth birthday. She wanted to go out with her friends, and their parents had rules—rules she thought were stupid. He'd thought they were stupid when he was her age, too, but by the time he went to college, he'd seen the wisdom. Their parents only wanted to protect her, and so did he. She'd felt ganged up on, and the next thing they knew, she ran away after a particularly bitter argument.

He spoke with his dad a few more minutes, then hopped in the shower. After changing into jeans and a Seahawks sweatshirt, he drove to Daniel's house, a small ranch on the east side of Seattle.

Daniel's wife, Sandy, came to the door with Milo in her arms. The beautiful redhead had flour on her cheek and chocolate frosting at the corner of her mouth. She thrust the baby at him. "Here, take Milo. I've got to finish the cake before our parents get here. Someone just shoot me now."

Milo patted his face and gave him a toothy grin. The kid was cute as a button and sported eight teeth now. His white-blond hair was like his dad's, and his big gray eyes had everyone gaga over him. Including Lance. He put Milo's present on the gift table, then hoisted the toddler to his shoulders. Milo grabbed his hair and squealed with hysterical laughter. This was a favorite game of theirs. He romped to the living room with a giggling Milo and found Daniel frantically stuffing baby toys back into a tub.

"Sandy is ready to kill me for getting home too late to watch Milo while she finished cooking. By the way, some hits came in on Bailey Fleming, and I stopped by the office to print them out."

"What did you find out?"

"The sheriff in Rock Harbor, Michigan, is looking for her in connection with a shooting."

Whoa, Lance hadn't been expecting that. He lifted Milo down from his shoulders and settled him in one arm. "Can I see?"

"After dinner. Everyone is arriving and if I spoil Milo's first birthday, I'm toast."

The doorbell rang and Daniel groaned. "Here we go."

"It'll be fun." Lance handed Milo a toy car and the baby squirmed to get down to roll it. Cars were his favorite.

Would he ever have a family of his own? It probably wouldn't happen until he found Ava.

❧

Mac let herself into Jason's house with her key and walked through the unlit rooms to the living room, where she found Jason sitting in the dark in his recliner by the fireplace. The television's volume was so low she could hardly hear it.

She flipped on the light and set a thermos of chili on the table beside the chair. It hurt to see him unshaven and in food-stained sweats. He'd always been so meticulous about his hygiene and appearance. "I brought you some dinner."

"I'm not hungry."

She paid no more attention to his usual response than she did any other night. She fetched bowls and spoons from the kitchen and grimaced at the sink overflowing with dishes. Tomorrow she'd find time to come earlier so she could clean. The place was a pigsty, but she tamped down her irritation. He couldn't see any of the mess.

For the past two weeks, since they'd gotten out of the hospital, she worked at showing him how sorry she was for everything. The divorce had been her fault, and if he hadn't been trying to rescue her from her own stupidity, he wouldn't have been injured. He deserved better than she'd given him. But no matter how much she tried to help him, he stayed surly. Maybe he would never forgive her.

She carried the bowl and spoon back to the living room and poured out the chili, then touched the side of a bowl against his right hand. "Here you go. Lots of jalapeños as you like it."

Chili was his favorite dish, but she still expected a token refusal at first. But his fingers closed around the bowl, and he took it from her hands. He balanced the bowl on his lap and felt around the rim for the spoon. Handsome with his sun-streaked brown hair, Jason Yarwood had always been one of the strongest people she'd ever known. He and her sister, Ellie, owned a house-flipping business, and he could heft large beams on those broad shoulders with ease. Ever since hitting his head during her rescue from terrorists, those gorgeous brown eyes were sightless.

Would he ever look at her with love again? She hadn't loved him when she married him, but she'd been wrong, so wrong.

"You eating too?" His voice was gruff.

"Yep." She picked up the other bowl of chili and settled onto the sofa across from him.

The spices and tomatoes hit her tongue in a wave that sharpened her senses. He lifted the spoon to his mouth with care and winced when the bite of soup spilled onto his sweatshirt. Maybe soup hadn't been such a good idea. A sandwich was easier to handle.

She set her empty bowl aside on the table next to her. "Did your mom take you to see the doctor today?"

"I'm still blind. No change."

The next thing she knew his bowl flew through the air to shatter against the fireplace. Red splatters of chili dripped like blood off the mantel and onto the wood floor.

She shot to her feet with her fists clenched. "What if I'd stood just then and you hit me with the bowl?"

"I can hear where you are. Only my eyes are broken, not my ears." He glowered, and his strident voice held an edge. "How do you think it makes me feel to know I'm helpless here, Mac? Why do you come so often anyway? To feel sorry for the poor blind guy? Save your pity. I've only ever wanted your love, and you saw fit to kick me to the curb. What's the point?"

She longed to confess her changed feelings, but he was in no frame of mind to receive that kind of confession. He'd think it was only because of pity. "I want to see you well, Jason. We might not be married any longer, but I care about you."

"Yeah, guilt is an emotion. I get that, but this wasn't your fault." The anger drained from his face, and he rubbed his forehead. "What am I going to do if I never see again?"

She knew he wasn't asking about money, but about living a productive life. Jason always had a thing about taking care of her. His mother too. He was the caregiving type.

"The first thing you can do is learn to be self-sufficient, no matter what. A nurse is coming to help you with that. She'll teach you how to care for yourself, how to cook, how to navigate. At least for now."

He raised his head, his nostrils flaring. "What have you done, Mac?"

"It's just until your sight returns. It can't hurt to learn how to get around in the house."

"I don't want a nursemaid!"

"She's not. She's had experience teaching this kind of thing. I think you'll feel better about yourself if you're not so dependent."

He chewed his lip, and his brown eyes held anguish. "I don't like being a burden."

"You're not a burden. Not to me and not to your mom. But I know you, Jason. This will help you. Give her a chance, okay?"

He shrugged. "I'll see."

And that was the best she could hope for under the circumstances. She went to fetch a bucket of water and a rag to clean up the chili mess.

## *Chapter 7*

The house felt secretive and spooky without lights, and Bailey left the bedroom door open in hopes that the heat and glow from the dying fire would creep inside the room. Without knowing the status of the chimney, she didn't dare go to bed with a fire blazing, though she would have loved to be warm. Using a flashlight from her car, she found extra blankets in the hall closet and piled the bed high with them, then went to the bathroom to wash her face.

Of course there was no water. This far out of town, there would only be a well, and the pump needed electricity. Her reflection in the mirror was dim and ghostly. She already hated her purple hair, but she'd read somewhere that if you wanted to hide, changing your hair color to something gaudy was helpful because that's all people would see. Purple had seemed best to go with her dark hair, but the color startled her every time she caught a glimpse of it.

She pulled out the burner phone she'd bought in Minnesota. Dare she call one of her stepbrothers? She felt so alone, but what if Mom's killer had tapped their phones? It wasn't safe. They'd be able to triangulate her location by tracing back a call. Though she wasn't yet used to Pacific time, she wasn't sleepy and she desperately wanted to talk to someone.

Maybe she could call the sheriff and see if he'd found out anything. The killer wasn't likely to be watching the sheriff's phone. Her mother had said not to go to the police, but she felt too isolated and vulnerable. She had to know what was happening.

It was only ten back home. Surely that wasn't too late to call. Before she could change her mind, she placed the call.

"Sheriff Kaleva." He sounded alert.

"Um, Sheriff, it's Bailey Fleming."

"Bailey, what happened? I've been worried about you."

"I had to get away. Mom's killer is after me. Have you arrested anyone? Is the autopsy back?"

"Where are you?"

"I can't tell you that. Please, don't ask any more questions or I'll have to hang up."

He cleared his throat. "We still don't have any clues to the murderer's identity. Do you have any idea who this is? Did your mother talk about being in danger?"

"We always moved around a lot, and Mom left a note telling me to hide, so that's what I'm doing." His lack of progress fueled her decision. She wouldn't tell him she planned to investigate and find out who had killed her mother.

"Look, it's not safe for you to be out there by yourself. Wherever you are, contact the police and have them call me. I'll corroborate how much danger you're in. We can arrange for police protection."

She knew how that worked—the killer would just lie low

until the police pulled off the protection detail from lack of funds. "I'm okay. I just wanted an update. I'll be in touch." She ended the call before he could object, then switched off the phone.

What did she know about all this? Her mother had to have left some clues over the years as to her background. Bailey had always been told her mother's parents were dead, but was that even true? What was this house? The neighbor said it was owned by a holding company. Did that mean Kyle was involved in something illegal?

She wouldn't put it past him, but the bigger question was, why would he own a house in the same town where her mother grew up? Had she known Kyle somehow? Maybe that was why she had been in favor of the marriage.

In the light of day tomorrow, she'd search through everything in this house. Maybe clues were hidden somewhere as to Kyle's plans. It was even possible her connection to Kyle had caused all this. She couldn't overlook anything.

All these questions made her head hurt. She took off her shoes, and still wearing her clothing and socks, she crept under the thick stack of quilts. Her body heat soon warmed the sheets, and she drifted off to sleep.

When she awoke, moonlight streamed through the windows, and she lay there with her heart pounding. The loud crash that had awakened her still reverberated through her chest. She sat up and heard muttering down the hall. It sounded like someone in the living room. She had no real weapons, only bear spray. Her inclination was to huddle under the covers and pray whoever was out there departed, but if it was the killer, he'd find her.

She slipped out of bed and found her purse. Holding the car

keys in her hand like a knife, she tiptoed to the door and peered out down the hall and into the living room. A dark shadow moved jerkily around the room, and a swath of moonlight revealed the intruder's identity.

Her neighbor Lily.

Bailey exhaled and stuffed the keys into her pocket, then padded quietly into the room and watched the old woman for a while. Still dressed in her ratty bathrobe and muddy slippers, Lily pulled out the drawers in the side tables by the sofa and muttered under her breath.

"Where is it?" She stopped and raked her white hair out of her face. "I know it's here."

"Lily?" Bailey pitched her voice soft and low so she didn't scare her. "Can I help you?" Lily's blue eyes reminded her of someone, but this late at night she couldn't think who it was.

Lily whirled to face her. Her eyes were wide with terror, but they held more awareness than when Bailey had first met her. Her fingers laced together in front of her, she backed away.

Bailey stepped forward and touched her on the shoulder. "Don't be afraid. It's just me, Bailey. I live here, remember?"

Lily brushed Bailey's cheek with dry, wrinkled fingers. "I always knew you'd come back, Liv."

Who did Lily think she was? A daughter maybe? "Let me throw a quilt around you. You're cold."

Poor lady needed more help than she was getting.

❦

Wrapping paper lay strewn like confetti around the living room. Sandy had whisked a tired Milo off to bed as soon as the grandparents left, and Lance sat at the kitchen table with Daniel sipping a cup of coffee and eating handfuls of peanut M&Ms. He already had a sugar overload from the cake and ice cream, but the things were as addictive as crack cocaine.

He took a swig of already-lukewarm coffee. "Okay, tell me about Bailey and Baker Holdings."

Daniel shrugged. "The property was transferred out of Baker Holdings and into her name about two weeks ago."

"Is she on the board? Maybe she transferred it herself."

Daniel reached for a handful of candy and shook his head. "Not on the list."

"Who is on the list? Anyone we know?"

"You might say that. Alfred Jackson for one."

"Our Alfie?"

"It's possible it's a different Alfred Jackson, but it's enough to make me raise my eyebrows."

Lance crunched up an M&M. "Do we know who ordered the property moved into her name?"

"No, it was handled in Panama. Anyone on the board could have done it. There are six board members, but Jackson was the only familiar name."

Lance tried to imagine the young woman as part of a trafficking ring, and it didn't compute with the vulnerability he'd seen in her eyes. "I think maybe she's a patsy. She seemed scared when she answered the door. I got the distinct impression she's on the run."

"Maybe, but you have to admit it's suspicious. She shows up here out of the blue with the property in her name. Maybe she's here to run a brothel out of the cabin. Maybe she is one of Jackson's minions and will be managing where the girls go once they're brought in. Could be anything."

"Could be. Or maybe she really is an innocent."

"Then why'd Baker put the property in her name? There had to be a reason."

Lance had no answer for that question. Something about the green-eyed, purple-haired beauty had tugged at his heartstrings, and he wasn't easily moved by a pretty face. What was with the hair? She hadn't seemed the type to dye it an outlandish color, though he had to admit it looked good on her. She'd be a knockout even if she were bald.

"What?" Daniel asked. "You've got a goofy expression on your face."

"Just thinking about how she acquired that house. She lied to me, too, said she was just staying there for a while. That makes another mark in the suspicious column. Plus she was quick to say she'd pay me to check out the electrical. If she's only renting, why would she put money in the house? You mentioned a sheriff in Michigan is looking for her about a shooting. Did you talk to him yet?"

"Left a message for Sheriff Kaleva, but he hasn't called me back yet."

Lance's thoughts drifted to his sister again. "Any update from our haul in Seattle last week?"

"I was there when Sarah's parents came to get her. I nearly cried myself. It was pretty emotional. Makes what we do worth all the headaches. Well, partly at least."

"I'd like to have seen that."

He sometimes daydreamed about what his family would be like if Ava came home. His parents weren't likely to get back together, but it made for a pleasant dream. The likelier scenario was that Ava had moved on to a new life with that jerk she met.

Though he often tried to tell himself she wasn't lost in the trafficking underworld but had a happy home, deep down he knew better. Even if Ava had been furious with their parents, she never held a grudge long. And the two of them had been tight. If she could, she would have contacted him long before now. She was either dead or imprisoned in a living hell. Either way, he wasn't sure he could live without someday knowing. But how did he get to the truth?

He finished off the bowl of M&Ms and rose. "I'd better get some sleep. I have a cabin to repair."

"Good job on getting that in with her. You need me to hang around and keep an eye out?"

Lance shook his head. "See what else you can dig up on Bailey Fleming. Baker Holdings too. If we can uncover the connection between her and the holding company, we might be able to figure this out."

"If you can, take a stroll around the property and see if there's any sign they've moved girls through there recently. It's a perfect landing spot with the seclusion and that pier."

"I plan to. Let me know if you find out anything important."

Daniel walked him out, and Lance zipped his coat against the wind. November weather could be anything in the Olympic rain shadow. They could get an early snow or the temperature could hit sixty. One thing you could count on was the wind, and it howled down the mountain slopes to lift his hair and chill his ears as he walked to his SUV.

He slung himself behind the wheel and started the engine, then cranked the radio up to let Garth Brooks belt out "The Dance" and tried to ignore the blur of moisture in his eyes.

## *Chapter 8*

Lily stroked the quilt around her shoulders. "This is my favorite one. I made it when I was twenty."

"Did you used to live here, Lily?" Bailey guessed the cabin had been built in the fifties or sixties, but she could be wrong.

"Oh no, this was Liv's house." Lily's rheumy blue eyes stared off into the distance. "I made the quilt for her when she graduated from high school. My father built this cabin the year I was born—1936 it was. He used trees from this property and fitted every log into the place. I used to know every nook and cranny of it, and I had so many hiding places." Her giggle was that of a young girl's.

*Hiding places.*

Bailey touched Lily's wrinkled hand. "Could you show me some of the hiding places?"

"I'm tired. I think I'll go to bed now." Clutching the quilt around her neck, she rose and went to the ladder leading to the loft.

Bailey sprang forward. "Let me take you home."

"I am home. My bed is up there." She pointed to the loft.

Bailey hadn't been up there. The space might be inhabited by birds and mice, and she didn't trust the old woman not to fall and break her neck. "You live down the road now." She took her arm and tried to steer her toward the door, but Lily jerked away.

"I live here!" Her eyes were getting more confused by the moment, and her hands fluttered in agitation.

Bailey gave up the fight. "How about you sleep in the big bed?"

Lily's grin of childish delight beamed. "I get to sleep with Mama? I can only do that when Papa is gone."

"He's not here right now." Bailey led her to the bedroom and pulled back the thick layer of quilts. "Let's get you all tucked in." She pulled the covers up around Lily's neck and stepped back.

Almost instantly, the woman's thin lids lowered, and her mouth opened in a slight snore. Bailey tiptoed out and grabbed a quilt from the hall closet before making her way to the sofa. She stretched out on it with her head propped on the arm and tried to close her eyes, but her thoughts kept whirling around. Could there be secrets in this house, secrets that would lead her to the killer?

She wanted to believe it, but it might be hope talking and not reality. Tomorrow Lily might be clearer headed—or she might be worse. Bailey had taken care of enough people with dementia to know the clouds swept in when they wanted and departed when you didn't expect. She'd have to be alert for times when she might ask questions and get lucid answers.

The glowing logs shifted in the fireplace and settled with a soft *thunk*. She slid her gaze to the ladder to the loft. What was up there? The impulse to find out brought her off the sofa.

Flashlight in hand, she climbed the steps to the eaves and ducked under the wooden beams. The light's glow illuminated the hump of a large trunk, several armoires, and a space crammed tight with boxes. A tiny cot nestled beneath a beam, and it bowed under the weight of the boxes stacked on it.

It would take forever to go through all this stuff, but she itched to know what the boxes held, especially the trunk. She moved to it and flipped the latch on the lid. A squeak came from inside, and she snatched her hand back. On second thought, this would have to wait for morning. She didn't like mice, and the thought of coming face-to-face with a nest of mice or rats made her gulp.

Her head barely cleared the rafters and ceiling up here. Stooping over, she swept her beam around the space one more time, then descended the ladder.

Tomorrow the neighbor would return. He seemed a nice enough guy, the tall, dark, and handsome type, but his eyes had been serious behind his smile. She didn't know what that meant. Was he suspicious about what she was doing here? Did he know her mother or how this place came to be in Bailey's possession? She hoped to find out.

Settling back onto the sofa, she tried to close her eyes, but a light bobbed outside the window and she bolted upright. Though it was probably Jermaine, she got up and crept to the window. It looked like someone holding a lantern or a flashlight in the woods. Two other figures followed the first one, and the trio vanished into the shadows.

Hunters . . . or something more?

The ceilings soared to eighteen feet in the cavernous room floored with pink marble. Red silk draped the walls, and the golden glow of lanterns spaced around the perimeter illuminated the dancers dressed in lavish Khmer costumes, complete with the elaborate headdresses of the Apsara dancers. King sat in the middle of the front row with five clients on each side of him. For some of them, this would be the first time they saw his dancers.

The traditional Apsaras were female spirits of the wind and clouds in Hindu and Buddhist cultures, and he'd fallen in love with them the first time he'd stepped foot in Siem Reap, Cambodia, at the ancient temples of Angkor Wat. He'd spent hours at the bas-relief engravings and even more hours watching the Apsara dancers in town. Mythology said they seduced god and man and that they could change their shape at will. They ruled over the fortunes of gambling, and he'd instantly decided they would form the basis of his entire empire. His pleasure houses would be unique because of the Apsaras. He maintained ten of the most beautiful, most accomplished girls in his "court." And only the richest men were allowed access to them.

The fluid movements of the dance melded perfectly with the musicians playing traditional Cambodian instruments: the *sampho*, which was a type of drum played by hand, finger cymbals, a xylophone with bamboo keys, and gongs.

His other houses held Apsaras he'd deemed less perfect, less beautiful than these ten.

His gaze stayed fixed on Lotus. He'd wanted to call his Apsaras by their traditional Hindu names, but clients had asked for something easier to pronounce than names like Rambha and Urvashi, and he'd begun to call them by flower names. Lotus was always his best dancer and most beautiful girl. An hour with her cost ten thousand dollars, and an entire night would set the buyer back a hundred thousand dollars. One look at her usually had the man asking for an entire night.

His current Lotus had held the position for four years, and he saw no evidence that she was losing her extraordinary beauty. He made sure she didn't work more than once a week, just to sustain her value.

Her glossy black hair under the three-point crown was perfection, and the smooth caramel of her skin invited a man to touch her. She had been a lucky acquisition several years ago. He'd spied her when she was sixteen and had authorized one of his minions to lure her in. It had taken a year to break her and train her. Even now, he often caught a rebellious expression in those beautiful dark eyes, but she'd never voiced her displeasure. She'd learned wiser ways.

The Apsaras' movements were meant to be hypnotic, and it was hard for anyone to look away. He was particularly fond of the flexed foot and graceful hand gestures.

The dance ended, and three men bid on Lotus. He ended up selling her for a quarter of a million dollars for the night. All his clients knew they weren't allowed to hit or abuse his girls in any way, but he didn't like the look in the eye of one of the men and had him discreetly removed and drugged so he wouldn't remember this place.

Lotus locked gazes with him, and a plea sparkled in her eyes that he had to ignore. He'd do most anything for her except refuse that kind of money. She was his cash cow, and he'd do whatever it took to milk her for the most money possible.

## *Chapter 9*

Shauna knew the Whitewell mansion nearly as well as she knew her own. She parked in the big circle drive and got out when Taylor didn't come bouncing out the door. Shauna had babysat for Taylor when she was little, and now Taylor was old enough to watch Alex. Full circle.

She rang the bell, and the housekeeper answered the door with a welcoming smile. In her fifties, Rafaela had only a little gray in her black hair, and her brown eyes were as lively as ever. "Señora, you look lovely this morning, bright and happy. Marriage agrees with you, *sí*."

"Thank you, Rafaela, I couldn't be happier." Shauna stepped into the massive marble foyer with its soaring ceilings and great light. "I'm here to pick up Taylor."

"*Sí*, I know this. The *chiquita* is not quite ready. The hair must be perfect." She shook her head and smiled.

Rafaela Fletcher had worked for the Whitewells for as long as Shauna could remember. She'd started as a young woman when her husband took over managing the large, elaborate grounds, and she had kept everything operating like clockwork in the house. With the help of two part-time women, she did all of the cleaning and most of the cooking.

At the clatter of heels on the marble floors, Shauna greeted Gina Whitewell with a smile. Her dark hair was perfectly styled in a sleek bob that grazed her chin and accented her high cheekbones. She wore slim-fitting jeans and a V-neck sweater that accented curves that had grown more pronounced over the years. In spite of a few pounds, she was still beautiful and turned plenty of heads in her forties.

She held out her arms. "You're a sight for sore eyes. Hawaii must have been amazing. We went there on our honeymoon, and I used to nag Harry to go back. I might just have to go by myself since he works so much."

Shauna embraced her and inhaled the scent of her Joy perfume, a fragrance she'd worn forever. "Thanks for loaning me Taylor today. Marilyn has to go to Seattle, and I have some appointments about the airport expansion. I should have her back home by midafternoon."

"She's looking forward to it. She adores Alex. And you. We might have a budding helicopter pilot on our hands." Gina gazed past Shauna to the sweeping staircase. "Here comes our sleepyhead."

Taylor bounced down the stairs with a smile. The fourteen-year-old had done occasional babysitting for Alex since she was thirteen. Responsible and mature for her age, she loved all things that had to do with flying and had begged for flight lessons. Shauna was tempted to teach her, but so far her parents had been reluctant to allow it.

A beautiful leggy blonde, Taylor resembled her dad more than her gorgeous mother. Fair skin, hazel eyes, and hair as yellow as Rapunzel's, she had no idea yet of her beauty. She gave Shauna a boisterous hug. "Sorry I kept you waiting. Are we late?"

Shauna hugged her back, then released her. "Not at all. I was just chatting with your mom."

Taylor spun around to her mom. "Did you tell her?"

"I didn't get a chance." Gina's smile widened, but her hazel eyes held a touch of reserve. "I've talked with Harry, and we'd like you to start flight lessons with Taylor. If you're willing, of course."

"Aw, that's great!" Shauna knew Taylor had been dying to learn. "I promise I'll take good care of her. You'll have to learn on a plane first, Taylor. The helicopter will have to come much later. You need to learn about aerodynamics and gain some experience in the air."

Taylor bounced on the balls of her feet, the excitement flowing off her in waves. "I'm okay with that. When can we start?"

"Maybe this afternoon if I get back in time. It's all bookwork at first."

"I can't believe it!" Taylor gave her another exuberant hug.

Smiling, Shauna headed toward the door. "We'd better get going."

Taylor followed her to the truck. "Are you ever going to trade off that old truck?"

"Not if I can help it." Shauna buckled her seat belt and made sure Taylor did as well.

Shauna started the engine and pulled out onto the road. "How's school?"

Taylor rolled her eyes. "Okay. When did you start dating?"

Uh-oh. "I was sixteen."

"That's how old Dad says I have to be. It's ridiculous! All my friends are already dating. I'm *fourteen*, for Pete's sake. Get with the real world."

"You have a guy in mind?"

Taylor toyed with her hair. "Well, there's this one guy. I haven't met him yet, just on Instagram. He's been asking me to meet him for coffee. Want to see his picture?" Without waiting for an answer, she drew out her phone and showed Shauna the screen. "Isn't he cute?"

Shauna widened her eyes at the scruff on the young man's chin and the expression in his eyes. "Honey, he's much older than you. I'll bet he's in his twenties."

Taylor frowned and shut off the phone's screen. "Oh no, he's not that old. He talked like he was in high school."

Unease rippled up Shauna's back. An extensive article appeared in a magazine recently about how men used the internet to lure in young girls and prey on them. That was how many of them ended up taken into the sex trade against their will.

"I want you to show this guy to your parents. You haven't yet, have you?"

Taylor frowned and shook her head. "They'd freak, Shauna. I can't show them his picture."

"When we get home, there's an article I want you to read. Promise me you will?"

"I guess." Taylor crossed her arms. "Sheesh, you're making a lot of fuss about nothing."

Shauna could only pray it was nothing. If Taylor didn't tell her parents, she'd have to. The judge would not be happy.

Lance made the drive from Seattle to Lavender Tides and parked in Bailey's drive. After studying the structure, the old cabin had more problems than he'd first thought. Chinking around the logs on the porch needed replacing, and the stain on the upper-level cedar was nearly gone. Several cedar shingles stuck up on the roof at odd angles, letting in moisture.

Lance strapped on his tool belt and grabbed his tool chest and thermos. With his jeans and ball cap, he looked the part of a friendly handyman. When he approached the front door, he found it already open with just the screen door in place. An elderly woman's voice came from inside, but he only heard something about "no coffee."

He rapped his knuckles on the door. "Did someone say coffee?"

Bailey turned at his voice. She wore her purple hair on top of her head, and little wisps trailed across her cheeks. Dressed in the same jeans and long-sleeved red T-shirt, she was adorable. His gaze lingered on her full lips. What might it be like to kiss her? He stamped that troublesome thought into the ground.

She held open the screen door. "Coffee is the password."

Lance stepped inside and went to the dusty table. He pulled two disposable cups from his toolbox, then poured coffee into them. The older lady took hers and slurped it, seemingly not bothered by the hot temperature.

Bailey must have caught his quizzical gaze. "You're probably wondering why Lily is here so early. She spent the night."

Lily must be a neighbor. "Good morning, Lily."

Her white hair didn't appear to have seen a brush in several days, and bits of twigs littered it as well. Lily grunted and continued to drink her coffee, then handed the cup back to him. "More, please."

"Sure thing." He filled her cup again. "I brought donuts too."

Lily eyed the white pastry bag he pulled from his toolbox but waited until he opened it and offered her a caramel Long John. She devoured the donut in three bites, and he gave her another. Poor lady was much too thin. Did she have anyone looking after her? He needed to get a better feel for who lived out here or he'd blow his cover.

Bailey nibbled on her donut. "Good of you to bring us breakfast. Lily, um, she showed up after I went to bed. I found her poking through the living room. She didn't want to go home, so I put her to bed here."

Was Lily somehow involved in all this? She seemed at ease with Bailey and this house, too, but he didn't know what to make of this situation.

He set the donut bag on the table with the thermos. "Well, I'll take a look around at what needs done. Help yourself to more breakfast."

"Thank you," Bailey called after him as he glanced around the interior.

The cabin was small, probably not more than seven hundred square feet including the bedroom and loft area. The living room was about fifteen by twenty and connected to a small kitchen that held six feet of cabinets, an ancient stove, and a small fridge. Years of smoke from the fireplace darkened the logs on the inside, and the wood floors showed scratches from decades of use. He suspected the old velvet sofa was original as was the rounded fridge and wood-heat range.

It was cute though. In their investigation they'd found traces of cocaine on the old wooden table and some used syringes in the trash buried out back. Dozens of used condoms had been recovered in the downstairs bedroom, and he shuddered at the thought of the old lady sleeping in that bed. Bailey, too, for that matter. He could only hope she'd changed the sheets. The place had been nasty before the FBI had taken everything as evidence.

He worked on nailing down floorboards on the front porch first. About an hour later, he paused to grab a bottle of water from the cooler and heard voices out back.

He followed the sound to the back porch that faced the water. "Wow, beautiful view from here." Rainshadow Bay peeked through the trees, and he saw the ferry steaming past. "Careful." He pointed out a rotted board before Lily stepped onto it. "You need to have some of this replaced."

Bailey frowned down at the rotted wood. "Would you be interested in this job, too, or could you recommend a carpenter?"

"I've got time to do it. The roof needs tended to first. It's been leaking. Some of the logs need chinked, and this decking needs shored up."

"How much will that cost?"

He had no idea of the going rate for carpentry. "If you buy the supplies, I'll work for a hundred dollars a day."

Her nicely shaped black brows rose. "That sounds pretty cheap."

"It is, but you're a new neighbor and I'm between big jobs right now. I've got about two weeks, and I think I can get most of it good and sound by then." Lying didn't come easily to him even after three years with the Bureau.

His suspicions might be groundless, but if there was any

chance this woman and this place would connect him to Alfie Jackson, he had to follow the leads.

Her troubled expression cleared. "Okay, I'll take you up on your offer. I'm going into town to see if I can get the electricity switched on. The utility probably isn't open, but I thought I'd at least stop and check out the hours. What should I buy for the repairs?"

"I'll pick it up and bring you the receipts. That'll be easier. I'll run to the lumberyard and get started today. Do you mind leaving the door unlocked so I can get in if I return before you?"

"I shouldn't be gone long, but I'll leave the key under the rock by the mailbox post."

"Sounds good." Maybe he'd get a chance to look around before she got back.

# *Chapter 10*

Bailey stopped at a stop sign and directed her attention down Main Street at the Victorian storefronts with their painted lady exteriors. Brick sidewalks lined the street, and she spotted an antique shop she wanted to check out. She first stopped at the bank and opened an account to deposit the cash in her purse. It made her nervous to carry so much money. Lily flipped through a magazine while Bailey took care of business.

As soon as she stepped outside, she saw the public utility sign, but she doubted it would be open on a Saturday. She might be without power for the weekend.

Lily hummed tunelessly and stared off into space.

"Come on, Lily, we need to go in here for a minute." Bailey took her arm and tried to steer her to the door to the utility office, but Lily shook her head and planted her feet. Bringing her to town hadn't been Bailey's best idea, but when she'd tried to drop Lily at home, the elderly woman protested and refused to get out of the car.

Bailey pointed out a bench by a display of fading roses. "You wait here for me, okay?"

Lily settled on the bench and plucked at the strings on the sleeve of her robe. "Curse of Cain. Devil's spawn."

Bailey sighed and hurried to the door. She yanked on it. Locked.

"They're not open until Monday."

Bailey shifted to see a woman pulling weeds from the planting bed.

"Is Lily with you today?" The woman, middle-aged and graying, gave her a sharp glance.

"Yes."

The woman put a hand to her back and straightened. "She's never been the same since her husband died five years ago. You'd never know it now, but she used to be perfectly turned out every time you'd see her—every hair in place, the latest style of clothes, shoes, and handbags. She went downhill fast after he died. She probably should be in a nursing home, but no one seems to know where her daughter has gone. She used to check on her occasionally, but I'll bet it's been a year or more since she came to town."

Bailey's heart squeezed. No one should be abandoned in their old age like that. She had to try to find that daughter. "Thanks for the information."

The temperature was in the fifties today but felt warmer with the sunshine beating down. Bailey frowned. Lily had left the spot where she'd been sitting. She was just here a minute ago. "Lily!"

Several people glanced her way when she shouted, and one man pointed toward the antique shop. "She went in there."

She thanked him and ran across the street to go inside. Lily stood by a beautiful old trunk. Her long fingers caressed the worn wood. She opened the top of the trunk and tried to lift out the tray inside. Was she looking for something?

Lily spotted Bailey. "My music is gone. It was here just a minute ago."

An Asian woman with long black hair and a friendly smile shifted toward her. "Are you with Lily? I didn't see anyone come in with her."

"Yes, I'm her neighbor Bailey Fleming. I hope she hasn't harmed anything."

"I didn't see her do much except explore the trunk. I stopped in with some lavender the owner ordered." She held out a slim hand. "Michelle Diskin, Jermaine's wife. He said he met you. It's sweet of you to look out for her. I stopped by to see her this morning, but she was gone. I was worried."

Bailey told her about her late-night visit from Lily. "Did she own my cabin at one time? She seems to think she used to live there."

Michelle's smooth forehead furrowed. "Not that I know of, but we've only been in town about five years. It's possible her family owned the entire tract of land out that way. I've heard the Norman family was one of the founders of the town, so she'd know a lot of history about this place."

And it was all locked in her brain.

"Jermaine said you're leaving on vacation soon."

Michelle moved her brightly colored skirt out of Lily's way as the elderly woman moved to examine a desk. "Tomorrow actually. I'm finishing up a few errands before we go."

"Have a great time. I'll look after Lily."

"It will ease our minds. She's a sweet little thing. Before she got . . . sick, she used to bring the kids cookies and fudge. She'd play hide-and-seek with them, and we'd often have her over to dinner. She went downhill so fast. It's sad."

Bailey's gaze strayed to Lily again. "I wish she could tell me all the history. This seems like a wonderful town."

"It is. People here care about each other."

"I've found that out. A neighbor has already offered to put my dilapidated house in order, and everyone is making sure Lily is all right. I'm used to bigger cities. Well, except for the last place I lived, which is a lot like this."

"You told Jermaine you had experience with the elderly. Are you a nurse?"

Bailey nodded.

Michelle eyed her. "I don't suppose you're looking for a job?"

The part-time job probably wouldn't be enough long term. "I might be."

"My friend's son had a brain injury that left him blind. It might be temporary, but so far nothing has changed. Helen's interested in having someone come by a few hours every two days to check him over, help him orient himself and shower, that kind of thing." Michelle named a generous salary. "I told her I'd be on the lookout for someone suitable. If you're interested, I can give you her number."

"Would it be for Jason Yarwood?"

Michelle's beautiful black eyes widened. "It is."

"I met his ex-wife when I arrived in town yesterday. She pretty much hired me on the spot."

"I wondered if those two would get back together after all they went through. Glad to hear she cares enough about Jason to hire you." She smiled and glanced over to check on Lily, who was focused on a fireplace mantel. "Where'd you come from?"

"A little town called Rock Harbor, Michigan. I've forgotten all the places when I was in grade school, but I went to four different schools before I was in the sixth grade."

"Goodness, you need to stop and catch your breath." Michelle tipped her head to one side and studied Bailey's face. "You remind me of someone, but I can't put my finger on who just yet. I think it's the eyes." Her gaze shifted over Bailey's shoulder. "No, Lily, that might break." She sprang past Bailey to take a lamp out of Lily's hands.

"I'd better get her home," Bailey said. "I want to give her a bath and wash her hair."

"You say that like you've had experience caring for the elderly."

"A little bit." Bailey smiled and clasped Lily's hand to lead her to the door.

---

Lance had brought his yellow Chevy C-10 pickup instead of his Acadia so he could pick up supplies, and he'd been careful to put out a tarp to protect his baby's bed. He drove carefully to the cabin but left the stack of lumber in the truck and got out into overcast skies and a cold wind that ran down his spine. He grabbed a sock hat and gloves, then zipped up his jacket to take a stroll around the outside before Bailey got back. She wouldn't take kindly to him poking around out here when she'd hired him to repair her house.

He walked over soft, uneven ground and entered the woods at the back of the property. The red cedar, Sitka spruce, and western hemlock formed a canopy over soft mosses, yellow skunk cabbage, and deer fern. The air held the odor of moss and mold mingled with grass. Lance examined the understory of vegetation for tracks and paths—and struck pay dirt. Most of the vegetation had been trampled through here. He followed the path down to the water where the grayed pier stuck out into the calm water.

This was a perfect landing place. A fairly large boat could get in here with cargo and be unseen. Hardly anyone lived out this way and the cabin sat on ten acres, so there was plenty of privacy. He walked onto the pier and inhaled the briny scent of the sea. An eagle soared overhead and landed in a tall red cedar. Several sea otters chattered along the shore, then dove into the pristine waters.

Everywhere he looked wildlife abounded. This would be a conservationist's dream, probably because no one had lived here for so long. He walked out on the pier a little ways, noting where several planks needed replacing. The pier felt fairly sound though and didn't wobble when he walked.

He retraced his steps and headed back toward the house. As he got closer to the road, he heard the whine of a chain saw. He followed the noise through the woods and across a mostly downed barbed-wire fence to where the trees grew thicker, and he had to climb over several fallen trees.

He recognized the man as Jermaine Diskin, the next-door neighbor. He'd spoken with him a few months back when he'd checked out this property. He waited for Diskin to notice him and shut off the chain saw.

Diskin nodded. "Agent Phoenix, isn't it?"

"You have a good memory, Mr. Diskin."

"Comes with the job."

Lance knew Diskin was a paramedic and took care of kids

his boss transported by plane from Alaska. Admirable work, and he'd liked the young man the moment they'd met. "You have a new neighbor."

Diskin removed his wool hat with its earflaps and wiped the perspiration from his forehead. "I met her yesterday. Seems nice enough. You're not investigating her, are you?"

He would have to keep Diskin from alerting Bailey to his investigation. "Just keeping an eye on this place. You know much about her?"

"Just that she's a nurse and immediately offered to look in on our elderly neighbor. That makes her tops in my book."

In Lance's too. "Anything else?"

"Not really. She talked like she wasn't sure how long she was staying. I have to admit I was curious how she came to be here, but something about her made me keep my mouth shut. She seemed scared, but maybe I'm reading more into her manner than I should."

"I noticed a path through the property down to the pier. Looked like someone had been through there recently. You happen to see anything?"

Diskin shook his head. "I didn't see anything, but I heard a scream a few days ago. I got up to investigate, but I didn't see anyone, so I thought maybe an owl got a rabbit. Didn't like it though. The next morning I drove past the little cabin, but everything seemed the same."

A scream? That put Lance on high alert. "Anything else you've noticed?"

"Not until Bailey arrived. I sometimes stop and peer in the windows just to make sure everything is okay. I've never seen anything off inside or out."

"Thanks for the information. I'd appreciate it if you don't tell Ms. Fleming I'm an FBI agent. I'm going to poke around for a few days and make sure she's okay."

"Sure thing, Agent Phoenix. I'll be out of town with the family for about ten days, so I won't be around to blow your cover. In fact, if you need to use my house for anything, help yourself. The key's under the wheelbarrow in the shed. There's a spare room on the second floor. I'd hate for anything to happen to Bailey. I have the feeling she's here looking for somewhere to hide."

"Nice of you to offer, Mr. Diskin. Have a great vacation."

Lance walked back the way he'd come and exited the woods into the front yard of the little cabin. Every time he was in this area, he marveled at how kind people were.

His phone rang, and Daniel was calling. "Hey, buddy, I was about to call you."

"Yeah, well, we've got a tip on wily Alfie's whereabouts. I'm headed there now. Someone called it in a few minutes ago and told us he had four girls at an apartment in Port Townsend."

Lance's gut tightened. "I'll head that way now."

"I've got a replacement to help me already. Chief says to stay there and see what you can find out about Baker Holdings. We're not positive this tip is real, so don't blow your cover by rushing off. I'll let you know what I find."

Though he knew the orders were the right thing to do, Lance chafed at being left out. What if one of the girls was his sister? The likelihood was slim though, so he ended the call with Daniel and headed to unload the truck.

## *Chapter 11*

Even from the road, Bailey noticed the derelict appearance of the large cabin. She parked in the drive at Lily's house. It was a cedar-log home, too, larger than Bailey's, and hidden in the woods down a nearly impenetrable dirt drive. She pushed inside to find the house in total disarray. Dust lay thick on the wood floors and tables, and heaps of quilting supplies lay in several different areas. The dirty windows blocked most of the light struggling to get in. Lily's bedsheets were grimy, and the whole place smelled bad.

She'd tackle the house once she got Lily clean.

Lily didn't fight Bailey as she disrobed her and got her in the shower. She washed the elderly woman's dirty white hair, then wrapped her in a big towel and helped her dress. She combed out Lily's hair, then braided it so it would stay neat.

With a quilt on her lap, Lily curled up on the decrepit brown sofa and looked at her with bright, aware eyes. "I like you. Could I have some tea? I'm a little hungry."

"I like you, too, Lily." Trying not to notice the bits of food, dirt, and mud on the chair opposite Lily, Bailey perched on the edge of the cushion. Maybe she could get some information out of the woman now. "Do you have your daughter's phone number? I'd like to contact her, then I'll fix you some tea and lunch."

"Liv's number should be in my phone book in the kitchen."

Bailey left Lily in the living room and went through a doorway into the kitchen. Did Bailey dare to rummage through things? The stacks of dishes on the counter looked like they could topple over and kill her at any moment. A mouse squeaked and ran past her hand as she moved a tower of plates. She dropped the plates and stepped back with a shriek. Her heart pounded and her mouth was dry. This was so much worse than she thought.

"Are you okay, dear?" Lily called.

"Yes, I'm fine. A mouse startled me." She'd have to get some traps.

After taking a deep breath, she began to rummage through the kitchen again, but nothing looked like a phone book or address book. Shuddering, she moved things out of the sink, then ran hot water and dumped in a lot of dish soap. She loaded the filled sink with dishes and cutlery until she could find a space on the old Formica counter. She washed it and glanced in the refrigerator. Nothing but sour milk, a partial stick of hard butter, and various small containers of moldy leftovers.

No wonder Lily was so skinny. When did she last have a good meal? Probably when Michelle and Jermaine brought something over. This was a seriously bad situation. Bailey managed to find a box of macaroni and cheese mix in the cupboard and put water on the stove to boil. While it heated, she washed dishes and cleared away the trash on the counter.

By the time the macaroni and tea were ready, the kitchen

surfaces could at least be seen. She ladled macaroni into a bowl and poured a cup of tea for both of them, then carried Lily's lunch to her and returned for her own tea. By the time she came back into the living room, Lily had inhaled several bites of food.

"You were hungry."

Lily nodded. "Did you find the number?" she mumbled around a full mouth.

"Not yet." Bailey glanced around the living room. Built-ins appeared on both sides of the fireplace, and she spied picture albums and other books on the right side. She set down her tea, knelt in front of the shelves, and pulled out a stack of picture albums and books.

When she didn't find an address book, she flipped through the first album. The early ones were in black and white, and she recognized Lily only after she reached her teens in the family photos. The landscape looked like this area with the dock at the water, but it could have been a large lake also.

She flipped open the second album. These pictures were of Lily with a man, presumably her husband. Bailey carried it to the sofa and showed the elderly woman, who had practically licked clean the bowl of macaroni and cheese. "Is this your husband?"

Lily smiled. "That's Roger. He was a wonderful husband."

Bailey didn't want to ask how long Roger had been dead, so she moved to the next picture, one of the Normans with a little girl. "Is this your daughter?"

"Yes, that's Liv."

The child's sweet expression reminded her of dozens of other photos of other children. Bailey flipped to the next page and saw the little girl getting older. Then there were just ones of Lily and Roger.

"Why are there no pictures of your daughter any longer?"

Lily's smile faded. "Roger insisted she go off to finishing school after high school for six months. He wanted me to travel with him. I argued with him, of course, but once he had his mind set, there was no changing it." She lowered her voice to a whisper. "She was seeing someone most unsuitable, and Roger hoped some time away would squelch the romance."

"Did it?"

Lily shook her head. "She was quite infatuated with him."

Bailey closed the book and went to fetch the last. "When did she come home from finishing school?"

"She was twenty, such a beautiful girl. You'd have thought all that money we spent would have made her wiser, but she never had a good head on her shoulders. The man she took up with . . ." Lily snapped her mouth shut and stared down at her bowl. "Never mind."

Bailey opened the burgundy cover and glanced at the first picture. She blinked as she struggled to take in the reality of that photo, but she'd seen it before. Her mother holding a tiny baby who was maybe two weeks old.

She sank to her knees in front of Lily. "Is this Liv? Her name is Olivia?"

Lily smiled. "Yes, it's Olivia and baby Bailey. Isn't she beautiful? I wish Olivia would bring the baby to see me. I'll bet she's six months old by now."

Bailey closed her eyes and took several deep breaths. This dear lady was her grandmother. How did she go about discovering all the secrets she knew?

❦

When Shauna got home from her errands, she found the house clean and neat as always. The scent of garlic and cheese hung in the air. They had pizza for lunch. Taylor was a good babysitter.

She and Alex were playing Go Fish in the living room. "Hey, sport." Shauna ruffled his hair.

Her five-year-old son was the spitting image of his dead father, Jack, right down to his auburn hair and turquoise eyes. Alex's bear, Blueberry, was tucked into the chair with him. "Hey, Mommy, I beat Taylor two different times."

"Good for you! How about you go get a snack? I need to talk to Taylor a minute."

"She told me she's going to learn to fly. That's cool." Alex got up and trotted off to the kitchen.

Moments later the door to the microwave slammed and Shauna knew he was making popcorn. It was his favorite snack, and she and Zach could hardly keep it in the house.

"I've got some books for you to start reading." Shauna went to the bookcase and removed new flight primers, ones she'd used herself.

When she turned, she noticed Taylor was much more subdued than she'd been this morning. "What's wrong, honey?"

Taylor's troubled eyes flooded with tears. "I read that article you gave me. It scared me, and I called Dad. He's coming over here to pick me up. He's really mad, and he wants to find out more about Ryan, so now I'm not sure if I did the right thing."

Shauna clasped her shoulders. "You did the right thing." She gave her a comforting shake. "No normal twentysomething cruises the web looking for fourteen-year-old girls. You don't even use makeup, so no one would ever mistake you for even eighteen. There's something fishy going on with that guy. I'm proud of you. I didn't think you'd listen."

Taylor managed a watery smile. "I always listen to you, Shauna." The doorbell rang, and she spun around with her hand to her mouth. "That's got to be Dad."

"I'll let him in and the two of you can talk."

Taylor reached for her. "No! I need you to stay with me."

"Okay, I'll be here." Shauna opened the door to face Harry Whitewell.

In his fifties, he was handsome with blond hair that held only a little gray at the temples. He must have come from the golf course, because he wore khakis and a blue polo shirt. She had confidence he'd do something about that lowlife targeting his daughter.

The judge's mouth was set and strained, and his hazel eyes peered past her. "Taylor's here, isn't she?"

"Come on in. She's in the living room." Shauna shut the door behind him and hoped she was never the target of that stern expression. The scent of tobacco followed him.

He stopped in the entry. "Thanks for your wise counsel to Taylor, Shauna. You're a good friend, and I appreciate how you talked to her about this. I'm just sorry she didn't tell us about Ryan right from the start."

"No harm done, Judge. She hasn't met with the guy or anything."

His jaw flexed. "And she's not going to." He marched to the living room where Taylor stood with her hands behind her back and trepidation on her face. "I'd like to see this guy's profile."

Taylor handed over her phone without a word. "After I read that article, I checked to see if he was on Facebook. I don't use

Facebook, so I had to create a profile. He's on there, too, and he's been talking with lots of other girls."

The judge's face was thunderous. "Lowlife hood." He took the phone and sat on the sofa, then scanned through the posts and the man's profile. "He's got to be at least twenty-five."

That had been Shauna's guess too.

The phone chimed, and the judge frowned. "You got a private message. I thought you said you weren't on Facebook."

"I wasn't." Taylor went to sit by him and took her phone. She tapped the screen. "It's him. I made a profile with a different name and then found him and friended him about an hour ago."

"What's the message say?" her dad demanded.

Color ran up her face, and she handed the phone back to her dad. "It's all flirty. I think he's what you said he was, Shauna." Her voice quivered.

"Does he know who you really are?"

Taylor shook her head. "I never used my real name. He probably didn't either. I was so stupid!"

Shauna went to sit on her other side and put her arm around her shoulders. "It's not your fault, Taylor. You didn't know there were predators like that out there."

"I'm turning him in to the FBI," the judge said. "His profile says he lives in Port Townsend, but it's hard to say if he really does. Maybe law enforcement can track him down and see what he's up to. I hope he hasn't done any harm to anyone. I don't like the smell of this at all."

Shauna shifted uneasily. The world suddenly seemed very unsafe, and she feared for Alex as well. It wasn't just girls targeted by predators. She and Zach would need to watch Alex's internet usage closely.

## *Chapter 12*

If only her mother were still alive. Bailey's thoughts were a jumble as she cleaned Lily's house. While she didn't have time to do a perfect job, at least there were clean sheets on the bed, a sparkling bathroom and kitchen, and a vacuumed floor and furniture cushions. She'd come back tomorrow and do a better job.

But what would she do with this new knowledge? She wasn't alone in the world after all—she had a grandmother. Maybe aunts and uncles and cousins too. A world of possibilities lay in that direction. The first thing she needed to do was get power of attorney. She couldn't let her grandmother live in these conditions.

Why had her mother lied to her all these years? She claimed her parents were dead, yet Lily still lived in the same house where Mom had grown up. Mom even made an occasional trip out here to check on her. She probably covered it up by claiming it was a training class. Bailey twisted her mouth and gritted her teeth. She hated lies more than anything.

"Lily, I have to go home to check on the carpenter for a little while. I'll bring you back some dinner, okay?" She touched her grandmother's soft white hair.

Lily didn't respond. The clouds swirled in her eyes again, and her mouth hung slackly as she traveled some road in her past.

Bailey left her and went out into the overcast day. This changed everything. No longer was this place a stopgap hidey-hole, but it held the hope of sanctuary, of home. She couldn't leave Lily to fend for herself even if the killer tracked Bailey here. She longed for friends, someone to share what she was finding out. Some of Lily's friends might be around who could help piece together what happened and why her mom left. Why she never even told her she had a grandmother.

Her part-time job might not be enough. The only bills she had were utilities and food right now, but she would need to take care of Lily's food as well. If Lily required a nursing home, the fifty thousand dollars her mother had left her wouldn't go far. She should have searched for a bank account that told how her grandmother was doing financially. Was she not eating because she was destitute?

Before she started her car, she checked her email. There was finally a reply from the private investigator she'd contacted. She sent off a reply and asked him to look into her mother's past. At least now she had a real name. His retainer was a thousand dollars, and she sent him the payment via PayPal.

She started her car and drove toward home. As she passed the driveway into the Diskin place, she made a split-second decision to turn in. Maybe they would know something.

Jermaine was in the yard blowing leaves when she pulled in and parked. He shaded his eyes with his hand, then waved. He walked over to her as she got out. "Hello, neighbor, everything okay?"

"Yes, I just gave Lily a bath and cleaned up her place a little."

"She let you inside? She usually stops us at the door when we come by with dinner."

"It was pretty bad inside. I made some progress but there's more to do. How well do you know her?"

"Well, she's not easy to get to know with her dementia. We've just been here a couple of years, and she was already foggy when we moved in. I met her daughter once, but she wasn't very talkative either."

Bailey longed to confess what she'd discovered to this nice young man, but she bit back the words and smiled. "Does she have any friends, anyone I could ask about family?"

His forehead wrinkled as he thought for a moment. "Some of the church ladies stop by to check on her. One in particular is pretty agitated about her situation. Clara DeWitt. She lives in town in the assisted-living place, but she has her own car and comes over a couple of times a month. She's tried to get Lily to move into the same home, but Lily won't do it. Of course, most of the time she probably doesn't even know what Clara wants her to do."

Bailey wrote down the name of the home. "Anyone else?"

"The mayor's wife comes by once in a while. She's quite a bit younger, but I think she's friends with Lily's daughter. She might be able to tell you how to reach the daughter. I think her name's Olivia."

There was no reaching Olivia, not now. The sudden surprise of tears flooded Bailey's eyes, and she turned away before Jermaine could see them and wonder. "I guess I'd better get home and find out if my cabin is still standing. Have a nice vacation."

She got back in her car and headed for home. Home. She was already thinking of it with fondness.

❧

A car door slammed and Grayson looked through the big floor-to-ceiling windows to see his girlfriend exiting the old pickup she called Jaws. He threw open the door and embraced her as she stepped across the threshold. A stray lock of light-brown hair caressed a high cheekbone.

Ellie threw her arms around his neck. "Gosh, I missed you!"

He kissed her and she nestled close. Her slim, petite body fitted into his arms as if she'd been made for him—which he was beginning to think was the case. Their feelings had grown quickly in the danger swirling around them from a terrorist plot that had nearly taken her life.

He released her far enough to rest his hands on her shoulders and look her over. Her hair was down on her shoulders, and she wasn't wearing her glasses, probably just for him. She'd finally admitted they'd been a shield against the world getting too close, and since they'd started dating, she'd been more willing to embrace relationship.

Her eyes always mesmerized him—light brown with so many yellow flecks they looked golden. He planted another kiss on her mouth before steering her to the kitchen. "I've got spaghetti about done. You hungry?"

Her small hand curved trustingly into his. "Starved. Lunch should have been two hours ago. Is that coffee I smell? What about Bailey? Did you get any leads on her?"

His smile faded, and he shook his head. "Not a hint of where she went. I'm not giving up though. How's the house coming?"

"I've worked my tail off for hours. The house is done though."

He grinned at the triumph in her voice. She and Jason flipped houses, and they were good at what they did. She'd been working on the House at Saltwater Point for weeks, and its completion would mean a lot to her since she planned to keep it.

He released her hand and went to pour them coffee. "Congratulations! When are you moving in?"

"Right away, maybe this weekend."

"It's okay with Jason?"

Her smile dropped away. "He doesn't seem to care about anything. I sorely miss bouncing projects off him and his help with the work. If his sight doesn't come back, I'm not sure what I'm going to do."

"Is there anything he can do if he stays blind? Any job he could do for the business?

She took a sip of the coffee he handed her. "I did some research. There are some computer programs that will help the blind do accounting and that kind of thing. If he's willing to learn, I think I could come up with something. We've been talking about hiring some office help anyway. It would go a long way toward bolstering his self-respect too. Mac says he's depressed and angry."

"Can't really blame him." Grayson drained the spaghetti and dumped it in a bowl, then added the sauce before pulling the garlic bread from the oven. "Let's eat."

There were no easy answers about Jason. If his eyesight didn't come back, the future would be a hazy road to travel.

The cabin already looked better. Bailey parked her car and studied the repaired roof. Lily sat beside her with her wrinkled hands clutching the picture album in her lap. She hadn't let go of it since Bailey found the picture of Mom and baby Bailey. The clouds had swept into Lily's eyes and stayed there. Bailey couldn't leave her home alone, not in her confused state, so she'd bundled her into the car and brought her down for dinner.

She opened Lily's door and helped her out. "I got a few groceries and ice for the cooler. I thought I'd make turkey sandwiches for lunch. Are you hungry, Lily?"

When the old woman didn't answer, Bailey sighed and led her inside the cabin. She got her settled on the sofa, then checked on Sheba and found her sleeping under the bed. Bailey followed the sound of pounding on the back of the cabin where Lance knelt hammering new boards onto the deck. She watched him for a moment while he was too focused to notice her.

Nice-looking guy. Obviously muscular but not overly bulky—just the perfect amount of muscles. His big hands were making short work of the job at hand. His Seahawks sweatshirt made her smile. Were all guys sports fans? A lock of his nearly black hair fell over his forehead, and his dark eyes focused on his task.

He might have a bit of Asian blood in him, though it was hard to tell for sure. He seemed the dependable type, but she was clearly not a good judge of men. Look how Kyle had taken her in. Still, this guy seemed like the stand-up kind. She liked him.

She cleared her throat. "You made it back."

He smiled at her. "I've gotten a lot done already. I didn't notice any power coming on though."

"I can't get it on until Monday, just like we thought."

He swiped the back of his arm over his damp forehead. "Still a lot more to do. I've barely made a dent in this deck, but at least the roof will keep you dry."

"I'm about to make turkey sandwiches for lunch. You hungry?"

He dropped his hammer onto the deck and stood. "I could eat a horse. I meant to bring a sandwich but left it in the fridge. I appreciate your offer to feed me. It's not your fault I planned so poorly."

"I have an ulterior motive." She stepped through the back door he held open for her and gestured to Lily, who had fallen asleep on the sofa with the photo album clutched to her chest. "I wondered what you knew about her. How long have you been neighbors?"

He turned his back to her and went to sluice water over his hands from a bottle. It was several moments before he replied. "I live on the road the next mile over. I haven't run into her much. Sorry not to have more information, but I could ask around. Are you searching for her family?"

"Family, friends, someone who might be able to make a decision about her. She needs to be in full-time care. One of these days she'll wander off into the woods and not be found until spring. I'm surprised it hasn't already happened."

"She's that bad?" He faced her. "I haven't been around anyone with this kind of condition. Is it Alzheimer's?"

"Probably. Some kind of severe dementia, but a doctor would have to make the final diagnosis. I'd lay money on Alzheimer's though. I see it all the time at my work."

"Your work?"

"I'm a geriatric nurse."

He winced. "That takes a special kind of person to be willing to deal with that. What made you choose geriatrics?"

No one had ever asked her that before, and she felt tongue-tied to admit what had driven her in her heart of hearts. "I always wanted grandparents, so every time we moved, I found an elderly couple in my neighborhood to hang out with while Mom was at work. We moved so often many took me in and nurtured a lonely little girl."

His dark eyes shadowed. "That's hard."

She shrugged. "I grew to love elderly people. So much wisdom, so much unconditional love to share. That's the thing with the elderly—by the time they're facing their own mortality, they've learned the true value of love and acceptance. I often didn't feel that from my mom."

Her face heated, and she moved toward the stove. Why was she sharing such personal stuff with this guy? She didn't know him from Adam, but he had such a compassionate manner. It wasn't something she'd ever noticed in a man before. Of course they moved so much she hadn't gotten past the barely-getting-to-know-you phase.

"I think you're right. Good grandparents give you the ability to find your wings and reach for the sky," he said behind her. "My grandparents always encouraged me to trust my instincts and work hard."

So he did understand. She'd thought he would. What would he think if he knew the situation she'd left behind in Rock Harbor? She trusted her instincts when she fled here, but she'd made enough bad decisions that she wasn't sure her instincts were trustworthy.

# *Chapter 13*

When Lance dropped onto the dock, the sun hadn't come up yet. He rubbed gritty eyes as the first rays of gold and orange rose above the water. An early morning ferry motored across the water in the distance, and the smell of diesel mingled with the scent of salt and kelp. He huddled in his jacket from the wind and took out his phone to review his calendar.

The date hit him. November 10, Ava's twenty-first birthday. And he was no closer to finding her than he was at this time last year. There would be no big birthday bash for her, no presents. He'd told himself if he found her by her birthday, he would buy her a car and had saved money for it all year.

The bleakness of a lifetime spent searching for his sister and never finding her stretched out in front of him like a desert without water. But the not knowing was impossible to live with. He *had* to find her. Absolutely had to, no matter what it took.

His phone rang. He took it out of his pocket and winced. "Hey, Mom. How you doing?" The sob on the other end told him everything he needed to know. "I'm having a rough morning too." The sun's rays began to warm his chilled skin.

It was another moment before her choked voice came through the phone. "Did you talk to your father?" Even after all these years in the States, she still held on to a trace of her Cambodian accent.

"No, not yet."

Every birthday he dutifully called his parents to let them know he remembered, too, that he hadn't forgotten his quest.

"Any word today?"

"I feel we're getting closer."

"That's what you say every time I ask. We're never going to know what happened to her, are we? We never should have fought with her like that."

"And then what? You let her do whatever she wanted, go out with some older guy without a word? She'd still be gone if you did that, Mom. It's not your fault. Ava was young and stupid like every teenager. You can't fix that yourself. Only experience helps that teenage idiocy. I had it too."

"You never argued with us like that."

"No, I just sneaked out." He rubbed his forehead. "Let go of the guilt, Mom. It's ruining your life." There was no answer on the other end. "Mom?"

"I'm here. Listen, I have to go, Lance. I just wanted to hear your voice."

The call ended before he could say good-bye, and he sat staring at the blank screen. A sob built in his throat, and he choked it down until all that emerged was a strangled sound.

He picked up a rock and threw it as hard as he could into the silvery waves. He closed his eyes a moment, then took out his small pocket Bible.

Sheba bounded ahead of Bailey on the path through the woods, then romped back to circle her feet. Savannah cats loved exercise, and Bailey was always amazed at how far her cat could leap after the ball. The sunshine was hot on her arms today, warming the chill from last night's low of forty-five. Lily had been here for three nights now and was still sleeping when Bailey left the cabin to take the cat for a walk.

She'd trained Sheba to the leash, but the cat preferred the freedom of chasing small animals and leaves, so Bailey let her run free. Sheba never wandered far because she was so tightly focused on Bailey.

She hid and let Sheba find her several times before she walked down to the water. She heard a sound, almost like a sob, and stopped to listen. A flash of blue caught her eye, and she saw a figure sitting on the side of the dock. She squinted through the trees. Lance. He had his head buried in his hands, and the dejected pose tugged her forward.

She stepped out of the canopy of trees, and he straightened at the creak of her feet on the wood. "You okay?"

"Fine." His clipped voice warned her off. He tucked what appeared to be a small Bible into the pocket of his flannel shirt.

She stepped closer. "Sometimes it helps to talk to someone." Her heart clenched at the sorrow on his face. Whatever grief dogged him, it made tears well in her eyes too.

He rose and pivoted toward her. "You can't help with this, though I appreciate the concern. I was waiting until you were up before I got to work."

She examined his hooded eyes and pinched mouth. "Did you get any sleep last night?"

"I brought my nail gun today. That will make repairing the deck faster."

She wasn't going to pry it out of him, so she gave a mental shrug. "Sounds good. I have to go check on a new patient today."

Sheba gave a momentous leap from the ground to a tree branch, and Lance's eyes widened. "That's no house cat."

"She's bred from an African serval and a house cat. Her breeding is F1, which means she's a first generation. These cats retain more of the wild characteristics of a serval."

"Is she likely to hurt someone? She's big enough to do some damage."

"She's gentle and loyal. Savannahs are playful and very focused on their owners. Crazy smart too. She plays hide-and-seek and fetch. Now if you try to hurt me, she might take you on."

"I'll remember that. She's pretty with those spots."

He'd successfully steered the conversation away from his obvious distress, so Bailey hid a small grin and veered toward the house. "Lily is still asleep in the bedroom, but I'm sure she'll be up shortly. You can start whenever you'd like."

"There's only one bedroom. Where did you sleep?"

"The sofa."

"What are you going to do about her?" His voice was gentle.

She looked away, unwilling to tell him of the familial relationship yet. "I'm not sure. Try to find her family for one thing, maybe friends. I have some ideas on where to start. Someone needs to know about her condition. I can't just let her wander the wilderness. She'll end up dying of exposure."

"You just got here, yet you made it your business to take charge of her."

"There's no one else."

"That wouldn't matter to most people."

"And there you have why I became a nurse." She forced a chuckle. "I'm a busybody and get involved when I shouldn't."

"I didn't say you shouldn't. You put the rest of us to shame."

She tilted a glance up at him as they walked through the fallen leaves toward the house. "I don't think you would have ignored her plight. You were on my doorstep offering help before I barely had a chance to look around the cabin. We're two of a kind."

He glanced away as if her praise made him uncomfortable. "Lily's up."

She followed his gaze and saw the elderly woman wandering the yard. She had a mug in her hand, probably the old coffee Lance had left in the thermos. Lily made a beeline for an old shed and tugged on the padlock. "What's she doing?" Bailey picked up the pace.

When she neared Lily, the older woman's tugging had become frantic. "What's wrong, Lily? That's just an old shed."

"She needs me to let her out." Lily yanked on the door again.

Bailey fished the keys out of her pocket and unlocked the padlock. "There's nothing inside but yard tools." She'd peered in the window, so she already knew what it held. The door swung open, and air thick with the odor of grease and gasoline rushed out. "See? The mower and trimmer are right there. It's just tools. No one's in here."

Lily slid a blank stare around the space, then clutched herself and backed away. Her gaze began to clear of the clouds. "It's you, Bailey. I thought you were calling me. I'm hungry."

"Let me make you some breakfast." She glanced at Lance who'd been standing quietly behind her. "You hungry?"

"I wouldn't say no to breakfast. I had a protein bar about an hour ago."

She wrinkled her nose. "That's not enough. I found a propane gas cooktop yesterday. I'll fix eggs." She whistled for her cat, and Sheba made a low growl. Bailey frowned. "What's wrong, sweet girl?" Sheba made many odd sounds, but she rarely growled. The cat had her golden eyes fixed on Lily.

The older woman backed away, then bolted for the house. Sheba leaped down and chased after her. Bailey ran to try to stop the cat, but Lily reached the door safely and slipped inside with the screen door banging behind the dirty hem of her trailing robe. The cat, big ears pricked forward, came bounding back to Bailey as if she'd done what she set out to do.

"You leave Lily alone," Bailey scolded. "You'll scare her to death."

Lance put his hands in his pockets and grinned. "So much for being gentle. She chased Lily like a rabid dog."

"She wouldn't have hurt her. I don't understand what got into her." But if that behavior continued, it could cause problems with caring for Lily.

So much to do today. King sat at this desk with the sunrise gilding the rhododendrons and trees with an early morning dress of red and gold. Just like his Apsaras. Friday night's take had been stellar, the best night so far, all thanks to Lotus's beauty.

The door opened, and Chey stepped inside with a tray of coffee and bagels. "You're here early, sir."

He accepted the coffee Chey offered and took a sip. "Did you dispose of the bodies?"

"Not yet. I dispatched a couple of men to handle it, but they reported that a couple of FBI agents are hanging around the area. I gave orders to cease moving any of the girls through there until they're gone."

King spooned Rainier cherry jam onto his bagel. "Any idea why the FBI is nosing around?"

"No, but it may have nothing to do with us."

Or it could. King frowned and took a bite of the bagel. He didn't reach this position by ignoring possible threats. He'd see if the sheriff had any idea of what was going on out on Red Cedar Road.

He picked up his coffee mug. "What about Bailey?"

"She still hasn't surfaced."

He slammed the mug onto his desk, and coffee sloshed onto the polished surface. "You need to find her now. If the police find her first and she blabs any of her mother's business, it won't be good."

Too late he realized he shouldn't give Chey too much information. He grabbed a napkin and mopped up the coffee. "Never mind. Just keep looking for her. She could be an asset."

Chey nodded and slipped back out of the room. When the door closed, he leaned back in his chair and stared out the window. Where could she have gone?

## *Chapter 14*

While Lance worked on her cabin, Bailey took Sheba with her to meet her new patient while Lily stayed behind with Lance. The cat would be out of Lance's way, and Jason might even be interested in hearing about her unusual pet. She made a quick stop and paid to get the utilities activated, then headed for Jason's house.

Her GPS led her to a white cottage trimmed in green with a brick path leading to the front door. It looked vaguely Craftsman with its roofline and the shape of the pillars on the front porch.

A small church on a hillside had a clear view of his backyard. Maybe next week she could try it out.

With Sheba in one arm, she rang the bell and waited. The distant sound of canned laughter told her he was watching TV. When no one answered the door, she rang the bell again, then pounded on the door with her fist. "Mr. Yarwood, it's your nurse, Bailey Fleming."

Still no answer. She tried the doorknob. It turned under her fingers, and she pushed open the door. "Mr. Yarwood?"

"In here." His voice was gravelly and held more than a hint of irritation.

Sheba stiffened at the gruff tone and hissed. Bailey stroked her soft fur. "Shh. Don't get us thrown out," she whispered.

The inside of the home was just as charming as the outside—or at least it would be if it were clean. Shoes and clothing lay scattered on the lightly stained oak floors and dirty coffee mugs and soup bowls covered every table surface in the living room. The furniture was pale-gray leather and probably expensive, but drips of coffee and milk spotted the cushions and the armrests. Of course Jason couldn't see to clean up any spills, but she was surprised Mac hadn't hired a maid service to come by once a week. Or maybe it was time for a cleaning, and this was how it appeared after a week.

She made a mental note to talk to Mac about it. Cleaning house was outside her nursing duties.

Studying the man in the gray recliner, she was shocked to see he was so young. Probably in his late twenties. Muscles rippled under his T-shirt and jeans, and he had sun-streaked brown hair that gave him an attractive, boyish look. His brown eyes stared off into space in the direction of the TV.

Bailey picked up the remote and muted the TV. "Mr. Yarwood, I'm Bailey, your new nurse. Did Mac tell you I was coming by? Look at this place. You ever hear that 'God is not a God of confusion but of peace'?"

He merely grunted. "I don't need someone to show me how to live blind. This"—he waved a hand over his eyes—"is going to end any day." His voice held a touch of desperation.

She fell silent, marshaling her thoughts. "Mr. Yarwood—"

"Call me Jason. Sheesh, I'm not my dad."

"Jason, this place is a pigsty. With a little direction you can keep it clean and take care of yourself. A big, muscular man like you must hate being dependent on anyone. I can teach you to take charge of your life while you're waiting for your sight to return. What could it hurt to learn some new skills? They might come in handy if you're ever trapped in a dark cave." She chuckled to try to lighten the moment. Sheba struggled to get down, and Bailey tried to shush her noises.

Jason tipped his head to one side. "You have a kid with you or something?"

"I brought my cat. There's some work going on at my house today, and I didn't want her to get out. She's worth too much money, plus she's my baby." Bailey approached him and took his hand to place it on Sheba. "She looks like a cheetah with spots and long legs. She's a special breed called a Savannah. She's bred from a wild serval cat and a domestic cat."

He ran his hands down the cat's sleek coat and tall ears. "Those ears!" His fingers continued on down her long legs. "I can kind of picture her. Coloring just like a cheetah?"

"Yes, she's a golden. Some of the Savannahs come in different colors. There are whitish-gray ones with black spots, black ones with darker black spots, brown ones with black spots."

"Isn't that something." He continued to pet the cat, and Sheba's loud purr started. "I think she likes me. Can I hold her?"

"Sure." Bailey placed the cat on his lap and went to sit on the chair opposite his.

The strong scent of perspiration told her he hadn't bathed in a while, so that task should be the first one of the day. "I thought we'd get you showered, and then I'd show you how to organize your closet so it's easy to dress yourself. You're still in pajamas."

"I live in pajamas." His mouth flattened into a tight line. "I'm not having a woman give me a bath."

"I don't plan to. I'll get your shower ready, lay out things where you can easily find them, then step out unless you need me."

"That might be all right. Mac would be the last person I'd ever ask for help. She'd as soon stick a knife in my gut as help me."

Bailey raised a brow. "If she didn't care about you, she wouldn't have hired me."

"She wants me to get well so she's rid of the guilt. I was injured saving her from her own bad choices."

Whoa, interesting backstory there. It was none of her business, but she couldn't help but wonder what he meant. "Well, regardless, I'm here and I'll teach you to get along by yourself as much as possible. I'll let you keep Sheba while I get things ready in the bathroom."

She didn't wait for him to object but found her way to the master, a large room that held a king bed and two dressers. Clothing and toiletries were strewn all over the bed and the floor. A door led into the master bath with a large walk-in shower and separate soaking tub. Toiletries, coffee mugs, and saucers covered the double vanity top. She'd have to clean this up first.

She made quick work of stacking dishes and putting away toiletries, then poked her head in the shower. There was a ledge for shampoo and soap, but it was several steps away from the showerhead, which wasn't ideal. The floor wasn't the best place for it either. Maybe the other bathroom had one of those shelves that hung from the shower. She went back into the hall and found the second bathroom. No shelf unit there either.

They'd have to make do today with putting the shampoo and shower gel in the niche. Now to beard the lion in his den.

❧

It had taken forever for Jason to disrobe and shower. Bailey spent her time organizing his bedroom. She moved underwear and socks to logical locations and put pants with matching shirts, organized by colors, on hangers in the closet. The sheets didn't look like they'd been changed in a while, so she stripped the bed and found clean bedding in the hall linen closet.

By the time Jason emerged from the master bathroom to stand in the doorway, the room appeared 100 percent better than the way she'd found it.

Jason ran a hand over his glistening hair. "I can't see if I parted it straight."

"Looks pretty good. You need any hair product?"

He shook his head. He wore jeans and a T-shirt but was still barefoot. "I feel better though. You were right." His tone held a bit of grudging admiration.

"I'll show you where to find everything. Come to the dresser. Count your steps from the bathroom door to my voice."

His eyes were bright as he did so. "Twelve steps."

"Good, remember that. I'm going to take your hand and show you where I've put things." She guided his hand to the top open drawer. "Underwear in the top drawer. Socks in the second drawer. Pajamas in the third drawer, and sweats in the bottom drawer. Got it?"

"Got it."

"Now I'm going to move to the closet." She went to stand in front of the open closet door. "Count your steps to my voice here."

He nodded and walked uncertainly her way. "Six steps, half the distance from the dresser to the bathroom."

He was figuring things out. "I've put a piece of tape on the bar between outfit colors. You pretty much have all blue, black, and red shirts, so from right to left you'll find black, then blue, then red. Feel the tape?" She guided his hand to the tape she'd put on the bar. "I'll bring actual dividers." She guided his hand to a T-shirt. "Black shirts have no safety pin on the hem. Blue has one safety pin, and red has two." She let him finger the hems. "Then you can hang up your own clothes."

He turned away. "You think I'm going to stay blind, don't you?"

"I don't know anything about your diagnosis, Jason, but you might as well be productive while you're waiting. This has to feel good that you can figure things out for yourself."

"I guess."

The doorbell's ring echoed down the hall. "I'll get that. Count your steps to the door from here, then down the hall to join me while I see who that is." She didn't wait for him to answer but went down the hall to the living room and opened the door. "Mayor Weaver, right?"

He smiled. "I didn't expect to see you here, Ms. Fleming. I thought I'd stop and see how Jason is doing."

"Come on in." She stepped out of the way so he could enter. "Mac hired me to help him learn to cope with his situation for the moment. He'll be right in."

The mayor followed her into the living room, and his craggy face didn't show any distaste for the disarray in the living room. Maybe he'd been here before.

Jason, his hand trailing along the hallway wall, approached them. "Nice of you to stop by, Tom."

His voice held the first genuine warmth Bailey had heard. They must be friends. "Can I get the two of you some coffee or anything?"

"Thanks, but I can't stay," the mayor said. "I thought maybe you'd want to get some dinner, Jason. The wife is out of town, and I don't want to go to an empty house tonight until I have to. Harvey's is having a big clam fest tonight with live music. What do you say?"

Jason ran his hand over his damp hair. "I'm tired of being stuck in the house, so maybe I'll take you up on it. It's not like I'm doing anything else."

"Great." The mayor headed for the door. "I'll pick you up around four. We'll beat the rush."

Bailey went to let him out and stepped onto the porch with him. "I think this is the best thing you could have done. You two are old friends?"

"He grew up with my son, Adam. The three of us have spent many hours fishing together. Adam died in a car crash a couple of years ago, and Jason has always been there for me. I want to be here for him too. Judge Whitewell and his kids usually go with us too."

Bailey recognized the grief behind the mayor's words and nodded. "I'll let Mac know where he is."

She went back inside and shut the door. There was much she didn't know yet about her new home, but it was clear people looked out for each other. She liked that.

## *Chapter 15*

The pungent scent of garlic and clams wafted in the air of Harvey's Pier and made Mac's mouth water. She hadn't eaten since breakfast, and it was four thirty. She glanced around the packed restaurant and didn't see an empty table or booth. She approached the hostess stand.

Kelly Willis looked frazzled with her blonde hair in disarray and a flush on her cheeks. She glanced at her seating chart. "It's going to be an hour, Mac."

Mac's stomach couldn't take an hour. She spied her ex-husband sitting with Mayor Weaver in a back booth. "I'll just join Jason and the mayor if that's okay."

Relief lit Kelly's eyes. "That would be great."

Mac threaded her way through the crowd past a boisterous table of college guys throwing back shots. Maybe coming here hadn't been the best idea, but she didn't want to be alone. Loneliness led to too many thoughts of all the mistakes she'd made. Ellie would have told her to come by, but lately Mac felt like a fifth wheel. Ellie and Grayson were the real deal, and she was happy for her sister, but it just made Mac regret the mess she'd made of her own life.

When she drew near the booth, she realized a woman sat on Jason's other side. Felicia Burchell, the sheriff's trophy wife, laughed up at him. The lights in her black hair and the sparkle in her dark-brown eyes made Mac's gut clench. Everyone knew Felicia was crazy about her older husband, but seeing the Asian beauty's charisma made Mac feel dowdy—not that Jason could see her.

She forced a smile. "Mind if I join you? The place is packed, and I didn't want to wait an hour for food."

Jason's smile suddenly shuttered. Was he drawing an internal comparison between Felicia and her? Mac kept her smile steady. Her sense of betrayal held no trace of reality. Nothing was going on between Felicia and Jason, so why was she feeling so down about it?

"Sure thing." Jason's clipped tone indicated the opposite of his words.

The mayor stood. "I have to go anyway. Duty calls." He didn't sound upset. "I'll take care of the bill on my way out. Have whatever you like, Mac. My treat for taking Jason home." He gave them all one last smile, then hurried away before any of them could thank him.

Mac slid into the booth. "That was an abrupt leave-taking. Everything okay?"

Jason felt for his glass of iced tea, and his fingers closed around the beaded glass. "He had a call a minute ago. Some hot crisis down at city hall."

Felicia smiled. "And I hate to be a party pooper, but I need to leave too. Everett texted me he was on his way home. I like to be there when he arrives after a hard day in the office."

Jason slid out to allow her to exit. "Nice to see you, Felicia. Thanks for keeping us company."

"It was good to see you out and about." She ducked her head when she said *see* as if she'd suddenly remembered Jason's blindness.

Jason felt for the edge of the table, then sat back down. "You checking up on me, Mac?"

"What? Of course not! I had no idea you were here."

"Your new spy didn't call and tell you?"

"What new spy?"

"Bailey was there when Tom came by. She knew we were meeting for dinner."

Mac struggled to keep her tone even and calm. "I haven't talked to her. How did it go with her today?"

Jason shrugged. "She organized my bedroom and bathroom. I took a shower. Does that make you feel like your money is well spent?"

The bitterness in his voice tore at her heart. Had she killed all the love he'd once had for her? "I hate seeing what I've done to you, Jason. I'm sorry. I never meant to hurt you." Did she dare tell him how she really felt? She drew in a deep breath. "What can I do to heal things between us?"

Jason lifted a brow. "Heal things? You smashed them beyond repair when you kicked me out, Mac. I don't want your pity."

"I don't pity you." The words *I love you* hovered on her tongue but couldn't make it past her lips. What right did she have to ask for forgiveness?

"Sure feels like pity from where I'm sitting." He took a gulp of iced tea. "You don't need to run me home. I can call an Uber."

"I want to take you home. I'd like to see what Bailey accomplished today."

"I wish you wouldn't come in. It's hard enough knowing

what we once had is gone, but to have you in my place now is setting too many precedents. Ones that will make it even harder on me."

A flutter moved up her spine. Might there still be a chance between them? She would have to tell him how she felt. But not tonight—not when he was so gruff and bitter.

Lance dropped the last piece of lumber onto the pile and wiped perspiration from his brow. Bailey had made a quick pit stop before going out again to check on Lily, and he hoped to have time to prowl the property before she returned. Two sheds were secured with padlocks, and he suspected more evidence might be found inside the house. Squinting, he checked down the road. No telltale plume of dust on the dirt road.

He couldn't cut the locks off and stay within the law. Since they were locked, she'd need to give permission for him to be inside. Maybe he could ask her to look for tools when she got back.

His decision made, he retrieved the key to the house and went inside. He'd barely shut the door behind him when Sheba growled and leaped onto his back. He danced around and swatted at her, but she hissed and bit at his hat. She succeeded in tearing the hat from his head, then dropped off him and pranced to the living room with her spoils.

"What the heck are you?" His back stung where her claws had dug in, and he studied the cat. The other day he hadn't gotten nearly as good a look as he would have liked since the cat had been hanging out in the shadow of the woods.

Long legs, spotted golden coat, with big black ears and intelligent eyes. The cat curled up with his hat, and even from here, he heard its loud purr. He squatted beside Sheba. The cat didn't flatten her ears, and her purr got louder, so he dared to lay his hand on her head and rub.

Amazing cat.

He stood. Where to even begin? The small place was so packed with furniture it felt claustrophobic in spite of the tall ceilings. The stone fireplace took up one full wall, and the sofa and chair close to it were oversized for the room. The bedroom would be the logical place to search for trafficking evidence. He stepped inside. Heaps of quilts lay on top of the bed, and Bailey's suitcase stood open on a chair. She hadn't brought much with her from the looks of it.

He found several condoms under the bed, so there had likely been some activity here since the search last year when they'd hauled away what evidence they found. The bed sat on a threadbare Oriental rug, and he eyed it. Could it hide anything? He lifted the corner of the rug and found nothing.

He heard the crunch of tires on gravel. She was back. He darted from the bedroom into the kitchen and out the back door, where he knelt at the worst of the rotten boards.

Bailey poked her head out the door. "Oh good, you're back. I see you bought a bunch more wood. Can I get the receipt? I don't want you to be out anything."

"Sure." He fished it from his shirt pocket and handed it to her.

His hand grazed hers, and he froze at the electricity sparking between them. Or was it just him who felt it?

"Where's Lily?"

"Sleeping at her house. She insisted on staying home, so I let her." Lance didn't know what to make of her and the care she was showing the old lady. Commendable. "Your attack cat is something else."

"Attack cat? You mean Sheba?"

"She jumped me and stole my hat."

Bailey smiled as she glanced at the receipt, then dug in her purse and handed him cash. "She's my baby. I hope she didn't hurt you."

"Nope." He'd spent over five hundred dollars on materials, and most people didn't carry that much cash on them. Another indication she might be on the run from someone. Traffickers? He stuffed the money in his pocket. "I'll get started on that other section of the deck."

The lights flickered inside, then flooded the interior of the cabin. "The power's on. Let me check around and make sure everything is okay."

He followed her inside and used his electrical tester to make sure current was flowing correctly to the outlets. Nothing smelled hot and he gave her a nod. "Looks like you're good to go."

She had her hands on her hips as she gazed around at the space. "This place is filthy. Without lights I had no idea how dirty it was, but it needs a good cleaning. I brought Lily's vacuum home with me, thank goodness. I'll leave you to your work while I tackle this."

The locked outbuilding itched at him. She didn't seem to be going anywhere, so he wouldn't be able to check it. Unless . . .

"If I were you, I'd start in the bedroom so you have someplace clean to sleep. Need me to help move out the furniture so you can give it a good going over?"

Her green eyes brightened. "That would be great."

"There's a clothesline in the backyard. I'll take the mattress and rug out for a good beating. It will get more dirt and dust out than a vacuum."

"Thank you. Will this affect getting the repairs made? I don't want the deck to cave in."

"It won't be much of a delay. This won't take more than an hour. There's an outbuilding where we could store some stuff. There might be tools I need there too. Do you have a key?"

She pulled out a key ring. "I found this in the kitchen drawer. A key to the sheds should be on it."

He'd hoped to look by himself, but she followed him across the yard to the shed, and he unlocked it, then pushed it open. The space was surprisingly neat with hedge trimmers, hammers, and various other tools hung on pegboards around the perimeter. A large trapdoor was in the middle of the floor. A slight odor of decay had him on high alert, and he moved to study the trapdoor.

"Whatever is that for?"

"Could be a root cellar," he said.

She frowned and lifted a brow. "In the shed? That doesn't seem likely."

"Only one way to find out." The door had a grip in it, and he reached down to yank it open.

Fetid air rushed out at him, and he couldn't control his grimace. "Nasty down there. Got a flashlight?"

"Right here." She retrieved it from the workbench and handed it to him. "Be careful. Those steps don't seem very safe."

He shone the light on them and saw where the treads were busted. "I'll be careful."

Watching where he put his feet, he descended into the dark hole. He had to duck once he reached the dirt floor since the floor joists were only about five feet above him. He swept the light around and recoiled.

In the corner were the bodies of two young women.

# Chapter 16

Bailey backed away from the stench wafting from the open shed. Dead rats maybe? She shuddered and hugged herself, then went to sit on the porch step. Lance would clean it out. She exhaled the horrible odor from her lungs.

It was starting to get dark. There was a heavy, weary tread to his boots as he exited the shed and walked across the grass. He stopped and stared at her. "I'll need to ask you some questions."

She didn't like his imperious tone. "About the repairs?"

"Let me make a call first." He whipped out his phone and turned his back to her.

Though his tone was low, she caught the word *bodies*. He was calling someone about rats or raccoons? Maybe a biologist or something.

He ended the call and pinned her in place with a suspicious glare. "I need to know how you came to be here. What is your connection to this place?"

She stiffened and studied the steely expression in his eyes. "This sounds like an interrogation. What's going on?"

He reached in his pocket and drew out a badge. "FBI agent. There are two bodies in that shed, Ms. Fleming."

*FBI.* Her gaze lingered on the official badge, and she gripped her hands together. "B-Bodies? You mean people?"

"Two young women, probably about fifteen or sixteen."

She fought a wave of nausea. "Oh no." His eyes narrowed as he stared at her, and the reality of his badge finally sank in. "You *lied* to me? You're not a neighbor at all."

"That's right. I'm working an organized-crime ring that includes sex trafficking. One of our satellite offices called me in Seattle to alert me to the activity they suspected was going on out of this cabin. You've got some serious questions to answer. What's your connection to Baker Holdings company?"

She'd liked him, trusted him. Would she never learn? Her judgment about men was seriously skewed.

She glared at him. "I don't want to talk to you. Leave me alone. This has nothing to do with me. And you *lied* to me. I hate liars!"

"Look, I can make this hard if you want me to. Answer my question or I'll have to arrest you. What is your connection to Baker Holdings?"

Arrest her? She shook her head. "I've never heard of Baker Holdings." She rose and clasped her hands together. His suspicious glare didn't fade.

Lance took a step closer to her. "There are young women murdered in that shed. Doesn't that matter to you? Families are grieving and longing to hear from their daughters, and you're standing here refusing to answer simple questions. Do you know who they are?"

She forced herself to think of the girls lying dead in that building instead of her own outrage. "Look, Lance, there is some kind of mistake." She exhaled. "This has nothing to do with me." She looked away from the strong planes and angles of his handsome face. "I-I made a really stupid mistake. I found out the man I married six months ago already had a wife. I left him as soon as I found out, but he's in the public eye. The press must have gotten wind of it, and a few reporters had called me. I didn't intend to talk about it, but Kyle must have been afraid I would. He showed up at work and wanted to bribe me to keep me from talking to the press. He put this house in my name as compensation. I only saw the deed to it after my mother was murdered."

His dark-blue eyes narrowed. "Murdered?"

She nodded. "Call Sheriff Kaleva in Rock Harbor, Michigan. He can tell you about it. He said her hands were tied behind her back and she was shot through the h-head." She gulped and swallowed hard. "She left me a note telling me to hide because the killer would be coming after me. I didn't believe it until someone shot at me too. So I ran. The only place I could think to come was to this house that I'd just found out was in my name."

Saying it all out loud sounded ridiculous, like something from a movie. How could this be her life? She was a simple nurse, and the most exciting thing she'd done up to this point was to get married.

He stared at her for a long minute. "Don't go anywhere. My partner has been playing phone tag with the sheriff. I'll call him myself."

"I've got his number." She stepped inside the cabin long enough to retrieve her phone. "Here."

She showed him the number and he put it in his phone, then walked away a few feet.

What was all this about? Nothing made sense. The FBI

would need to talk to Kyle about this. He wouldn't be happy about that, but she didn't care. If only her mother were still alive. She might be able to shed some light on this.

Her gaze lingered on Lance's broad back. His lies reinforced her belief that handsome men couldn't be trusted. He could have told her the truth and asked his questions the moment he came to the door, but lying was more convenient. And she'd *liked* him.

Never again.

He ended the call and faced her. "The sheriff corroborated your story."

"Of course he did. I don't lie, unlike most men." She curled her lip and turned to stomp up the steps to the cabin. "Leave me alone. I've told you everything I know."

Before she reached the door, he came after her and took her arm. "You don't know what you might know. There had to be some reason this Kyle put the house in your name. What do you know about your bogus husband?"

"Obviously not very much or I would have known he was already married. He's a singer." She shook her head. "I couldn't believe it when he singled me out at a concert and sent a roadie to give me a backstage pass."

"What did your mother think of him?"

"She didn't like him at first, but he won her over too. He asked me to marry him two months after we met, and I was hesitant, but she urged me to follow my heart. So I did, and look where it got me."

"Did Kyle ever see your mom alone?"

She stared at him as she thought about it. "Well, now that you mention it, he talked to her before he asked me to marry him. What are you thinking?"

"I don't know yet, but with your mom's murder, it would appear there might be some connection to organized crime. The sheriff said it looked like an execution. If Kyle had crime connections, maybe he ordered the hit on your mother. Any idea why?"

"He liked her. At least he said he did." A wave of nausea swamped her, and she rushed up to the edge of the woods and leaned over. Her stomach emptied in a hot rush, and she sank to her knees in the soft loam.

If only she could go back a year in time.

Daniel should have called by now. As forensic techs and law enforcement agents descended onto the property, Lance pulled out his phone and called his partner.

Daniel answered on the first ring. "I was about to call you. It was a bust. There was a brothel, but it used older prostitutes. We arrested the pimp, and we're processing the women now, but there's no sign of Jackson. This isn't his kind of operation either."

Lance watched a tech duck into the shed. "You won't believe what I found here."

Daniel whistled as Lance ran through the discovery of the two bodies. "You talk to the Fleming woman any more? Get anything out of her?"

"I asked to get into the shed, and she handed over the key without any objection. When I found the trapdoor, she didn't try to stop me from opening it. I don't think she had any idea what was down there."

"Interesting. You get any other info out of her?"

"Yeah, her mother was murdered. That's the shooting." He told Daniel what he'd learned from Sheriff Kaleva. "Then someone shot at her, and she ran."

"Wow. And this lowlife gave her the deed to the house? You have to wonder if that was all part of his plan. It's pretty remote. Wait a second. I have the list of board members here. There's a Kyle on the list. Kyle Boone."

"I'll talk to her a little more." He ended the call and went to find Bailey.

She was in the kitchen with the cat on her lap. The feline was so big that her legs hung over the sides of Bailey's lap. The cat followed him with her gaze and licked her chops.

"Your cat looks like I'm her next meal."

Bailey rubbed the cat's ears. "She's very friendly and loving. What are they finding out there?"

"Nothing more just yet. They're processing the scene and gathering evidence, but we won't know much for several days. They'll try to ID the bodies, get closure to the families. We might get lucky and find DNA we can identify." Slim chance of that though. "Was Kyle Boone the sleazebag singer?"

She shook her head. "Kyle Bearcroft."

"Maybe that's not his real name."

"Probably not. Nothing else about him was real."

Lance went to the coffeepot and poured himself a cup. "You want some?"

"No thanks."

Carrying his cup, he joined her at the minuscule table and sat in the other chair. "I'd like to ask you a few questions about your marriage to Kyle Bearcroft."

She rubbed the cat's ears. "You're FBI. You can probably find out more about him than I'll ever know."

"Let's retrace how this all happened, okay? Start at the beginning."

"I was at a concert at Michigan Tech. He had one of his roadies send out a backstage pass. I was flattered, of course. I'd been a fan since I was a senior in high school."

"He's older than you?"

She nodded. "He's about thirty. I'm twenty-four."

"So then what happened?"

"He told me he'd spotted me right off and couldn't take his eyes off me, then he asked to take me out as soon as he got changed. We went to a little bar restaurant in Houghton and talked until almost three in the morning. He had a break of two weeks between concerts, and we spent every evening together. He kept trying to get me to ditch work, but I wouldn't do that."

"You said your mom didn't like him at first?"

She shook her head. "She about had a cow about the age difference, but Kyle said he'd talk to her. They spoke for about two hours, and when I got home from work, her attitude was different." Bailey's fingers stilled in the cat's fur. "She seemed like she'd been crying though. I didn't want to ask her about it because I was afraid she'd still be against him." Her green eyes were luminous with tears. "If only I'd been smarter, wiser about all of it."

"A rock star like that—I'm surprised he wanted to marry you if he was already married. Didn't he know he'd be found out? And don't guys like that have groupies and women at every concert?"

Pink rushed to her cheeks, and she didn't look at him. "I,

um, I was saving myself for marriage. I told him that the first time he put the moves on me. I'm a Christian, and I have really strong feelings about that."

Well, well, well, what a rarity in this day and age. Lance kept his admiration to himself. "I see. So that's when he proposed marriage?"

"He swore me to secrecy and said we'd get married by a justice of the peace. I couldn't tell anyone because the media might get hold of it, and it would affect his popularity. I was okay with that. It seemed a sweet and secret romance." She blew out a breath. "I can't believe how stupid I was. I-I feel pretty worthless about now. And stupid."

He touched her hand. "It wasn't your fault, Bailey. It doesn't mean you're any less valuable either. You're a beautiful woman, both inside and out. Any man would be proud to be with you."

Her gaze shot up to collide with his. "It doesn't feel that way."

He cupped her face in his palm and relished the feel of her soft skin against his hand. "Feelings lie. What he did was awful, but don't beat yourself up about it. You took him at his word."

The moment between them stretched out until he either had to kiss her or drop his hand. He dropped his hand and cleared his throat. "How'd you find out it was all a ruse to get you into bed?"

She flinched, and the color washed out of her cheeks. "That's all it was, wasn't it? I kept trying to tell myself he loved me even after I found out the truth. But he didn't. He never did."

The cat jumped off her lap and came to sniff at his shoes. Apparently satisfied at his smell, she leaped onto his lap and purred. "This cat is something else."

"Kyle gave her to me. I about died when I found out he paid sixteen thousand dollars for her, but she's priceless to me."

Sixteen thousand dollars. Holy moly. "How did you find out?"

"We'd been 'married'"—she made air quotes— "for about a month. I overheard him talking to his real wife. He was soothing her about not making it home on his break and promised to come see her and the kids in a few weeks. He has two children."

"That's not been in the media?"

She shook her head. "No one knows his real name. He's super private. Though you asked me if it was Boone."

Lance had every intention of finding out the guy's true identity. It would make sense that he was the man on the Baker Holdings' board.

# *Chapter 17*

Lance tossed his car keys onto the desk in the motel. Driving back and forth from Seattle would take too much time away from his investigation, so he and Daniel had decided to stay in Lavender Tides a few days. The place smelled of Lysol and air freshener, which was a lot better than the odor of decay. As soon as they had the search warrant, they'd head back to the Cedar Cabin property.

He sat on the edge of one of the beds and took out his phone, but Daniel exited the bathroom before he had a chance to place another call to the Rock Harbor sheriff.

"Good work today." Daniel's blond hair hung on his forehead in a damp mess from his shower. He padded barefoot to the bed and grabbed his socks. "Man, that was a nasty scene. Even with a shower, the smell is still in my nose."

Lance planned to take a shower as well, but he had more pressing things to do. "We need to talk to Kyle Bearcroft. You find anything on him?"

"Nada. He's well known in the rock world, but I don't have anything beyond that."

"What about his real wife?"

"She seems clean. A childhood sweetheart from Idaho. She still lives on the ranch where Kyle grew up. His real last name is Boone, by the way, just as we suspected."

Lance grunted and took off his shoes. "Any friends we've heard about connected to him?"

"Nothing coming up in the databases."

"Not much to go on. You locate Bearcroft's current whereabouts?"

"He's on tour and due to sing in Seattle this Friday. What did you make of the Fleming woman's connection? You believe her story?"

"I'm not sure yet. Sheriff Kaleva spoke highly of her, but she's only been in town a couple of years. She and her mom moved around a lot, which is suspicious in itself. I wish we could question her mother. I think there's a lot there we don't know."

Bailey Fleming with her dark-purple hair and big green eyes intrigued him. She seemed to have a well of compassion for the elderly, but people weren't always what they seemed. For all he knew, she was in this with Bearcroft up to her pretty neck.

"Your wheels are turning," Daniel said.

"What if Bearcroft sent her here to handle something about to come down? She seems innocent enough, but we just don't know much about her. Not yet. Any matches to the girls in the missing persons record?"

"Not yet. Prints will come back first, and we might get a hit while we're waiting on DNA."

"I want to go over that property with a fine-tooth comb. We got a warrant to extend our search yet?"

Daniel put his shoes on. "Just came down. A courier is on his way out here with it. Should have it in another thirty minutes. We can hit it hard as soon as it's daylight."

"We should talk to the neighbors, too, see if they've noticed any activity. That place is pretty remote. You'd think they'd see something."

"There are ten acres surrounding the cabin, and it runs down to the water. The traffickers could easily access it by boat without being seen unless someone happened to be out in the woods."

Lance nodded. "I'll take a quick shower, then we can grab some dinner."

His phone rang as he laid it on the desk, and he glanced at the screen to see his supervisor's name. "Lance here."

"Where are you and Daniel?"

"Still in Lavender Tides. We're waiting on the search warrant. What's up, Scott? We have an ID on the bodies yet?"

"Got a hit on one of the girls. Chloe Wilson. She ran away after a fight with her mom when she was fourteen. That was two years ago."

Lance winced. At least the parents would have closure.

"There's more," Scott said. "Alfie Jackson is dead."

Lance stilled, and the room did a slow spin. Jackson was his best lead to Ava. "What happened?" His throat was almost too tight to speak.

"Shot, execution style. Police think he was killed last night around midnight. Witnesses heard what sounded like a car backfiring around 12:10. Single shot to the head. We're going through everything now. Maybe something will turn up to lead us to the rest of the ring. Let me know what you find in the search of the property."

Lance ended the call and faced Daniel. "Jackson's dead. Shot."

Daniel rubbed the back of his neck. "Man, Lance, that's not good."

"I'm not giving up. Jackson had plenty of snakes working for him. One of them has to lead me to Ava." But for all his bravado, he felt his grip on hope slip down a rung.

❧

It was nearly noon, and Bailey sat on the sofa in the living room while the tiny cabin buzzed with activity around her. Forensic techs and FBI agents swarmed the property to take fingerprint samples, look for blood spots in the house and on the property, and to question her. She'd answered the same questions over and over, but the suspicion hadn't left anyone's eyes.

And Lance had asked a zillion questions about her relationship with Kyle before leaving for the night. He'd come back this morning with a search warrant for the FBI to go over the entire property.

Her inclination was to get in her car and disappear, but that would appear even more suspicious. But was it even safe to stay? What if the killer came back?

Lance gestured for the remaining two techs to exit the cabin. "I'm sure you're exhausted."

She eyed him. His tone was entirely too placating after the way he'd grilled her earlier. The sun glinted through the window to stab her in the eyes. She shaded her face with her hand and waited for the next question.

"I think we're about done here."

"I can clean up?"

They'd gone through dressers, boxes in the closets, the stuff in the loft, and of course every square inch of the cellar space in the shed where the bodies were recovered. Her eyes burned at the memory of those body bags being carried off. Those poor girls.

"It's fine to clean up once everyone leaves. Sorry about the mess."

"I can clean it." At least he apologized.

Unexpectedly, her eyes filled and she looked away. Right now she wanted her mother and her house. She wanted the familiarity of her job and the sweet elderly people she loved so much. While the ocean scenery here took her breath away, it didn't compete with the wintery wonderland on the south shore of Lake Superior. People loved her back home. If anyone noticed her here, it was only to raise a brow her direction and pepper her with accusations.

She rose and went to stand at the window facing the front yard, where SUVs, cars, and trucks crammed the drive and lined the road. Her throat was a hot mess, and she blinked fiercely. She *would not* demean herself by crying. She was twenty-four, not two.

There was no one she could rely on right now. For the umpteenth time she mourned the fact she had no real family beyond her mother. It had been lonely growing up, but it was even worse now that she was an adult. If only her mother had opened up about extended family, she might have gotten to know her grandmother before she became lost to dementia. And her dad. Who was he? Her mother always refused to tell her, and her birth certificate listed him as unknown.

A warm hand settled on her shoulder, and Lance's low voice said, "Hey, you okay?"

"I'm fine." She gulped back the wobble in her voice. "I-It's just a little overwhelming. Do you know who the girls are?"

"We've identified one of them and the other's identity should come soon."

"Was it a kidnapping?"

"Probably sex trafficking." His words came out hard and bitter.

She turned around. His dark jeans and polo shirt hugged his muscles, and he reminded her of Ian Anthony Dale from *Hawaii Five-O* with his dark good looks. She guessed him to be in his mid- to late twenties.

"How'd you end up joining the FBI?" After she blurted out the words, she put her hand to her mouth. "Sorry, that was much too personal a question, especially when we've just met." Though he didn't feel like a stranger to her, and that feeling made his lie about his identity still sting.

He moved to the coffeepot and poured two cups, then handed her one. "I like you, Bailey. I like your honesty, and I'm really sorry I lied to you. Those girls were the reason though." Although he smiled, his eyes remained sad. "My sister has been missing for five years, and everywhere I go, I search for her. I cringe at the thought of finding her in a brothel, forced to work for some subhuman pimp. Or even worse, lying dead in some outbuilding."

He shook his head. "Look at me talking about this. I never discuss it. Most of my coworkers have no idea what drives me to find these animals who prey on kids. My partner and my boss know, but that's about it."

Her chest squeezed at the tragedy he dealt with. "Five years! I'm so sorry, Lance. That has to be hard."

His jaw clenched but his gaze continued to hold hers. "Hard doesn't begin to cover it. It's all-consuming. I have to find her."

"Do you know how she was taken?"

His jaw hardened. "She'd been corresponding with a guy online. Ava said he was her age, but I suspected he was older. The whole family had a fight about it, and Ava sneaked off to meet him after being told she couldn't go out. We never saw her again and later found out the guy was a known pimp. It changed our family. Our parents ended up fighting over whose fault it was and a year later they had divorced."

"So you joined the FBI to find her?"

He nodded. "I finished college in three years with a degree in criminal justice. With my dad's connections, I snagged an FBI internship my last summer. Mom is Cambodian and I speak fluent Khmer as well as Japanese and Chinese. My language ability helped me get a position with the Bureau. But I still haven't found Ava."

"Thank you for telling me. I forgive you for lying to me."

The smile reached his eyes this time. "I'm glad. I didn't want to hurt you. I'm pretty handy with a saw and a drill though. I plan to finish the job I started here. If it's okay with you, I'd like to camp out in the yard. The Rock Harbor sheriff told me about your attack. I don't like the idea of you being out here in such a remote location. I sent him a text and told him we were looking out for you."

She hadn't wanted to think about the attack. "Does he have any idea why Mom was murdered or what the killer wanted?"

"Not yet. He's concerned though, and so am I."

"No one knows where I went. Not even Kyle."

"Are you sure? What if he wanted to force you to come here?

For all we know he could have killed your mother, then arranged the attack so you'd run. Where else would you go except here?"

A wave of dizziness struck her. She pressed her hand against her forehead. "I should talk to Kyle."

"He's performing in Seattle on Friday. I plan to pay him a visit."

She put her hand on the hard ridge of muscles on his forearm. "I could arrange to see him if you want."

His dark eyes studied her. "It could be dangerous. Let me think about it."

"That's my life right now. The danger won't go away until we figure out who's behind this and why."

The dream of a normal life working with the elderly might come her way yet. She had to try.

"I'll think about it," was all Lance said.

## *Chapter 18*

The scent of decaying vegetation and fallen leaves lay heavy in the air. The glowering sky spit out a few sprinkles, and Lance zipped up his jacket and faced the wind. The rest of the team had departed, and he walked through the knee-high grasses and weeds in the acreage behind the cabin with Daniel.

What had possessed him to tell Bailey about Ava? That showed too much weakness on his part. He couldn't afford to let personal situations have a bearing on his work. Not cool.

Daniel whistled through his teeth. "Take a look here." He pointed out drag marks in the grass from the shed down to the pier. "Those girls might have already been dead when they were stashed in the shed. We already know the traffickers smuggle the girls in by boat. This could be their landing spot."

Lance knelt and examined the evidence. "This depression could've been made from heels being dragged along."

"Yeah. The girls could have died on board the boat or tried to escape and were killed. When the traffickers found them dead, they just may have decided to park them here until they figured out what to do. This place has been used a lot. You can tell by the evidence in the bedroom we found last year."

"They probably won't be back once news gets out that we found the bodies. They'll know we're watching the place. So we need to gather as much evidence as we can now. I don't think there will be more."

Not really sure what he was hoping to find, Lance wandered over the area again. This time he concentrated on a different section. It appeared to be a simple wooded lot with a small stream running through it. What had made this property so appealing to the traffickers? Its seclusion maybe? A recent heavy rain had left the ground soft, and he saw where animals had been digging near the base of a fallen tree. Mushrooms sprouted in the roots that had been torn from the ground.

Wait a minute, those weren't mushrooms. Upon closer examination he whistled for Daniel. "Call the team. We have another body."

The bones of a hand gleamed white through the tangle of roots. This person had been dead a long time from the look of the bones. They'd have to call in a forensic team to recover the remains. If not for the rotten tree falling, the victim's fate wouldn't have been known, even now.

Daniel knelt beside him, and they fell silent for a moment of respect.

"Old bones," Daniel said. "Completely skeletonized."

"Yeah." Lance studied the tangle of vegetation and tree roots again. "Check out the cranium." He took out his flashlight and shone it into the shadows where he'd found the head. "Bullet hole through the forehead."

"Female?"

"Wish I knew." Lance rose and went over to the other side of the tree to see if any other bones lay exposed.

From this angle he saw a gleam of metal on a finger. He needed to wait for the techs to get here, but he stepped a bit closer and trained the flashlight on it. "Looks like a ring here, Daniel." He pulled out his phone and took a picture. Though dirt marred the ring, he saw what appeared to be a Corvette emblem with a honking big diamond in it. "This ring might help identify him."

"Oh, it's a him now?"

"Male ring, so yeah, I'm taking a stab at that one." Lance grinned at his partner. "Makes you wonder what this place is all about. This murder is maybe decades old, and we find two new bodies today. It's like the place has been used for evil for a long time."

"We need to find out who originally owned this property, examine its history."

"What's going on out here?" Bailey's voice came from their left.

Lance moved to block her view as several agents scurried their way. "We've got another body—one that's been here awhile."

Her green eyes went wide. "How long?"

"Don't know yet. This one appears to be male though."

She clasped her arms around herself. "This place. I don't even know what to say about it. It's creepy."

"It's definitely seen its share of violence."

"Listen, can I talk to you?" She glanced over at Daniel. "In private."

Lance exchanged a glance with his partner. "Sure. Want to go inside? I could use some coffee."

She nodded, and he followed her across the soft ground to the back of the cabin. Avoiding the rotting boards, they went in the back door, and he smelled coffee as soon as he entered. She poured them both a cup of coffee, then handed him his and gestured to the sofa.

He cradled the mug in his cold hands and perched on the edge of the cushion. "What's wrong?"

"I haven't known what to make of all this, but there might be a connection between my mom and everything that's going on."

"You think your mom's murder is related?"

She flinched. "Maybe. I just found out she grew up here."

"I thought your bogus husband gave you this house."

"He did, which makes everything even more bizarre. You've met Lily. I found out on Saturday that s-she's my grandmother."

Not much ever surprised Lance, but at this revelation, he gaped before he recovered his composure. He listened as she told him about finding photo albums. "You've never been here?"

"I found pictures of me as a baby but nothing beyond that. I have no memory of ever visiting. My mom told me my grandparents were dead, that all my family was dead. She never brought me on any of the trips when she came to check on Lily."

"It was as if she was trying to protect you from this place."

She nodded. "I don't know what it all means, but I thought you should have that information. I'm going to the school tomorrow to review yearbooks."

He took a gulp of coffee. "Thanks. I'll see what I can find out about Lily."

"I hired a private investigator to look into it too."

"Save your money. I'll get to the bottom of it. Let's start at the school."

The old high school was a stone building with Victorian touches. Bailey felt an instant connection to it. What would her life have been like if she'd grown up here?

She put her hand on the door handle of Lance's truck. "Thanks for coming with me." He'd been quick to offer yesterday when she told him her plan.

He looked devastatingly handsome in the royal-blue shirt he wore. "I can't really let you go wandering around by yourself. There's already been one attempt on your life."

"I get it. Everywhere I go I see death. The cabin had seemed so sweet and welcoming when I first arrived, but now I want to run far, far away."

Lance opened his door. "I'm not sure perusing yearbooks will get us anywhere."

She shoved open her door and got out. "There has to be some connection between my mom and this place. Her history here seems the logical place to look."

He didn't answer, and they checked in at the office to be directed to the library. The place smelled like every high school she'd attended: floor wax, kids, and gym. The odors smelled like loneliness. She and Mom had moved around so much Bailey hadn't made many friends, and she'd walked many a hall by herself.

Nondescript brown carpet covered the library floor, and tables held students studying while others perused the library shelves. The librarian, an attractive brunette with bright-red lipstick, directed them to the shelf of yearbooks dating back fifty years. If her mother was really born in 1969, then her senior year would have been 1985 or 1986. She pulled out three yearbooks from 1984 to 1986 and handed one to Lance. They carried them to an empty table in the corner, and she opened the 1985 one. Before she went to the Clubs and Activities sections, she looked at the class pictures and spotted her mother on the third page.

"Here she is. She's a junior." She rotated the book around to show Lance her mother's smiling face under an enormous cloud of hair.

"Wow, big-hair era. Olivia Norman was hot."

"She still was when she died. She didn't look fifty, and she always took care of herself."

"Did she date at all?"

"Not once she was widowed when I was five. Men stared at her a lot though. She claimed all she needed was me." Bailey's throat tightened, and she blinked at the sting in her eyes. "I want to see what clubs and activities she participated in. Maybe I can track down a friend or two."

She flipped back to that section and began to look at every picture. "Here she is on the student counsel, so she must have been fairly active in school. And well known."

He pointed out another picture. "Smart too. She was in the National Honor Society."

She jabbed a finger at a man beside her. "Isn't that the mayor? Thomas Weaver?"

"I haven't met him."

"Oh right. Because you're not really a neighbor." All the feelings of camaraderie and working toward the same goal washed away. "I'm sure it's him. We could talk to him about Mom and what he remembers about her. He might know who her best friends were."

"The mayor's office is down the block. We could go there when we leave here."

The woman who had directed them to the yearbooks moved their direction, and Bailey realized she wasn't watching how loud her voice was. She sent her an apologetic smile. "Sorry, we'll be quiet."

"No, that's okay. I heard you mention Olivia Norman and that you wanted to know about friends of hers. She was my best friend in high school, and we still get together for coffee whenever she comes back to see her mom. I can give you her number." The woman held out her hand. "Kim Johnson."

Bailey's stomach dropped to her toes. She would have to tell this sweet-faced woman with soft brown eyes that her best friend was dead. "I'm Bailey, Olivia's daughter."

Kim's smile widened. "I should have recognized you. I've seen a thousand pictures, but maybe not so many since you're all grown. And the purple hair distracted me. Is your mom here with you?"

Bailey's mouth went dry, and she shook her head. "S-She was killed, Kim. Shot. About two weeks ago."

The color leached from Kim's face, and she grabbed the back of a chair for support. Lance leaped up and eased her onto the seat. "Put your head between your legs." He pushed Kim's head down, and she didn't resist.

After a few moments, she raised her head. "I-I don't know what to say, Bailey. I loved your mother very much. Was it one of your stepbrothers who shot her?"

"What? No. Why would you think that? We haven't seen them in ages. They basically vanished from our lives when their dad died."

Kim pursed her red lips. "That's what your mom told you?"

Bailey wanted to say she knew more about her stepbrothers

than this stranger, but she was beginning to realize she didn't know her own mother nearly as well as she thought she had. "We never saw them or heard from them very often over the past few years."

"She probably wanted to keep their threats from you."

"Threats?" Lance raised his eyebrows. "What kind of threats?"

"Eric left Olivia all his money, and the boys wanted their share. She tried to be fair and gave both of them a third of the substantial cash, but that wasn't enough for them. They wanted her to divvy up his 401k, but she refused to do that. She wanted to keep it for her own retirement someday, and you can't blame her. She didn't have to give them anything."

"What kind of threats?" Lance's voice was sterner this time.

"Threats to take her to court, to make her pay for their financial situation. Some of it was vague stuff, but Scott showed up once in Phoenix waving a gun around. She called the police on him, but she was a little afraid he'd snap someday."

Bailey tensed. "She never said a word about this. I should let the sheriff in Rock Harbor know. Maybe Scott killed Mom."

"What about your mom's will?" Lance asked.

"Everything came to me on her death. I haven't reviewed her estate yet. It didn't seem important."

But nothing was unimportant in this labyrinth of lies and secrets. Bailey would have to call her mother's attorney and see what she could find out.

## *Chapter 19*

The building, a drafty fortress like all the other houses where Ava had stayed, felt different today. She had a sense that others were coming, and she steeled herself for new girls. New girls who would have to be shown the ropes and helped as much as she could. This was one of the worst times, when she faced the shock and despair of confronting her circumstances all over again.

Her gilded cage would go from holding one trapped bird to two. She rose and faced the door as footsteps came her way.

Her bedroom door opened, and a teenage girl tumbled inside, pushed by heartless Maly. The door slammed and locked behind her.

The girl, probably about fifteen or sixteen, scrambled up from the floor and ran to the door. She twisted the knob. "Let me out! I want my mom!"

Ava went to her and touched her shoulder. "They make those doors out of solid wood. You can't escape. I've tried."

The girl flinched, and no wonder. A large bruise covered the side of her face. Alfie wouldn't be happy to see someone had marred the merchandise.

"I won't hurt you. What's your name? I'm Ava, though I'm

not supposed to use my real name. They call me Lotus." She scowled. "At first I refused to answer them when they called me that, but t-they have a way of breaking you down." She stared again at the bruise.

The girl wiped her streaming eyes. She was beautiful with her blonde hair and hazel eyes. "Where's Charlie? He has to come back for me." Her hand went to her cheek, and her eyes welled with tears again. "Where is this place?"

Ava didn't want to tell her. Usually they "broke in" the girls first and didn't just toss them into the stable. She'd been like this girl though, noncompliant and defiant. This one wouldn't be an Apsara dancer. Her coloring was wrong, even if they dyed her hair. "What's your name?"

"Jessica Penn." She tucked a strand of hair behind her ear. "Where is this place?"

"I'm not exactly sure. I don't recognize the area. I think we're in Seattle, but I wouldn't swear to it. They only let us into the backyard under guard, and we can only see the sky and the privacy fence."

Jessica's eyes widened. "How long for you?"

Ava had lost track. At first she'd made marks on the floor under the bed, but they'd moved her so many times, she'd lost her markings. "I'm not sure. Maybe five years. I know it was October a few weeks ago because I heard someone say it on the boat, but I've lost track of what year."

The color washed out of Jessica's face, and her eyes were huge. "Years?" She licked her lips. "I-Is this like a-a brothel?"

"Yes, I'm sorry." Ava rubbed her forehead. This was always so hard and brought all the horror back afresh. It made her want to pound on the door and scream at the top of her lungs.

She swallowed the bile burning the back of her throat. "Let me take a stab at how this happened for you. You were fighting with your parents who didn't understand you at all, right? You met this really great guy online who listened to all your problems and commiserated with you. He met with you a few times, and you liked how he was older, mature, and handsome. He took you to nice dinners and said all kinds of words you wanted to hear. When he suggested you run away with him, it seemed a dream come true."

"How'd you know that?"

"It's their method of luring in teenage girls. Most people think trafficking happens when a girl is kidnapped, but that's rare. It's much more common they play on our own discontent. They lurk on all the social media sites and target girls they think will bring in the money. We're inexperienced enough to fall for it."

"That happened to you?"

Ava nodded. "I'd give anything to see my parents again, my brother." Her voice went husky. "His name is Lance."

"Can't you get a message to him?"

Ava shook her head. "I've tried so hard. It's hopeless. Our captors would say I'm fortunate. They elevated me to their elite club where I dance for the men, but it's almost worse to be forced to watch them watch me and then to hear the bidding."

She showed the girl the lotus-flower tattoo on her ankle. "This is a reminder that there's nothing I can do." She'd thought she might escape a couple of weeks ago when she was moved by boat along with some new girls. Several of them had gone overboard and tried to swim to freedom, but it had all ended badly. Very badly.

Since then the last of her hope had swirled away. She was stuck here until she grew old and ugly.

She rarely cried anymore, but for some reason her eyes filled. She angled away so Jessica couldn't see her tears.

"What happens next?" Jessica's voice trembled.

Ava well remembered that first day when she realized she'd been duped—the fear, the loathing, the frantic need to escape. But there would be no escape today. Or ever.

"They may leave you alone today, give you time to adjust. One of the guards or Maly will come in and give you "the talk" where the punishment is explained. If you try to ask a john for help or try to escape, you'll be beaten and locked in a scary room in the cellar. Pleas for help are bad for business."

"You mean, t-the men who come don't care if we're here against our will?"

"Nope."

She'd thought that once too—that all she'd have to do was tell one of the men that she was a prisoner. All she got for her trouble were welts up and down her back and a gash in her head. The monsters who used girls this way knew it was wrong, and they just didn't care.

The gulls swooped and landed at Bailey's feet where she had tossed bits of her sandwich for them from the town pier. The sound of the waves lapping at the rocks and the toot of a ferry heading to one of the islands should have given her a sense of comfort, but she was a mess of jangled nerves.

She zipped up her jacket against the chill of the wind, then pulled out her phone and found Ursula Sawyer's cell number. Her finger hovered over the call button, but she couldn't bring herself to punch it.

Lance tossed some bread to the gulls. "Want me to talk to the attorney?"

He hadn't left her side, and she had been very aware of the way he watched every passing car and stared at every bush that lined the park where they sat. He was a man used to protecting, and she was able to relax a bit and think.

He was still waiting on an answer, and she forced herself to focus. "No, I'll call her. I doubt she'd tell you anything even if you are an FBI agent." She hit the button to connect the call, then put it on speakerphone.

"Ursula Sawyer."

In her fifties, Ursula was the best attorney in Rock Harbor, and Bailey had met her at church the first week she'd arrived in town. "Ursula, this is Bailey Fleming."

"Bailey! I've been so worried about you. Where are you? Wait, never mind. I don't want you to risk telling me anything. You're all right?" Her Yooper twang came out stronger as she showed her agitation.

"I'm fine. I have an FBI agent right here with me."

"FBI. What's this all about, honey?"

Bailey's heart clenched at the concern in Ursula's voice. She'd felt so alone for days, and it wasn't likely to get any better. "Did you know my stepbrothers had threatened Mom?" She told her all that had happened and what she'd learned about her mother's background so far.

"She told me there was some bad blood between them over

their dad's will, and she wanted to make sure everything was buttoned up tight for you. I made sure it was."

"Did she leave a lot of money? I didn't get a chance to talk to you about her will."

"Well, it's not chump change. About half a million dollars, most of it in Eric's 401k. There's also a house in Lavender Tides deeded to her about ten years ago that's occupied by her mother, your grandmother Lily. It's probably worth close to two hundred thousand." Ursula must have heard Bailey's sharp intake of breath because she paused. "What's wrong?"

"You knew about Lily?"

"Of course. What do you mean?"

"I was always told I had no other family. I'd never met Lily until I got here to Lavender Tides."

"I don't understand. You're *there*, yet you didn't know anything about your family?"

Bailey told her how she came to have the deed to the house. "Do you know if Mom was acquainted with Kyle before I married him?"

"She never mentioned it if she was."

"Have my stepbrothers contacted you since they heard Mom died?"

"Oh yes. The day after your mother's murder, Scott called on behalf of both of them and asked what she'd left them. When I told them nothing, he cursed and hung up on me."

"He told me they wouldn't attend the funeral, but at least he seemed solicitous." Bailey rubbed her head and watched Lance take notes.

"You don't have a will, Bailey. If you died without one, the money would go to your stepbrothers since Eric adopted you. You should get that taken care of as soon as possible. If either of them had something to do with your mom's death, you could be the next target."

Bailey's gaze connected with Lance's, and he raised his brows. "Which would explain why someone tried to kill me a few days later."

"Yes, of course. I'm worried about you. You want me to handle a will for you? I can get it done and send it to you via email. You can get it notarized and mail it back."

"I don't even know who I would leave my possessions to," Bailey said. "There's no one left. I'll have to think about it. Maybe a geriatric organization. I'll get back to you once I've figured it out."

"Don't take too long. If your brothers are involved, the sooner they know hurting you can't help them, the safer you'll be. Keep me posted, Bailey. I'm here for you."

"Thanks, Ursula." Bailey ended the call and looked at Lance. "What do you think?"

"I'll check them both out, see if they have an alibi. Where do they live?"

"In Chicago."

He nodded and rose from the picnic table to walk to the edge of the water. He squatted at the ocean's edge. "There's a tide pool here. My sister loves them."

Bailey knelt beside him. "I've never seen one. I've never lived near the beach before, at least not an ocean beach. What are all those things?"

"There's a limpet and an anemone." He pointed out each creature.

A rock seemed to move. "Is that a hermit crab?"

"Yep. And a small starfish. These creatures are all different from each other but share the same small pool in harmony. There's no fighting over who gets to occupy the small spaces. Makes you wonder about humans, doesn't it? I'm sure it hurts to think that your stepbrothers might want you dead." He brushed the sand from his hands and stood.

"I'm not quite sure I believe it." She walked with him to his SUV.

She slid into the vehicle beside him and glanced at his strong profile. At least it felt like someone was on her side. "Let's go talk to the mayor."

## *Chapter 20*

The mayor's office was in a new building on the edge of town. Black shutters complemented the gray brick and red door. The large oak tree in front had lost most of its leaves, and its barren branches whipped in the wind that had freshened in the last few minutes. Bailey had a feeling they wouldn't get far with the mayor. He'd be able to confirm he knew her mother, but that wouldn't tell them much.

Lance held open the door for Bailey, and she stepped into a space smelling of cloves and cinnamon from an essential-oil diffuser buzzing away on the receptionist's desk. The young woman with a red nose and watery eyes directed her back to the mayor's office as soon as Lance flashed his badge.

Mayor Thomas Weaver smiled at them from behind his desk, a massive cherry monster with ornate Oriental carvings on the front. "It's not every day I get a visit from the FBI." His gaze slid from Lance to Bailey. "Have a seat and tell me how I can help you today."

Lance introduced himself. Bailey perched on the edge of a leather armchair, but Lance crossed his arms and stared at the desk. "Nice desk, Mayor. Where'd you get it?"

Weaver's gray brows winged up. "Southeast Asia a few years ago. I bought some pieces in Cambodia and had them shipped here. You came here to ask about my choice in office furniture?"

Lance ran one hand over the shiny surface. "It must have set you back a pretty penny. Shipping alone would be costly. What were you doing in Cambodia?"

"It was a missions trip. A bunch of us from church went. I've been several times and love the country and the people. What's this all about?"

Bailey wanted to know as well. She had no interest in Asian furniture, but she kept her mouth closed and let Lance follow his rabbit trail. She already knew him well enough to realize he had some reason for the strange questions.

"You ever see Apsara dancers when you were there?"

The mayor's puzzled smile flattened, and his eyes narrowed. "Sure, up in Siem Reap. There's a dinner theater that puts on a nice show."

Lance gave a slight nod. "Uh-huh. You ever see anything like that here?"

"The Royal Ballet of Cambodia comes to the States once in a while, and my wife and I planned to go to Seattle a couple of years ago to see it, but we couldn't get tickets. Look, Agent Phoenix, I'm losing my patience here. These are strange questions."

Lance stared at him for a long minute. "That's it?"

"That's it."

"I'm investigating a trafficking ring that exploits women they've trained in Apsara dance."

"Operating in Lavender Tides?" The mayor's voice rose. "That's ludicrous. I would have caught wind of it."

"Not operating here but running some of the girls through

the county." Lance told him about the bodies discovered at Bailey's cabin.

The color drained from the mayor's face, and he leaned back in his chair. "I'll do whatever I can, give you whatever resources you need."

Bailey glanced at Lance and he nodded her way. "We actually came to ask you something personal. I'm looking into my mother's background, and I saw you in a picture with her in the school yearbook. Olivia Norman."

The sheriff's frown only deepened. "You want to ask me about Olivia but you're here talking about human traffickers and prostitution? I doubt Olivia would ever have anything to do with that kind of thing."

"She's dead. Murdered a couple of weeks ago, and I'm on the run after an attempt on my life as well. I'm finding out I didn't know my mother, not really. What can you tell me about her, and how well did you know her?"

"I took her to the senior prom. I had a mammoth crush on her, but she never went out with me again. She only let me take her to the senior prom because she couldn't get her boyfriend to go, and I was enough of a sap to hope she'd see I was a stand-up guy she could trust."

"Who was her boyfriend?" Lance asked.

Weaver picked up a pencil and twirled it in his fingers. "I never knew. No one did, but she was crazy about him. When I asked her out again, she said she was taken. I always thought it was an older guy—someone she thought her parents would disapprove of. I never found out though, and I even followed her a couple of times." He flushed and dropped the pencil. "That's not as nasty as it sounds. I was just curious."

Lance rested his hand on the back of Bailey's chair. "Did she see you?"

"Maybe. She drove all around, then went into a restaurant and managed to disappear. I went inside but she wasn't there, and when I came back out, her car was still there but she was gone. I'd guess she went out the back and got in his car."

Bailey's pulse zoomed. "If we could figure out who that was, maybe we could find him and talk to him."

"Good luck with that. I asked her best friend Kim and she had no idea. She was a little hot about it, too, because Olivia was being so secretive."

"Kim Johnson? We already talked to her at the school this morning, but I didn't ask her who Mom was dating. Maybe she knows now. They kept in touch."

Weaver shrugged. "She didn't date anyone else until she up and left here."

"Well, I was born here as far as I can tell," Bailey said. "I was born in September 1995 and Mom left town around then. So she must have been seeing someone."

Weaver stared at her and shook his head. "She was never pregnant when she lived here, Bailey. I saw her several times a week when she was working as a paramedic. I saw her the day before she left town and she wasn't pregnant. She was working the day of the earthquake."

A wave of nausea roiled in Bailey's stomach. "What earthquake?"

"A big one that killed a lot of people. She was trapped in a grocery store for about thirty hours with other shoppers. She was hailed as a hero for helping out in the rubble. The town wanted to give her an award, but she left out of the blue."

Bailey had heard of women giving birth when they didn't realize they were pregnant. Could that have happened to her mom?

She rose and zipped up her jacket. "Thanks for your help. I'll ask Kim if she knows who Mom was seeing."

Weaver rose and came around from behind his desk to open his door. "If you leave me your card, I'll contact you if I think of anything else."

"I don't have a card."

"I do." Lance took one out and handed it to the mayor. "Thanks for your help."

Back out in the cold wind, she stopped and asked Lance, "You think the mayor has something to do with your sister's disappearance?"

"I don't know. Cambodia isn't a popular vacation destination. I've been there many times because my mom is Khmer. I'm going to do some digging and see."

She pulled out Kim's number, then placed a call, but her mom's friend didn't know who her mother had been seeing then. Like Weaver, she claimed Olivia wasn't pregnant.

It's not like Bailey hatched under a mushroom. It was so peculiar she didn't know what to make of it.

Lance didn't have much to say as he drove Bailey home, but then she was lost in thought herself. She sat in the passenger seat and stared out the window. The whole investigation into her mom's past felt like a dead end to him when he wanted to bring down the traffickers and find his sister, but Bailey had no one else to help her. He darted a glance her way. How had he come to care about her in such a short time?

He parked in the drive and started for the back of the house. "There's still some daylight. I think I'll work on that back deck awhile."

Bailey swiveled toward the road and shielded her eyes from the sun with her hand. "Looks like we've got company. I'll leave you to deal with him while I check on Lily." She went to her car, then slid inside and drove off.

A swirl of dust blew behind a pickup heading this way. He lifted a hand and went to stand by the road as Daniel parked his truck and got out. It must be important or a phone call would have sufficed.

Daniel slammed the door shut and approached him. "We've got a few key bits of evidence back." He shivered in the wind in his polo shirt. "Can we go inside? I forgot to grab my jacket."

"Sure." Lance strode to the front door and they stepped into the small cabin.

"This looks a lot different. Bailey has worked wonders in here."

The wood on the floor and walls glowed with the dusting she'd given them after the techs left, and the kitchen appliances gleamed. Bailey had found a place for everything, and the tiny cabin felt bigger without all the clutter. Lance glanced at the loft and saw the boxes still in disarray. He had no doubt that space would be next.

They sat in the chairs by the fireplace. "So what's up?"

Daniel's gray eyes held compassion. "Stay steady, buddy. This is going to rock you."

Lance inhaled. "One of the bodies was Ava?" Dizziness struck and bile marched up his throat. He was going to throw up or scream and bash the wall.

Daniel held up his hand. "No, no! But there were some fingerprints in the cellar on some of the items down there. Ava's fingerprints."

The wild thumping of Lance's pulse settled. "But she's not one of the victims?"

"She's still alive, Lance. She was in that cellar two weeks ago."

His pulse surged again. "Two weeks ago? The medical examiner dated the deaths. How do you know she was there two weeks ago?"

"Let's take this one step at a time. We've got IDs back on both bodies. One girl was fifteen and one was sixteen."

Alive. Ava was alive. Lance couldn't process it. Against all hope, deep down he'd believed she was in a shallow grave somewhere or sold to some buyer overseas where she'd be better off dead.

"Cause of death?" His voice sounded like it was coming through a tunnel, and he fought to keep his focus.

"Drowning, if you can believe it. The ME thinks the girls might have tried to escape overboard and drowned. The pimp would have retrieved the bodies to prevent them from being found and identified."

"Makes sense." The thought of those young girls fighting for their lives in the water, only to drown and be hauled back into the boat made his heart hurt.

But Ava. Where was she now? He guessed she was close by. If she was still in Washington after five years, he didn't see the pimp moving her out of state. But he could be moving her to another country. International waters weren't far, and smuggling people wouldn't be any harder than smuggling drugs or guns. Residents in Lavender Tides had narrowly averted an EMP bomb a month ago. Lance had had a small hand in that as well.

"We're still processing the contents of the cellar, but we did find something else, though it's not a clue to her whereabouts." Daniel reached into his shirt pocket and pulled out a picture that he handed to Lance.

Before he reached for it, Lance could tell it was old and creased from frequent viewings. It was the size of a school picture, just a small snapshot. He looked down into his own face, a high school yearbook picture when he was a senior. "Ava," he breathed. "This is hers. Where was it found?"

"Placed under a tin pail in the cellar. It had to be deliberate. I think it was a message to you, a way to tell you that she was alive. And look at the back. It's dated October 31. She probably didn't think about her fingerprints being in the cellar, so she was trying to reach you the only way she knew how. She's had it all this time, and it probably hurt her to let go of it."

Lance flipped the picture over and immediately recognized his sister's handwriting with neat, large block letters. He turned the picture back around. He used to be idealistic with his chin up as if nothing could ever rock his world. But her disappearance had been a seismic convulsion that had shaken the foundations of everything he knew and believed. Until that moment he'd believed the world basically a good place, a safe place. He'd found out there were shadows everywhere, and it had propelled him into doing what he could to bring light into the darkness.

She'd tucked the picture in her wallet as soon as he gave it to her and had said something about showing off her hottie brother to her friends.

His baby sister. She was out there somewhere.

His chest squeezed and he rose to pace the floor. "I need to tell my parents."

"Tell them to keep it quiet. We don't want anything getting out about this. If it hits the news she might be punished."

Lance winced. "I'll make sure they understand. I can't keep this from them, not when it's the first ray of hope we've had."

"No, I agree as long as they don't blab it." Daniel rose and slapped his hand on Lance's shoulder. "We'll find her, buddy."

Lance gritted his teeth. "I'm going to find her, and those animals will wish they'd never been born."

## *Chapter 21*

When Daniel left, Lance went out on the back deck and dropped into one of the weathered wooden Adirondack chairs. The wind carried the briny scent of ocean to his nose, and the breeze ran down his back in a bone-chilling touch.

Who to call first was like walking through a minefield. Better to have Dad's complaints than Mom's tearful recriminations. He called his mother's number.

"Lance, what a nice surprise. You usually call on Sundays."

"Well, I have news, Mom." The lilt in his voice came in spite of his effort to sound dispassionate. It was impossible to hide his hope and joy. "I know for sure Ava is alive."

She gasped and choked out a sob. "Oh, Lance, you've seen her?"

"No, but we found her fingerprints at a cabin. And she left that old school picture of me as a senior in high school and dated the back two weeks ago. The picture was hidden, and I think she left it to me as a sign."

The only answer was a soft sobbing sound. He waited patiently for his mom to gather herself. There would be more questions. There were always more. He watched an eagle soar to a nearby alder tree and perch to watch him with beady golden eyes. Around him the woods were alive. The sounds of animals and birds going about the business of living was a reminder to him that hope existed even when he couldn't see it.

He would find Ava. He had to.

His mother's sobs tapered off. "Have you told your father?" Her voice held an edge.

"Not yet. I called you first."

"Thank you." The roughness in her voice smoothed out. "What's next?"

"Next we find out who was in the shed. We're combing through all the fingerprints hoping for a lead to who she was with."

"I just can't believe it. Hope after all this time!"

"I know. It's pretty amazing. I have to admit I didn't think I'd ever find her. And I still haven't," he hastened to add. "But I will. And you can't tell anyone. Not *anyone*, Mom. If what she did gets out, she might be hurt. Or worse."

"I won't say anything."

He chatted a few more minutes with his mother and promised to call the moment he had any more information, then ended the call. Now to contact Dad.

The phone rang so many times he thought he might get his father's voice mail, but his dad picked up. "Lance? What's up?"

"News, Dad."

He launched into the find in the shed cellar, this time leaving nothing out. His father was a former Seattle cop, and he understood the details Lance couldn't tell his mother.

"They drowned, you say? Rather an odd way to dispose of drowned bodies. Why didn't they sink them in the strait?"

"I'd guess they had nothing to use to weight them down, so they stuck them in the cellar and planned to come back for them. Or maybe they were just offshore and knew the place was unoccupied. Maybe they'd seen the cellar and didn't think it would be disturbed. We don't really know yet."

"Ava's a smart girl to leave that picture. If she's held on to it all this time, it was probably difficult for her to part with it."

"I thought that too. This might have been the first chance she had to leave a clue somewhere she hoped it would be found. Or maybe it's the only time she's been out of the brothel."

He didn't even like saying the word *brothel*. It hurt to think of what his sister was going through, but once they found her, they'd work on helping her get past the pain and degradation.

"You'd better call your mother."

For a moment he was tempted to say okay and hang up, but his dad would probably hear about it. "I did already."

"Of course you did. Mama's boy." His dad's voice shook with disgust. "I told you to call me the minute you had any news."

"And I did. I just called Mom first. She's hurting too. Look, Dad, now that we're on the brink of finding Ava, the two of you need to mend your relationship. I'm not talking about getting back together, but just being civil."

"There's no way I can talk to that woman. She's seeing another man, did she tell you that? Some mother she is. Moving on with her life when her baby girl is out there somewhere crying for her parents."

Dad's obsession was what had split the marriage apart. He'd blamed Mom and she'd blamed him. In typical law enforcement behavior, he'd thrown himself into following every lead, knocking on every door. He'd arrive home after midnight, exhausted and angry at himself for his failure. It hadn't been pretty.

Luckily, Lance had been away at college and had missed most of the drama. His first clue something was badly wrong was when his mother showed up in his dorm room. She was crying and nearly hysterical. He'd taken her to a motel and sat with her all night while she poured out a bitter laundry list of affronts against his dad.

He loved them both and being in the middle hurt.

"You need to have a life, too, Dad. It's been five years. What did you expect Mom to do? Waste away to nothing in the house? There was never any guarantee we'd find Ava, and you know that as well as I do."

"She needs to be there for Ava."

"And she will be, whether she's dating again or not. She'll drop everything to be with Ava. You have to know that."

So the base of all this was jealousy. That explained a lot about how the angry rhetoric had increased in recent months. He wanted to ask when Mom's relationship had started, but he didn't want to rub salt in his dad's wounds.

"You still love her, Dad. Why sit back and let another man have her? Go after her."

When his dad didn't answer, Lance looked at the screen. Dad had hung up on him.

Lily was outside when Bailey reached her house. She hadn't expected to find Lily digging in the garden wearing only a lightweight pink silk nightie. Especially not in this wind. Bailey parked in the overgrown driveway and jumped out.

"Lily, what are you doing?" Bailey touched her and found Lily's skin like ice and her lips blue. "Let's get you inside and warmed up."

Lily continued to dig through the dirt. "I was looking for my house keys. I know I put them somewhere."

Bailey lifted her to her feet and guided her toward the open door. "I don't think you planted them. I'll help you search. Let's make some nice, hot tea and get you into warmer clothing."

The interior was still a mess, and Bailey knew it wasn't going to change unless she cleaned it herself. Life had been coming at her from every direction, and there hadn't been time. But she would have to make time.

A pair of sweatpants and shirt lay draped over a chair, and Bailey grabbed them. "Let's get these on you." She helped Lily dress in warm clothes, then hurried to the kitchen to make tea.

Lily's teeth clinked together as she followed Bailey to the stove. "I like the Earl Grey. I have a tin of it." Her blue eyes were clear and lucid again.

"I'll have some with you. Have you eaten anything today?"

"Eaten?" Lily blinked, then looked down at the floor.

"I'll fix you some eggs and toast." She knew Lily had some eggs, bread, and a few other items because she'd brought them herself.

She found a clean skillet and fried up some eggs, then fixed toast with slabs of butter. Lily licked the butter off the toast before she ate the rest of the food. Bailey sat beside her at the table and watched her dip her toast into the soft centers of the yolk, then gobble it down. Lily took dainty sips of the tea and gave an appreciative sigh on occasion.

The food was gone in minutes, and Bailey took the plate back to the sink. "I can make you more."

"That's enough, my dear Bailey. It was quite good."

She turned at the calm note in Lily's voice. She'd called her by name too. Should she tell her who she really was? It had been such a shock to see the pictures that Bailey hadn't been able to form the words to explain herself. She'd wanted to do it when Lily seemed to be herself. The clouds had scattered in her eyes, and she looked placidly back at Bailey.

Bailey went back to the table and sat by her, then took her hand. "I want to tell you a secret, Lily. Do you like secrets?"

"Oh my, yes. I'm very good at keeping them too. I never told anyone about the body buried in the yard. You can tell me anything you want and I won't tell anyone."

*Body?* Bailey needed to talk to her before more clouds rolled in. Lily's hand was birdlike, the bones small and crushable in Bailey's bigger hand. "When's your birthday, Lily?"

Lily's white hair stood on end from the wind, and she seemed even smaller and frailer in the sweats. She smiled and squeezed Bailey's hand. "That's not a secret, honey. It's February 29. I only have a birthday every four years. Guess how old I am." Her smile was as wide and delighted as a child's.

"Are you thirty?"

Lily giggled. "Wrong. I'm eighty."

Eighty. How was she living on her own all this time? And what was Bailey going to do about it?

Lily leaned forward. "I know the secret."

"You do? What is it?"

Lily's gaze wandered to the window and out to the trees

blowing in the wind. "I met a rock star. He said he's my daughter's friend. I didn't like him much. Devil's spawn. Curse of Cain."

Bailey set her cup back on the table. "Do you know his name?"

Lily stared over Bailey's shoulder out the window. "Roger said he'd take care of those pesky squirrels, and they're still out there." She rose and went toward the stairs. "Roger! Get down here right now and take care of those squirrels before they destroy my garden."

Bailey saw no squirrels and no garden. Lily was lost in the clouds again, so she couldn't be left here alone. She'd have to come home with Bailey to Cedar Cabin.

A rock star. Could it be Kyle? And why would she say Kyle was a friend of her daughter's? Mom didn't know him all that well, only through Bailey's relationship with him.

Or was this more of Mom's secrets coming out?

## *Chapter 22*

King stood at his office window looking at the leaves rolling in the wind. Bailey Fleming still hadn't turned up, and he would have bet half his bank account his men would have found her by now. They'd disappointed him. Alfie had disappointed him, too, by targeting the wrong girl. King had made sure he paid for it though.

A knock came at the door. "Enter," he called.

Chey entered as noiselessly as always, his fine leather shoes making not a sound. "Sir, I have some unsettling news."

Chey rarely used the word *unsettling* and the fact he did so now made King go to his desk and sit down. "Tell me."

"The bodies were found. The girls we disposed of temporarily in the cellar are in the custody of the FBI."

He cursed and leaped to his feet, then picked up a paperweight and threw it against the wall, where it dented the drywall, then fell to the floor in pieces. "I told you not to leave them there long. They should have been disposed of a day or two later. It's been two weeks."

"Yes, sir. I make no excuses."

His ire cooled. Chey had been doing his best to find Bailey, and his forces had been spread thin. This changed things though. There might be all manner of clues the FBI might discover—clues that would lead the Feds right to his door. "It might be time to cut our losses for now, concentrate on other avenues of income. Our arms smuggling has been going well, yes?"

"Yes, sir. It's bringing in more than the girls at the moment."

"Think you can find buyers overseas for the girls? I'd hate to have to figure out how to dispose of that many bodies."

"I'm sure I can. There are several clients in Saudi Arabia I've had particular success with—and China, of course. The oldest one we have is Lotus, so they're all young enough to dispose of easily."

China was hungry for women. After disposing of so many girl children, they'd found there weren't enough brides for the men.

King knew all the girls, but his gut clenched at losing Lotus. She'd been kept only for him at the beginning, but his eye had eventually fallen on a new girl who'd been brought in from Oregon. He liked to rotate the girls out so none of them were older than twenty-one or twenty-two. He'd found buyers all over the world for his merchandise, so they were easy to dispose of.

King gave a heavy sigh. "See to it then, as soon as you can."

"It's likely to take a couple of weeks to arrange for the sale, the transfer of money, and to transport the girls. I may have to move some of them again too."

"Do whatever you have to."

"Of course. Oh, and you have a visitor."

"Oh?"

"Kyle Boone."

He curved his hands into fists. "Send him in."

Chey nodded and exited the office. Moments later Kyle stepped through the door and shut it behind him, then approached him with his hand extended. "Uncle! Good to see you."

King ignored the outstretched hand and leaned back in his chair. "Sit."

The *uncle* moniker was just to try to soothe him. Kyle was his wife's nephew—not his. And because of that he'd had to put him on the board.

Kyle's smile faded, and he sat heavily in the leather chair across from the desk. From the corner of his eye, he glanced at the shattered glass globe on the floor. "Look, I get that you're mad, but it wasn't my fault. Bailey overheard me on the phone. Two days later and I would have been out of there, no harm done."

"Where is Bailey now?"

"I don't know. I've tried calling her phone, but I think she's changed her number."

"You surely have some idea where she might have gone. Did Olivia have a summer house, relatives or friends Bailey might have contacted?"

"Not a summer house, but I did give Bailey the deed to Cedar Cabin. She was so mad that I'll bet she tore it up after I left."

"You *what*?!" He rose and leaned over the desk. "What made you think you could do that without talking to me about it?"

Kyle stuck out his bottom lip. "I have a share in Baker, too, you know. I'm on the board, and I have the authority to do something that minor. My lawyer thought we needed to sweeten the pot to get her not to talk to the press. She wasn't interested though, and she agreed not to say anything."

"I don't care anything about the media, but that property is mine." That property couldn't fall into the wrong hands or what he'd done might come back to haunt him. "You little twerp, you'd better get that deed back to me. Find her and return my property."

Kyle flushed as his steely words echoed off the walls. "I-I'll try, Uncle, but I have no idea where's she's gone. If I could only talk to her, I'm sure I could get her to sign it back over to me. Can you find her for me? Your goons have great resources."

King wasn't about to tell Kyle about their lack of success as well. "You made this mess—you can fix it. I shouldn't have intervened for you with Olivia. That was my mistake, and I won't make it again."

Kyle leaned back in the chair and crossed his ankles. "It was a pretty cool thing to see though. Olivia went from ordering me out of the house to being sweet as candy. What did you tell her to get her to abandon her objections?"

"She owed me. If she didn't do what I told her, I promised to make sure Bailey ended up in a brothel."

Kyle chortled. "Man, that was cold, but it did the trick. Why'd you order the old broad dead though?"

That was a secret that would never get out. He rose and turned back to the window. "You can let yourself out, Kyle. Don't come back without that deed."

Was it possible Bailey had gone to the cottage?

The lantern light glowing out the window of the cabin winked out, and Lance shifted in the seat of his truck while Daniel had his head tucked into the collar of his jacket like a turtle. Their breaths had fogged the windows in the cold night air. "I don't think anything is going to happen tonight. Not with Lily there."

Daniel poked his head up a bit. "Bailey seems harmless enough. You picking up any vibes from her? You've spent more time with her than me."

Lance shook his head. "I didn't like lying to her though. I'm glad the truth about who we are is out."

"Part of the job."

It might just be part of the job in other investigations, but this one felt more personal because of Bailey. He liked the way she quieted a space when she came into it. His mom would call it good energy. She had a way of listening as if she really cared about people.

Daniel yawned and rubbed his hand over the foggy window. "We'd better take a stroll around the property or I'm going to fall asleep."

Lance glanced at the dim glow of his watch. Nearly eleven. "Yeah, let's take one excursion around the place before we head to the motel."

Uneasiness rippled down his back at the thought of leaving, but they couldn't stay here twenty-four hours a day. The traffickers probably knew the bodies had been found and would be making themselves scarce.

He eased his door shut, and his boots crunched on the cold gravel as he followed his partner deeper into the woods. His cell phone vibrated in his pocket, and he pulled it out. He didn't recognize the number, but he walked deeper into the woods to answer it anyway. The scent of crushed pine needles wafted to his nose as he stepped away from the house.

"Phoenix," he barked.

"L-Lance, is that you?" The female voice trembled, then ended on a choked sob.

He froze. He knew that voice. It cried out for help in his dreams. Ava was right there on the other end of this call.

He gripped the phone in tight fingers. "Ava? Where are you? I'll come get you right now."

His eyes wide, Daniel swung toward him. He stepped closer to Lance and pulled his phone out.

She gave a soft sob. "I don't know where I am. It's by the water, but that's all I know. Is it really you, Lance? Did you forget me?"

He swallowed hard. "Never, Ava. I've been looking all this time. Hang on." He changed the screen to reveal the number and showed it to Daniel. "*Call in a tracer,*" he mouthed. "You there, Ava?"

"I'm here. Oh, Lance, you have no idea of the trouble I'm in, what they've made me do."

"I know, honey. We're going to find you. Stay on the line, and we'll get a fix on your location. I'll come right now." He only had one bar on his phone, so he stayed where he was in case movement would make the call drop.

"It's been so long since anyone has called me by my name. They call me Lotus here. I want to come home. This is the first time I've managed to get hold of a phone. T-The last client left it behind. He didn't know it fell out of his pocket, and I didn't tell him. I wasn't sure you had the same number, but I hoped so."

Lance clenched his fists at her volley of soft sobs. It was really Ava. She was alive. Lotus. He shuddered at the moniker. He'd heard of the elite Apsara-dancer brothel. Lotus was their premier dancer.

"It's okay, honey. I'm coming." He looked at Daniel, who gave him a thumbs-up. "We've got a fix, Ava. We're sending in anyone who's close, and I'm on my way too."

He prayed fervently for the connection to hold as he ran for his truck with Daniel on his heels. He motioned for his partner to take the driver's seat. He wanted to hang on to the sound of Ava's voice.

Ava's sobs grew harsher and louder. "I want *you* here, Lance. I can't stand much more."

He'd barely slammed the door behind him when Daniel floored the accelerator, and the truck spit gravel from under its tires. "Calm down, Ava. Don't let anyone hear you." His pulse pounded in his chest at the thought of her being discovered with a phone. They'd punish her.

He heard something slam on the other end. A door maybe or a cupboard. A voice shrieked in Khmer. "Ava?"

When she didn't answer, he looked at the screen. The connection was gone, and he wanted to throw something.

Daniel did a fist bump. "We got her!"

"What was her location and how far away are some agents?"

"She was in Seattle, about two miles from our closest agents. They're on their way." The back end of the truck fishtailed as Daniel took the corner fast.

"Two miles could take too long if traffic is bad." And he was hours away. "Can we head for the airfield here, that Hurricane Roost one just down the road? Maybe we can snag a chopper to Seattle."

"Yeah, the owner had posted his number on the billboard for emergencies. See if you can find it online before we get there."

Staying focused took Herculean effort when Lance's mind wanted to run to all the things that might be happening to his sister. He called the number he found, and a man answered in an alert tone.

"Zach Bannister."

"Zach, this is agent Lance Phoenix with the FBI. I need a ride to Seattle right away. It's life-and-death."

"Hold on." The line went quiet for what seemed like hours. Then Zach came back on the line. "My wife will take you in her chopper. She'll be at Hurricane Roost in fifteen minutes."

"Thank you so much." Lance ended the call and stared out the windshield toward the lights of town.

The airport was five minutes away, but what was happening to Ava? His sister was *alive*. He'd felt it in his gut all these years, but to have it verified felt like a dream he might awaken from. All he could do was pray as Daniel hurtled the truck toward the airport. They had to get there in time. He refused to accept any other possible option.

## *Chapter 23*

Lance pointed out the chopper window. "Can you put us down in that field?"

Most of the buildings were dark, but streetlights shone enough light to reveal an empty space between a warehouse and a big block building with no lights.

The pilot, Shauna Bannister, nodded. She reminded him of someone with the widow's peak in her black hair and her facial structure, but he couldn't concentrate enough to figure out who she resembled. All he wanted was to get out of this bird and rush to the door of the house. The closest agents had been broadsided by a pickup truck en route, and they were both on their way to the hospital instead of this location. The delay might be deadly for Ava, but Lance couldn't let his thoughts go there.

The chopper's runners bumped to ground, and Lance had his harness off and his door opened before the helicopter really settled. Shauna shouted something at him, but his feet hit the ground, and he ducked under the rotors to run toward the massive stone building to his left. Daniel was right behind him.

The stink of helicopter fuel followed him as he ran over

rough ground to the back door of the building, and he caught the odor of rotting garbage from the Dumpster by the alley. He motioned for Daniel to go around front, then waited until his partner was in position.

Glock in hand, Lance went up the concrete steps to the metal door and pounded on it with his fist. "FBI, open up!"

A startled cat, ears laid back, darted past his feet and vanished. He pounded again and heard Daniel do the same. When no answer came, he tried the door. The knob turned in his hand, and he opened the door with a protesting screech. The scent of patchouli incense floated in the air, and he felt for the light switch on the wall. Light illuminated a laundry room, and he caught a glimpse of the elaborate gold costumes and headdresses of Apsara dancers.

This was the right place. Crouching down, he kept his Glock ready and moved to the front door through what appeared to be some kind of ballroom with a stage. "I'm unlocking the door," he called to Daniel. He let in his partner and gestured to the stairs. "You check the rest of the rooms down here. I'm going up there."

He didn't say what they both felt. This place felt as empty as a discarded candy wrapper. His heart rate kicked up a notch as he mounted the steps and cleared each room. Lavish silk tapestries in rich colors covered the walls and gleamed on the marble floors. A large bed with the same tapestries took center stage in every room, and the closets held more of the Apsara costumes plus street clothes like jeans and T-shirts.

He reached the last room and pushed open the door. A coppery odor struck him, and he flipped on the overhead light to see blood pooling by the window. It was fresh enough that it glistened. A phone, its screen shattered, lay on the floor. This was the room Ava called from. Her blood?

The strength went out of his legs, and only his training kept him from sinking to the floor and touching the blood. He couldn't contaminate the evidence. *Please God, let her be okay.* The prayer ran over and over in his head.

He swallowed down the boulder in his throat and went to call to Daniel. "Up here."

Down the stairs he heard voices and knew more agents had arrived, probably crime-scene technicians as well. If they were very lucky, evidence would lead to where they took Ava and the rest of the girls.

It was after four a.m. by the time he and Daniel walked back across the weeds to the helicopter waiting for them in the dark. Shauna Bannister's eyes opened when he rapped on the window. She looked pale and her eyes were swollen with sleep. He felt a stab of guilt for keeping her out all night.

The men climbed into the chopper and fastened their harnesses. Her gaze flickered from him to Daniel and back again. "Not a good night?"

He shook his head. "Not so good." He couldn't talk about Bureau business, and he stared out at the lights of Seattle as the chopper took to the air. Ava was out there somewhere. The phone call from her couldn't be the last.

He'd find his sister. Where did he look next?

❦

This was not the kind of call King liked to get in the middle of the night. Swathed in a hotel robe, he stood in his suite and listened to Chey's explanations. "How did she get a cell phone? I've left instructions for the rooms to be swept every day." He moved to the bar and poured himself a scotch before facing Chey.

Even at four in the morning, Chey was dressed in an impeccably tailored suit and tie. His dark hair gleamed from a recent shower, and he ducked his head. "We think she hid it before Maly checked the room after her client left."

"Where is she now?"

"At the Citadel."

The Citadel was a stone structure up in the mountains where they trained girls. The place was cold and austere with no hot water, and the girls stayed there until they were ready to comply with orders. It usually didn't take long, but he suspected Lotus would be different. The hint of rebellion in her eyes had never really vanished but had gone underground instead. He doubted he'd ever be able to fully trust her, but he was still reluctant to get rid of her. She brought in way too much money to make a decision like that easy.

He sipped his scotch and let it warm him. "What's she saying?"

"She just missed her brother and wanted to hear his voice. According to her she listened to his voice mail message over and over but didn't speak with him. It's a lie, of course. Before we destroyed the phone, we saw she made one call that lasted ten minutes." Chey cleared his throat. "There's more bad news though, sir. Per protocol with a security breach, we evacuated all the dancers, but we barely finished in time. The FBI showed up and swept the place."

"FBI? How'd they get wind of it so fast?" He glanced at his watch. "It's been what—barely two hours?"

"Unfortunately her brother is with the FBI, sir. He mobilized forces immediately."

He set down his empty glass. "Traced the call for sure."

"We lost most of the Apsara costumes too. When our men pulled up to retrieve the contents of the property, FBI and crime-scene specialists crowded the place. Our people left immediately."

Costumes could be recreated but it would take time. He'd been thinking about changing his mind and keeping his Apsara dancers. "Did we save any of them?"

"One."

"Not enough to stay in business. Order more immediately and cancel the sale of my Apsara dancers. I'm going to move operations. With Lotus's brother looking for her, Seattle isn't safe. California would be a good option with its diverse culture, but maybe now is the time to move to China. My dancers will be a big hit there. My high-rise in Shanghai has a ballroom on the top floor. Let's get the place ready and move the girls there. It will likely need some small renovations like locks on the doors and some other things. You should be able to get everything in order within a week or two."

"We suspend operations in the meantime?"

"Yes. In the meantime gather all the girls and put them in the warehouse."

The warehouse was a remote property along the strait. The long, nondescript building held plain cells with showers for the girls and was where newly acquired women were held until they were ready to be put into service. Security was tight, and they'd never had a breach there.

King still had to deal with Lotus. "I'll see Lotus myself and assess what to do about her."

"Of course."

He studied Chey's face. "What aren't you telling me?"

Chey sighed. "I'd rather you talk with Lotus and decide for yourself."

"Tell me."

"When she was found with the phone, she bloodied Maly's nose and pulled out chunks of her hair. Security had a hard time subduing her. I'm not sure we'll be able to trust her, sir."

He pressed his lips together and went to look out at the lights of the Space Needle from the sliding glass door. He'd hate to destroy such valuable property, and he actually admired Lotus's spirit. Her determination and resolve reminded him a bit of Olivia, not that he'd ever entertained strong feelings for Lotus. Only one woman had ever evoked that.

"And Bailey? Any sign of her yet?"

"Yes, sir. It appears your hunch was correct. She's at Cedar Cabin and has been in contact with the FBI."

This bump in the road didn't mean anything. He'd eliminate the threat, then get back to business as usual.

## *Chapter 24*

Lance put the last nail in the deck while he waited for Bailey to return from town, then he climbed down and went to get coffee. He had to explain before he just took off. He couldn't sit back and wait for the traffickers to show up here, not with Ava out there. Close, so close. If it took prowling through every seedy neighborhood in the state, he was prepared to do it.

Bailey entered the cabin with her cat in her arms. Her dark-purple hair was a tangle around her face, and her cheeks were pink from the cold. Sheba's big ears flickered when she saw Lance, and she squirmed to be put down. Bailey set her on the floor, and the cat pounced on Lance's shoestrings. She untied them in seconds.

"Crazy cat." He scratched her big ears, and her loud purr started. "I'm all done here for now."

"I noticed the deck. It looks great."

"But the chinking will take longer than I have. You'll have to find a bonafide carpenter for that. I've had some unexpected news."

"Oh? You sound excited. You found the traffickers?"

"Not just yet." He told her about his sister's phone call and the subsequent discovery of the abandoned brothel. "I know she's alive." The knowledge kept shocking him all over again.

"Lance, that's wonderful!" She hugged him and didn't let go. "Were you upset about your sister when I saw you on the dock Monday?"

She fit perfectly in his arms. "Yes, it was her twenty-first birthday, and I realized she was probably dead. But she's alive!" He caught a whiff of the scent of her hair, something with vanilla and cinnamon. Though common sense told him to release her and step back, he couldn't make himself do it. It felt good to have someone to celebrate this news with, someone who seemed to really get how important this was to him. And he liked her, genuinely liked her. It didn't hurt she was gorgeous, but even more than that, she had such a sweet, caring soul.

He liked how forthright she was. He never had to wonder what she was thinking. When he was dating Kim, she often gave him the cold shoulder when he had no idea what he'd done. He could already tell Bailey didn't play those games.

She lifted her head off his chest, and he dropped his arms. She stepped back. "Sorry, I'll bet that's not standard FBI protocol. I was too excited to think straight."

"It helped to have someone to talk to. I haven't quite known how to take it. Ava wanted me to know she was alive, so that must mean she's still actively trying to get away."

She frowned. "Of course she is. Why wouldn't she?"

"Some of the women resign themselves to the life and work their way up the system. They eventually become supervisors over other girls."

Her green eyes did a slow blink. "I can't even imagine that."

"They've spent so long hearing they are of no value that they come to believe everything their captors tell them. Ava was always spunky and courageous. I didn't think she'd give up, but those are pretty intense situations."

Bailey took off her jacket, revealing slim-fitting jeans and a snug sweater that hugged her curves. "So what's next?"

"I start scouring the bad neighborhoods for any sign of a brothel."

"I figured you'd already been doing that."

"We have been, but you can't find all the lowlifes." He shook his head. "Most of the brothels are populated by women who chose to be there. The ones with innocents are harder to find. Until now I had no proof she was even still alive."

She went to the tiny kitchen and got fresh water for Sheba, who sauntered over to splash in the bowl. "I heard something interesting from Lily yesterday." She pivoted, twisting her hair into a knot and securing it with a pencil. "She says she met a rock star who was a friend of my mother's."

He frowned and tried to make sense of it. "Kyle was there?"

"That's what it sounds like. She didn't know his name, but the only rock star who would even know my mom's name would be Kyle. Before I could ask more questions, Lily drifted into the fog again and called him the devil's spawn."

Kyle had owned this place, and Ava had been here along with the dead girls. It made sense to see what he knew. "We're planning to talk to Kyle soon. If he's part of the trafficking ring, he may know where Ava is."

She frowned and tucked a purple strand of hair behind her ear. "It's hard for me to believe he'd be involved in something like that."

He raised a brow. She was defending Kyle after what he'd done?

"I see the look on your face. I'm not defending him, but he's got the world at his fingertips. Why would he be involved in something so seedy and shameful? It's not like he's hurting for money."

"Why did he do what he did to you? He has no respect for women and thinks he's entitled to anything he wants. That's exactly the kind of person who'd be involved with this."

She kicked off her shoes and padded in bare feet over to drop on the sofa and pull an afghan over her legs. "When you put it like that, I see your point. Have you thought any more about letting me talk to him with a wire?"

"It might be worth the risk if I can make sure you stay safe." Now that he knew Ava was alive, he was ready to consider any option. "Let me look online at his schedule and see what time he's performing tomorrow." He searched on his phone and found the information. "He's playing at eight in Seattle. Let me call his booking agent." He placed the call but had to bully the man a bit before he talked. Lance jotted down the information. "He's due in tonight. He's got a tour bus, but he's also booked a room at the Four Seasons. I'll text Daniel and have him stake out the hotel."

"Kyle's going to be livid the FBI is poking into his business."

"Good. Maybe we can poke him enough he'll spill what we want to know." Lance was itching to find out what Kyle knew. "Do you really think he'll meet with you again?"

"I want to help find your sister. I'm sure he won't tell me no."

"Let's not risk it. I'll find out which room he's staying in, and you can just show up. The shock might shake some truth loose."

He locked gazes with her and saw the goodness in her soul. Kyle Bearcroft should be shot for taking advantage of her trust and naivety. If he was involved in this whole sordid mess, he'd wish he'd never been born.

Bailey wiped sweaty palms on her jeans and stared at herself in the hotel mirror. Her hair was in an updo with tendrils of purple trailing against her cheeks. The lacy black top showed just enough cleavage to entice Kyle but covered enough that she didn't feel like a trollop. She wished it had sleeves though. She didn't like showing that much skin. The four-inch heels took some getting used to, but they gave her extra height.

The tiny microphone tucked in her bra gave her confidence. If Kyle tried anything, Lance and his men would bust into the room. The FBI had managed to find out Kyle was in the presidential suite on the tenth floor. He was there now, but he might not be for long. He was a bottom dweller, and he'd be out trolling for women tonight. She was sure of that.

She slicked on pink gloss and pinched her cheeks to bring a bit of color to them. Her hands trembled as she hooked hoop earrings into her ears, then put on a dainty cross necklace her mother had given her for her eighteenth birthday. It would bring her courage and remind her that God was with her. She had right on her side. Kyle needed to be brought to justice.

"I'm going in now." While Lance couldn't speak back to her, they'd tested the mic and she knew he heard her.

Her heels clattered on the marble floors as she held her head high and exited the room to find the elevator. She rode it to the top floor with a woman dressed in a suit and pearls who looked at her with an inquisitive gaze. Did she think she was a hooker? Bailey felt a bit like one. Skinny jeans and lace tops were not her style.

With a perfunctory smile, she got off on the tenth floor and found the suite. She took a deep breath and exhaled. *You got this.* She knocked on the door. Music blared from inside, and she recognized Kyle's distinctive smoky voice. He might be practicing or a CD could be playing. She pounded on the door again.

"Coming."

At the sound of his voice, her pulse stuttered and her breathing hitched. *Breathe, in and out.* The door opened and Kyle, clad in a white terry cloth robe, stood in the doorway. Slack-jawed, his gaze slid from her purple hair to the stilettos. He stepped out of the doorway and gestured her inside.

She kept a smile plastered on her face as she shut the door. "Surprised to see me?"

He ran his hand down the length of her bare arm. "Floored. And you're stunning."

She barely restrained the shudder at his touch. "Thanks." She moved away to look around the suite, and her heels sank into the plush carpeting. "This is spectacular." The cologne he wore made her queasy.

The space was huge, with white sofas facing each other, and two red leather chairs, all situated around a fireplace. Beautiful art hung on the walls, and the dining table would seat six.

His gaze never left her, and she could almost see him salivating. He would be disappointed he wouldn't be allowed to sample the goods. The thought of even kissing him turned her stomach. He'd already taken much more than he had any right to. Even being in his presence made her feel dirty and ashamed.

"How'd you find me?"

"It wasn't hard. When I discovered you were singing here, I knew you liked the best. I'd say this qualifies." *Please don't ask me how I found out the room number.* She couldn't lie, not even for Lance.

His mouth eased into a bemused smile. "Last time we met you said you never wanted to see me again, yet here you are. Can't stay away, can you, baby?" He took a step closer to her.

She wanted to run from this suite as fast as she could, but she forced herself to stand her ground. "I guess not. Did you hear someone killed my mother?"

His smile vanished, and he moved to pour himself a drink from the bar. "I heard that sad news. I'm really sorry."

"Thank you. Then someone tried to kill me, too, so I ran off. The funny thing is, I got to remembering how Mom was so opposed to me seeing you at first. Remember that? What did you say to her that made her change her mind?"

He shrugged. "I have a way with women of all ages. She couldn't resist my charm."

"Did you threaten her somehow, Kyle?"

"Did you only come here to grill me?"

She wished she could smack his face, but she continued to smile at him. Who knew she could be such a good actress? "I wanted to see you."

The wariness left his face, and he grinned. "I've missed you, babe. You look good in purple hair." He stepped close enough to stroke his fingers through the strands touching her cheeks. "I might not have recognized you if I hadn't seen those emerald eyes. They're one of a kind."

"Thanks."

His hand dropped and he scowled. "I-I need you to sign that deed to the cabin back over to me."

"What? Why? I like the place."

"You're living there?"

Too late she realized she'd let her location slip. *Stupid, stupid, stupid.*

He shook his head. "I really need for you to go with me to the attorney and get that taken care of."

"I'll be glad to do it if you answer me about Mom. How'd you bring her around? I'll know if you're lying to me, Kyle."

His gaze searched her face, then he nodded. "No skin off my nose, I guess. A, uh, friend called her. He made a few threats and she caved."

"What kind of threats?"

He shrugged. "The kind that make a mom run scared when they're levied against a really beautiful daughter."

"He threatened to take me and put me in a brothel?"

He blinked. "Whoa, where'd that come from? I didn't say that."

The alarm in his voice told her otherwise. She ran for the door, but he yanked her back by the arm. "You're not leaving, not now that I've found you again."

She swung around and smacked him upside the head with her purse, then yanked open the door and made her escape.

# *Chapter 25*

Ava shivered as she looked out the large window into the forest backlit by the setting sun. Frost limned the trees, and this new place held on to the cold. She clutched the blanket around her shoulders, but she still shivered. They were never allowed to open windows in case they cried out for help, so this large window was unusual.

Jessica lay curled up, napping under a comforter. At least while she was sleeping Jessica had the chance of a pleasant dream that would let her forget her circumstances. Her blonde hair spread out on the pillow, and she wore a smile. Ava knew there'd be no smiling when she awakened.

Jessica groaned and threw her arm across her eyes. "I don't want to be awake," she muttered.

So far Jessica hadn't been touched. For now. Tonight or tomorrow could be the day their captors decided she needed to earn her keep.

Ava touched the lump on her head Maly had caused when she'd been found with the phone. When she'd seen Maly's angry face, Ava had been sure she'd be the next one buried in a shallow grave, but she'd fought hard to live, to see her brother again. Had anyone found the picture of Lance she'd left? Maybe the bodies hadn't even been discovered yet, so her effort to hide it might have been worthless.

And she missed the picture. Somehow she'd managed to hide it from her captors all this time. They didn't like the girls to have any personal effects, nothing that reminded them of their previous lives that would inspire them to escape.

Jessica, her blonde hair in disarray, sat up and stretched. The strain came back to her mouth as she looked around the room. "I was hoping it was a nightmare."

"It *is* a nightmare, but it's also real. They'll be unlocking the door soon so we can go down for dinner. You hungry?"

"Not hungry, but coffee sounds good."

The keys clicked in the lock and the door opened, but it wasn't one of Maly's underlings here to escort them to dinner but Maly herself. The woman had probably been beautiful once with her black hair and chiseled features, but her life's work had taken its toll. Myriad lines creased her mouth and eyes, hard lines that spoke of disappointment, cruelty, and drugs. Ava had always wondered how Maly became the betrayer of the women here, but she'd never had the courage to ask her.

She was thin—too thin—and her flowing muumuu hid the ridges of bone Ava had seen in her other clothing. It was probably the meth she'd done over the years. She carried nothing, which was a good sign. The bad sign was that she was here.

She shut the door behind her and smiled, displaying stained teeth from meth. "No work today. Vacation coming for few weeks." Her Khmer accent and broken English were harder to understand since she'd lost a couple more teeth.

Once upon a time Ava had tried to speak Khmer to her, hoping to create a bond, but the woman just stared at her with her dark, soulless eyes.

Ava put her hands behind her and backed away a few feet. She didn't trust Maly's genial manner. "What's going on?"

"Nice trip overseas." Her gaze slid to Jessica. "Boss want the merchandise fresh so he not making you work. And you." She gestured to Ava. "You are too much trouble, but Boss moving you to new place when ready, far from here. Shanghai. All costumes lost so we make new. Photographer come take pictures. You wear dress in closet. Put on makeup, do hair. Pictures must be perfect or you punished." She pinned Ava in place with a narrowed gaze.

Ava's chest squeezed. This couldn't be happening. Jessica still looked uncomprehending, but Ava knew what this meant for her new friend. Sold to the highest bidder, either an Arab who had other wives or to someone in China. Beatings were common, and so was death. Poor Jessica would disappear into a landscape that would swallow her whole. Ava would be moved far away to a land where she couldn't communicate. How long before she was sold to a "husband" herself? Lance would never be able to find her.

Somehow Ava managed to nod. Somehow she managed not to scream. But inside, her head whipped from side to side. She would find a way out of here or die trying. She had to, especially now that she'd heard her brother's voice and knew he was still searching for her.

"Dinner now, but you come back, do as I said." Maly exited the room and shut the door behind her.

"I-I don't understand," Jessica said.

Ava's lips felt numb. "You're about to be paraded around as if on the auction block. Slaves. The buyer will take you to his country and do whatever he likes with you. I'll be forced to dance like always but in Shanghai, until they decide to sell me too." While she knew the truth was terrible to hear, she had often wished she'd known what to expect.

Jessica went white. "They can't do that."

"They do it all the time."

Tears filled her eyes as Ava rushed for the door and stepped into the dreary hallway carpeted with a fraying brown rug. *Lance, please find me.*

❧

Lance ran through the Seattle streets as fast as he could. Agents had followed Bailey, and she told him through the mic where she was heading. When he stepped into the café down the street from the hotel, he found her nursing an iced tea with lemon. Her face was white, and her hand trembled as she ran her finger along the condensation in her glass.

He dropped into the chair beside her. "He scared you."

"I hate him." Her voice shook.

"You did great, Bailey. At least we know your mom was threatened." He had been so relieved when he found her safe. She'd gotten under his skin somehow, and the thought of that lowlife hurting her had dogged him all evening.

Her green eyes were huge and tragic as she raised them to meet his gaze. "He definitely has ties with trafficking, but it didn't even seem to bother Kyle that his friend made such an outrageous threat to Mom."

Lance struggled to keep his calm. He didn't want his anger to fuel Bailey's agitation. "Knowing his connection to this is huge. We can track his known associates, get his phone records to see who he's talked to, and follow him to see if he'll lead us to that friend. And clearly your mom knew enough to be afraid of the man who called her. Maybe she even knew him."

Bailey stared at her glass. "He seemed scared that I'd leave without signing over the property. Why would he care about that? I didn't even know about it until he gave it to me."

"Makes me wonder if he'd given you that deed without permission from someone. If we could only discover who owns Baker Holdings, we might get somewhere, but it's too well hidden."

"What can I do now? See Kyle again?"

He put a protective hand on her shoulder. "No, I don't want you around him now that we know he's involved in trafficking. In fact, I don't think it's safe for you to stay at your little cottage. He knows where you are now. Can you think of anywhere else you could go?"

"I could stay with Lily. She needs more care anyway. I was thinking about fixing up the loft so I could sleep in it and bringing her to my cabin, but her place is larger. I could park my car in her garage. It's so remote, I'd be able to duck inside if I heard a car coming down the lane."

He frowned as a dozen dangerous scenarios played out in his mind. "They could come by boat and walk across though."

"Jermaine's place is between Lily's and mine. They might not go that far from the water."

She had a point, but he still didn't like it. "There's nowhere else?"

"I could rent somewhere or stay in a hotel, but I don't think moving to a different place in plain sight would slow them down for long. They might not think to look at Lily's."

He couldn't fault her logic. "Okay. I don't suppose there's room for me at Lily's?"

"It's a four-bedroom cabin, so there's plenty of room."

Was that hope in her eyes? He knew she was scared. Who wouldn't be with the danger lurking around her that seemed to increase every day. "I'll move in, too, then if you think it's okay with Lily. This connection to Kyle is my only lead to the traffickers. It will probably bring me more information than aimlessly walking the streets of Seattle searching for Ava."

"I doubt Lily will mind. I'll need to clean it first. The place is a mess. I can sleep in a hotel tonight, then go down and clean it tomorrow."

"I've got a two-bedroom condo here in Seattle. It's late. You can stay with me, and we'll both go back to Lavender Tides tomorrow. Or if you'd rather stay in a hotel, I can camp out there. I don't think you should be alone."

Her green eyes held his captive. He'd never seen eyes like hers, and he couldn't look away. It was as if she were seeing into his soul to test his motives.

She finally nodded. "I can stay in your spare room. I'm exhausted, quite honestly. But I didn't bring a change of clothes. As long as we go back first thing in the morning, it should be okay. Sheba will want breakfast. I put water out for her and fed her before I left the house."

"I've got sweats you can wear. They'll be big on you, but they're clean. And I even have a hair dryer and shampoo." He grinned and signaled for the server. "Let's have some dinner first. I'm famished."

"Me too, now that I'm away from Kyle's cologne. I used to like it, but now it makes me want to throw up."

He glanced at the menu as the server, a college girl from the looks of her, came their way. "I think I'll have a burger and fries."

"Sounds good to me. Red meat to strengthen my backbone. Put avocado on mine, please."

The server jotted down their order and left them alone again. Lance studied Bailey's face and the way her long lashes lay on her cheeks as she gazed down at her hands. "Have you always had purple hair?"

She looked up and smiled. "I dyed it on the drive out here. I'd read that if you want to hide, pick a really bold and outlandish style. People will notice the hair or the clothes and not you."

"I don't think anyone could avoid noticing you, purple hair or not." His face heated. He couldn't believe he'd just said what he was thinking. "I mean, you're a striking woman. You can't hide those eyes. Your mom had green eyes too?" *Nice save. Deflect the topic to something safe.*

She shook her head. "She had blue eyes and much lighter hair. I don't know where I got my coloring. Maybe my dad, but she would never talk about him. I don't even know his name." She reached up and pulled the pins from her hair. "My head hurts." Her hair tumbled down onto her shoulders, and she ran her fingers against her scalp. "That feels better."

He was more attracted to her than he'd thought. There was more to her than her beauty. And everything about her intrigued him. Staying close to Bailey might be more dangerous than he'd thought.

## *Chapter 26*

Bailey should have felt nervous being alone with Lance in his condo, but she wasn't. They stepped into the spacious condo. The light wood floors and gray walls enveloped her with tranquility the moment he shut the door behind them. A faint odor of Pine-Sol hung in the room, and the place seemed spotless.

He showed her around the condo, including the spare room, which held a queen bed covered with an all-white quilt decorated with ocean-blue pillows. The walls were a pale blue, several shades lighter than the pillows, and a seascape rug softened the hardwood floors. "This is beautiful."

"There's a lock on your door." He pointed it out and held her gaze. "Just in case you're nervous."

"I'm not. I trust you." She shouldn't, not with her track record, but the man made it hard to hold on to her armor. His steady dark-blue eyes inspired total belief in his abilities and his character.

He smiled. "Your bathroom is just across the hall." He flipped off the lights to the guest room as they exited.

She peeked inside the spacious bathroom. The marble top held two sinks, and the huge tiled shower looked inviting.

He pointed to his right. "My room is at the end of the hall."

The door he referred to was closed. "I don't get to see if you're a slob?"

She didn't expect him to open the door, but he did. She peeked inside from the doorway to a king bed neatly made with a blue quilt, no pillows. The dresser had nothing on top of it, and the bedside tables held only lamps. Neat as a pin.

"Are all FBI agents neat freaks?"

"I'm a minimalist." His eyes gleamed. "I'm probably the exception and not the rule among agents. Daniel's place would give you a heart attack, but he's got a toddler in the house."

"Aw, he has a baby?" She followed him to the comfortable living room with its overstuffed leather sectional and dark-wood tables. "How old?"

"Milo just turned one. I was at his birthday party, and it was bedlam. I wanted to pick up all the wrapping paper and corral all the toys. Milo is cute though, and I'm sure he's worth living in that mess."

She sank into the welcoming embrace of the couch cushions. "I'd love to have half a dozen kids." The words were out before she realized it. "Sorry, we're treading into personal ground again, aren't we?"

"I think we're beyond a victim and law-enforcement type of relationship. Why so many kids?"

"I grew up alone. You know about my stepbrothers. I always wanted a little brother or sister. Since I can't have them, I hope to someday fill the house with laughter and kids." She fell silent and stared down at her hands. "I've always wanted a real home.

We bounced from rental to rental most of my life. I don't even have any cousins. No family at all now that Mom's gone."

She cleared her thickening throat. This wasn't the kind of thing she usually shared with anyone. He watched her intently. His half-smile seemed approving.

She forced a lighter tone into her voice. "How about you? You have a girlfriend who'll come hunting for me because I stayed here?"

His eyes crinkled at the corners, and he barked out a laugh. "There's not a lot of time for dating when you're with the FBI. I got through school in record time by taking as heavy a load as I was allowed, and I took summer school too. I got engaged my first summer out of school, but she didn't like playing second fiddle to my obsession to find Ava. I had what seemed a credible lead the weekend of my engagement party and went to check it out. She called off the wedding the week before the ceremony."

"You're kidding! A party isn't worth Ava's life."

"That's what I thought, but Kim had a different view. And I found I was okay with it. Looking back I realized it was always about her. Kim had little interest in my family, and it was always difficult to get her to visit my parents. I doubt we could have made a marriage work. But if life ever settles down, I wouldn't mind having a bunch of kids. I could about eat up little Milo."

"Driven," she said.

He nodded. "Guilty as charged. I wanted to find my sister."

"I can't imagine how hard this has been."

"Pure torture," he agreed. "So you moved a lot and you always wanted siblings. What else? How'd you get into nursing?"

She smiled and pulled her legs up under her on the sofa. "I gravitated to older people in the neighborhoods we moved to.

I told you about always looking for the missing grandparents. When I was thirteen, we lived in an apartment building in Phoenix. There was a sweet little old lady next door who used to have me over for milk and cookies after school. She started failing, and her daughter asked me to keep an eye on her. I cooked for her, gave her medicine when it was time, and spent a lot of hours with her. I loved her so much. I found I liked taking care of people." She shrugged. "Sounds lame."

"It doesn't sound lame. You care about other people. That's a rarity in this world."

His soft words caused her pulse to thump in her chest. "I'm not one to play games, Lance. I find it hard to hold back on talking about something when it's staring me in the face, and I feel like there's something between us. Something different—and maybe even special. It could be my imagination, but I like being around you. You're—different. I don't have a great track record though, so I have to tell you I'm terrified at the way I'm feeling."

The gentle expression in his eyes intensified. "Shew, you don't pull any punches, do you?" He chuckled. "It's not your imagination, Bailey. I like being around you too. Probably more than I should when I'm supposed to be concentrating on finding my sister."

"I want to help you do that."

"I know you do. And once she's found, I'd like to ask you out."

She held his gaze. "I'll say yes."

His gentle smile came again. "That's a load off my mind."

He was nothing like Kyle. This was a man she could trust with her life—and that's exactly what she'd been doing for the past few days. If anyone could find out what was happening, it was Lance.

❧

His secretary had started the coffee, and King inhaled the aroma of his Guatemalan coffee, then sipped a cup as he took care of signing various paperwork she'd left for him. He had several meetings in Seattle today, so he'd have to wrap things up quickly, then make the two-hour drive to the city.

He smiled. Life was good, and his business had never been better. The big arms purchase he'd just landed would bring in several million.

Chey knocked, then came on in. "Sir, I have the new pictures of the girls, both the ones we're selling and the ones who will be dancing in Shanghai. Would you like to see them, or should I forge ahead with arranging sales?"

"Let me take a look." He enjoyed this part of the business. His merchandise was always the best quality.

Chey crossed the walnut floors and handed him a sheaf of glossy photos. Lotus's photo was on top, and he stared at her full lips and exotic eyes. "She's as beautiful as ever. She'll be a big hit in Shanghai." He flipped to the next picture, a young blonde. "She's very attractive. I haven't seen her before. How long have we had her?"

"Just got her a couple of days ago. She hasn't been with any johns yet."

He pursed his lips. "Excellent. Let's advertise her as a virgin. She'll bring in a lot of money."

He went through the other pictures, some American, some foreign. Many of the girls in his stable were plucked from countries like Cambodia, Thailand, and Romania, but the Apsara-trained dancers were the most valuable to his organization. "Looks good. Let's get rid of all of them but the dancers until the heat's off. We can also snatch more girls in a few months and start over with the lower-class brothels."

"Yes, sir." Chey accepted the stack of photos and headed for the door. As he opened it, Kyle burst into the room.

"You've got to do something!" Kyle's hair was mussed, and he had dark circles under his eyes. The shirt he wore was wrinkled like it had been slept in. If he'd slept at all.

"What's going on?" He motioned for Chey to close the door behind him. "Get some coffee and calm down."

"I don't want coffee." Kyle raked his hand through his disheveled blond hair. "Bailey came to see me last night. She's been staying at the cabin, and I think the only reason she visited was to grill me about her mom."

Kyle was such an idiot that he'd likely spilled information he should have kept buttoned up. "What did she say?"

Kyle paced the floor. "She wanted to know how I'd gotten her mom to change her mind and favor the marriage. She'd evidently been thinking about it and remembered how opposed her mom had been at first."

"What did you tell her?" He kept his voice deceptively calm, but he curled his hands into fists in his lap.

"She startled me so much that I told her the truth. That a friend had threatened her mom. She somehow made the assumption the friend meant to put her in a brothel, so I think she knows something about the sex trafficking."

"You idiot! Why did you tell her that?" Under the desk, he reached for the secret door with the gun. He'd like to shoot Kyle himself.

"I didn't give her your name, of course. I didn't even tell her you were my uncle."

That was something at least. "She must have called the FBI, and that's how they found the bodies. Did you check her for a wire?"

Kyle blinked, then frowned and dropped into the chair. "Why would I even think she was wearing a wire? She just showed up at my hotel room dressed to the nines and looking hot. I thought maybe she wanted to get together."

"Probably to soften you up." The boy was such an idiot. And a liability. If the FBI happened to find the older body, it could lead to all kinds of trouble.

Kyle would have to be eliminated. A pity, but he'd always known he'd have to kill him sooner or later. He didn't want to share the business. He'd built it to this stage, and it belonged to him.

He put his hand on the desk and drummed his fingers. "Where is Bailey now?"

"Back at Cedar Cabin, I assume. She ran out of the hotel room when I asked her to sign the cabin back over to me."

"So you failed in that simple task as well."

Kyle shrugged. "I'm sorry, Uncle, but she wasn't listening to much of anything I said."

"I need the property back. I can't get rid of her unless I get that deed. Otherwise it would go to her next of kin."

"She has no next of kin. Could I produce the marriage certificate and show I'm her husband? As long as it didn't hit the news, no one would contest that."

"That might work." Which meant he'd have to let Kyle live just a little longer. At least he now knew where to find Bailey.

# *Chapter 27*

Lance hadn't slept much last night. Bailey's sweet words kept ringing over and over in his head. *"Something between us."* That felt like an understatement. The moment the words left her mouth, they'd lodged in his heart. He'd been trying to ignore the pull he felt toward her, but she dragged it right out into the open.

One thing about Bailey—you'd always know where you stood with her. She didn't play games, just like she'd said. How many women could say that? Once the traffickers were behind bars and their captives were free, he'd find out just where this relationship might go.

At the first streaks of sunlight through his blinds, he rose, showered, and pulled on jeans and a sweatshirt. When he stepped into the hallway, he nearly collided with her coming out of the bathroom, and he set his hands on her shoulders to steady them both. Her hair was up in a towel, and she wore a white terry-cloth robe he kept in the spare-room closet for guests. Her skin smelled heavenly, a mixture of vanilla shower gel and warm woman.

"Sorry." He couldn't seem to take his hands away. Her arms were warm and pliant under his fingers.

Her green eyes huge, she looked up at him with a smile. "I thought I heard you stirring. It's only six."

"I couldn't sleep."

"Me neither."

What would she do if he leaned down and tasted those plump, kissable lips? He couldn't tear his gaze away from them.

He didn't have to wonder long, because she stood on her tiptoes and brushed her lips across his. She started to pull away, but his hands moved to her waist and he pulled her back against him for a better taste. Her kiss was like honey, sweet and innocent. His fingers tangled in her damp hair, and the towel dropped to the floor. Her wet hair tumbled onto her shoulders, but he didn't care. He could drink of that sweetness all day long.

She made a small sound, and he instantly let her go. Her fingers went to her lips. "Um, that was supposed to be a thank-you kiss."

"I'd take another thank-you like that anytime."

"Maybe one more." She stood on her toes again and wrapped her arms around his neck.

He pulled her back into his arms and was shocked to find the second kiss even better than the first. Passion sparked between them, and he forced himself to release her. "I'll fix us some breakfast."

"A man who cooks. Can you get any better?"

"I whip up a mean omelet. Or pancakes, whichever you prefer."

"Omelets sound good. I'll be fast." She sent him one last glance, then stepped into the guest room and shut the door.

He exhaled. Wow. Feeling a little shaky, he stumbled to the kitchen and got out the fixings for omelets. Mushrooms, spinach, jalapeño, broccoli, bacon, and cheese were his favorites. He'd see what she liked when she came out. He put some sausage links in the skillet and began to cook them, then got out another skillet and put it on a burner to heat.

He heard the patter of her bare feet on the wood floor only minutes later. Her hair was still wet but up in a messy bun. She wore the same skinny jeans and lace top from last night. "I have clean sweats if you need them. Not that I'm complaining. You look stunning."

She smiled. "These weren't really dirty. I can change when I get home." She perched on a bar stool at the island where the cooktop was located. "I like your kitchen. Dark cabinets, marble counters—just beautiful."

"It's why I bought it. Nice, masculine kitchen. What do you like in your omelets?"

"The works. Whatever you're having. There isn't much I don't like."

He nodded and assembled the first omelet. "Want jalapeños?"

"Doesn't everyone? The hotter the better."

He slanted a grin her way. "Like your kisses."

She flushed. "I'd say that was your department."

So this was what dating banter was like. There'd been nothing like this with Kim. He was already in trouble when what he really wanted to do was let the omelets burn while he kissed Bailey until they were both breathless again.

*Focus.*

He cracked the eggs into a bowl with cream and whisked them to a froth, then dumped the mixture into the vegetables.

In moments he served up a fluffy omelet dripping with cheese. He slid it across the counter to her. "There's sour cream in the fridge if you want any. Avocado too."

"This looks perfect. A restaurant couldn't have done a better job." She grabbed the pepper mill and ground some on her food, then tucked into it. "Yummy. I was starving." She stared at the forkful of food. "This pepper is good."

"It's Khmer pepper. Best pepper in the world. When I use it, I think of Ava. Our mom is from Cambodia, and she looks just like Mom, while I have more of our dad in me. Using the pepper is one small way of being close to her."

"That's a lovely thing to do."

He finished cooking his omelet, then took sour cream out of the fridge and carried it to the counter. They ate in companionable silence as the coffee brewed.

When the coffeepot beeped, he poured them both a cup. "Cream?"

"Black."

"The perfection just keeps on going." He put the coffee mug in front of her.

Her smile faltered. "I'm far from perfect, Lance. If my mother were here, she'd tell you. I speak my mind. I'm opinionated, bossy, and I like things to go my way."

"Don't we all." He reached over and curled a strand of loose hair around his finger.

She batted his hand away. "I'm serious. I fail the Lord every day. Which reminds me, I haven't even asked how you feel about God. That's a nonnegotiable as far as I'm concerned. I didn't ask Kyle about it because I was too awestruck. I won't make that mistake again."

He grinned. "I'm auditioning for the role of boyfriend? I can tell you with total truth that I love the Lord. I may not be perfect either, but I try to follow the path Jesus laid down for me. At least your mom raised you right."

She shook her head. "It had nothing to do with Mom. She didn't have much use for God. I started going to church with one of those neighborhood grandparents I found. I've been a Christian since I was nine. Mom was horrified when I told her, but at least she didn't forbid me to go."

"I was ten."

She relaxed. "I'm glad. I would have hated to break up with you before we even got started."

"It would have been a tragedy." He leaned in closer. "How about one more kiss? Then we have to behave ourselves."

A dimple appeared by the corner of her mouth. "Just one more."

---

Bailey's spirits were high as she drove to check on Jason. Sheba had been all over her the minute she walked in the door, so she brought the cat with her again. Jason had liked Sheba.

Another car sat in the drive when she parked. The wood door was open but the screen door was shut when she approached with the cat in her arms. She heard the sound of voices.

"Hello," she called. "It's Bailey."

"Come on in," a woman replied.

Bailey stepped inside and put squirming Sheba on the floor. The cat pounced like Tigger across the floor and leaped onto Jason's lap. The place looked bright and airy today. Someone had done a major housecleaning job, and she smelled cleaner and lemon wax.

Jason scratched Sheba's ears. "You brought my friend back to see me."

He seemed to be in a good mood today. Bailey walked into the living room. Mac, her employer, sat in a chair. "Well, hello again."

"Jason tells me you have him on the straight-and-narrow path to independence," she said with a smile.

"It's early days yet. I have much more torture in store for him."

He laughed. "I think I'm scared. She's quite the disciplinarian, Mac. You don't know her very well."

"But I'd like to know her better. I was going to call you today, Bailey. I'm having a crab boil on my ship tonight and I'd love you to come. Some of my friends will be there."

"I'd love to. What's a crab boil? And do you mind if I bring a guest?" She told Mac about Lance. He wouldn't want her to go anywhere without him.

"The more the merrier. And you'll find out what a crab boil is when you get there." Mac rose and went over to touch Jason on the shoulder. "I'll pick you up at five, and you can help me."

His expression darkened. "A lot of help I'll be."

"You just wait. I'm going to put you to work." She wiggled her fingers at Bailey as she went out the door.

"What's going on with you? You're actually smiling," Bailey said. "And someone's cleaned the house."

He kept his face averted. "Mac came yesterday."

"You seemed a lot angrier at her the other day. Not that it's any of my business."

"Yeah, well, she apologized when she came by. We're going to try to get along. So what's on the agenda for today?"

"The kitchen. I'm going to organize it so you can find things easily. And I brought your cane and some other supplies. Let me get them out of the car." She walked back outside and retrieved the cane.

He was still playing with the cat when she brought the cane to him. "I want you to try this. Move it back and forth in small sweeping motions in front of you. If it knocks against something, you'll know there's an obstruction and can find a way around it."

He put the cat down and rose. She placed the cane in his hand and showed him how to move it. "Let's go to the kitchen. I'll tell you what I'm doing and why." She carried her box of supplies.

He made a pretty good job of moving slowly with the cane into the kitchen. "Start counting your steps and mapping out the walls and distance in your head. It will become second nature eventually."

She touched his shoulder and ran her hand down to his fingers. "The chair at the breakfast bar is to your right. Three steps."

She guided him to it and placed his hand on the seat back. He fumbled awkwardly onto the seat and leaned the cane against the counter.

"Great job. Okay, I'm going to put rubber bands on your canned goods as I organize them. Let me see what you've got." She opened the pantry and perused the contents. "Vegetables, legumes, soups, sauces, canned meats. Here's what it's going to look like. You'll find one rubber band on vegetables, two bands for black beans, three for canned meats, four for soups. So it goes by plants, then meats, then soups. Think you can remember it?"

"I think so."

She pulled open a drawer. "You've already got dividers for your cutlery. Do you know how they're organized?"

"Knives on the left, then forks, then spoons."

"Right! I'm putting your spatulas and things like that in a bucket. All you'll have to do is feel for what you want. And I'm putting your pots in the drawer to the right of the stove. The skillets are in the tray under the oven." She busied herself for a few minutes rearranging things.

"Now to your stove. Luckily it's electric. I'm putting little tactile dots by the different temperatures from low to high. One dot for low, two for medium, and three for high. Sounds easy, right?"

"Yeah." He was beginning to sound a little interested.

"Almost done. Stay with me." She opened the refrigerator door and nearly fainted. It was packed with fresh food. "Mac's been here, too, I see. I'll buy some special containers to store different types of food in, but for now, she's got your vegetables in the veggie tray and the fruit in the fruit tray."

"Why are you doing this?" he blurted out. "Have you heard I'm not going to see?"

The desperation in his voice tugged at her heart. "Not at all. But new skills are never wasted. Maybe by the time you learn all this, your sight will be back."

"I sure hope so." He hopped off the chair and stumbled over his cane, crashing to the ground. She rushed to help him, and he waved her off with a grimace. The bleakness on his face pained her.

# *Chapter 28*

With Bailey gone to check on her patient, Lance walked with Daniel out onto the pier. He sat on the far edge and dangled his legs above the waves to watch sea otters frolic in the water. The sounds of birds in the trees mingled with the rustle of leaves from the wind. He liked the smells too—the salty brine in the air and the rich scent of the forest all around him. This place was special with its varied wildlife and sea animals. He wished he could sit here for hours and let his cares slide away.

Daniel dropped down beside him. "I don't know if or when we'll get any kind of ID on the skeleton. I did some research on the background of this house." He pulled out his phone. "Before Baker Holdings acquired it, it belonged to Lily Norman. Her parents built it in the twenties. At the time they owned the property where the Diskin house sits too. According to utility records her daughter, Olivia Norman, lived here starting in 1993. She left in 1995, just days after an earthquake damaged the town, including this cabin. Lily couldn't afford to have it repaired, so when Baker Holdings offered to buy it, she sold it. She sold off the undeveloped land between her house and this one at the same time, also to Baker Holdings."

"Do we know who approached her to buy this?"

Daniel shook his head. "It would help if she could remember that."

"When she's having a good day, I'll see if she remembers anything." Though Lance had never seen one of those good days yet, he hadn't been around her as much as Bailey.

"Once we date the skeleton, we'll be able to figure out who was living here."

Daniel glanced at his phone. "We do have a hint about that. I called the ME before I came out here. He found a folded-up paper in the vic's pocket. The paper was mostly decayed and in tatters, but he used some kind of technique to read bits of it, enough to get a date off it. He couldn't read the month or day but the year was 1995. So he thinks it likely the person died about then. It's a male. That's about all we know so far."

"That's when Olivia left here, after the earthquake. Coincidence? Maybe, but maybe not. It's possible she killed the vic, then vamoosed."

Daniel nodded. "A good chance of it, I'd say. Too bad she's dead and we can't talk to her."

"But we can investigate those who were her friends when she lived here. Did anyone go missing back then? Was there any talk of her being involved in something shady, that kind of thing?"

Daniel put his phone away. "Olivia's at the heart of all this somehow. If we could just connect all the dots."

"Yeah. Learned some interesting stuff last night." Lance told him about Bailey's talk with Kyle. "While he didn't say she'd be sold into the sex trade, when Bailey jumped to that conclusion, he didn't deny it and seemed shocked she knew. So something's there. Kyle knows who's behind this. Which means he knows who has my sister." Lance squeezed his hands into fists. It had been all he could do not to charge in there and throttle Kyle when he'd heard what he said. And his tone. He clearly knew something.

Daniel grimaced. "Maybe we should bring him in for questioning."

"I don't want to spook him and scare off whoever has Ava. She's somewhere nearby—I can feel it. The leader of this might decide to cut his losses and dispose of the girls. We can't let that happen. Any results from the wiretap and the tail on him? Maybe he will lead us to the kingpin."

"I had a bit of trouble getting a judge to sign the warrants, but we're on him as of last night. What's next for Bailey? I have to say I'm not really comfortable with her staying out here by herself. It's too remote."

"I already told her the same thing. She's going to stay with Lily and so am I. Where she goes, I go for now." He grimaced. "Except to a crab boil. She invited me, but I'm not crazy about them."

"It would do you good. You're too obsessed. Go and have fun tonight."

Was Daniel right? Lance rubbed his face. It had been ages since he'd done anything for fun. "Maybe you're right."

"I can take a turn keeping watch over her tonight."

Lance tossed a leaf into the water to watch it swirl in the eddies. "You've got a little guy at home who'll be disappointed if you're not there. I can handle it by myself for now. You know I sleep with one eye open."

"You're like a cat." Daniel nodded. "So where's Bailey now?"

"Checking on her patient, the guy who was blinded in the takedown of the EMP bomb threat last month."

"He's still blind? I heard it would be temporary."

Lance rose and brushed off his hands. "Yeah, it hasn't lifted yet. But it still might. She's showing him how to get around and do things for himself. Bailey's making headway."

Daniel rose too. "We've been friends awhile now."

Lance lifted a brow and waited. His buddy had something to say. "So?"

"You like Bailey."

"Well, sure. Don't you?"

"I don't watch her like a drowning man grasping for a floatation device."

"Hey, neither do I."

Daniel grinned. "You haven't seen yourself, my friend. Watch yourself. A damsel in distress is hard to resist, especially one as pretty and vulnerable as Bailey."

"We've had our share of damsels in distress." Lance chuckled, hopeful the diversion would work.

"I'm serious, Lance. You don't know much about her yet, and you're planning on spending even more time with her. You could fall hard really fast."

Did he dare tell his friend it might already be too late? One look into Bailey's green eyes had started the slide. Maybe he'd go to that crab boil after all.

---

The evening couldn't be more perfect for a meal out on the water. Bailey stood with Lance aboard the ship in the dimming sunshine. She'd never been on a tall ship before, and *Lavender Lady* was beautiful. Mac had Jason at work husking corn, a job he seemed content to do. After his dark mood earlier today, she wasn't sure how he would act tonight.

She'd asked Lily to come, but her grandmother just wanted to sleep, so Bailey left her at the house snoring in bed.

Bailey smiled at Mac. "We're the first ones here?"

"Yep. My sister and her boyfriend, Grayson, are coming. Also a good friend and her husband, Shauna and Zach Bannister. You'll like them. Shauna has a five-year-old boy, but he's at his grandmother's for the weekend. They are very close. Her first husband, Jack, died in a climbing accident, and his mother, Marilyn, is crazy about Alex. So it's all adults tonight."

Lance looked up. "Shauna Bannister? The helicopter pilot?"

Mac's eyes brightened. "You know her?"

"She helped me out the other night. Nice lady."

"The best." Mac nodded.

"I don't suppose Grayson's last name is Bradshaw?" Lance asked.

"It sure is. You know him too?"

Lance grinned. "Yep. I consulted with him on the EMP threat last month. We've been colleagues a long time."

"At least you'll know a few people," Bailey said.

Mac looked beautiful tonight with her brown curls contrasting against a brightly colored top. The wind kicked up and Bailey tugged on her zip-up sweatshirt. The temperature had hit sixty today, but when the sun set, it was going to get cooler. Voices from the shore snagged her attention, and two couples headed down the dock to the other boat tied up there.

Mac returned their waves. "There they are, right on time."

Bailey leaned against the railing and watched the big man row them out. She was eager to make new friends here and was beginning to think she didn't ever want to leave this place. Lavender Tides held a special charm that had quickly ensnared her.

The couples laughed and talked as they climbed the access ladder. They looked to be in their twenties or thirties, and Bailey hung back a bit as they boarded the ship.

The first woman to step aboard smiled at her. "You must be Mac's new friend. I'm her sister, Ellie Blackmore."

In her mid- to late twenties, the young woman had unusual eyes that were almost golden. Her friendly expression set Bailey at ease. "Pleased to meet you, Ellie."

In quick succession the rest of the party boarded and stood waiting for introductions. Lance and the big man Bailey assumed must be Grayson Bradshaw had clapped each other on the back and immediately began to talk shop.

Mac pulled Bailey forward to stand by her. "Guys, this is my new friend. She's a nurse and has been helping Jason so much. You'll see he's here tonight. She's brought him out of his cave."

"You're forgetting her name. We can't just call her nurse," Ellie said.

Mac grinned. "Sorry, I'm a little airheaded tonight."

"Tonight?" the other woman said. She had black hair and wore jeans and a sweatshirt. Her friendly smile came quickly as she stepped forward. "I'm Shauna Bannister, and this is my husband, Zach."

Bailey took her hand and felt a warm sensation of instant liking. "Bailey. Bailey Fleming."

The woman's eyes went wide, and it was only then that Bailey realized they were a vivid green, just like hers. Lance would have to admit he was wrong. She wasn't the only one in the world with that shade of eye color.

Shauna sought the big guy's gaze. "Grayson?"

Grayson was easily six six with shoulders like a linebacker. He stared down at Bailey with his mouth dangling open. His gaze traveled from her hair to her face and back again. "Um, did you used to live in Rock Harbor, Michigan?"

"I did. I arrived in town a few days ago. Are you from there? Have we met?"

Shauna let out a gasp and took her husband's hand, then reached for Bailey. "We've been looking for you. You colored your hair, which is why I didn't recognize you immediately."

She took a step back. How would this woman know she'd colored her hair? "I don't understand."

Grayson stepped closer to Shauna. "Shauna is my sister." He stared down at Shauna for a long moment with an appeal for assistance on his face. "Um, I just got back from Rock Harbor, and the sheriff told me you'd left after someone tried to kill you. We weren't sure we'd ever be able to track you down again."

Bailey took a step back and locked gazes with Lance. He hurried to her side and took her hand. What was going on? "This isn't making any sense. I've never seen either of you before. Why would you want to track me down?"

Shauna's green eyes glimmered with tears, and her smile beamed out. "You've seen us but you wouldn't remember because you were only minutes old."

Bailey had to swallow before she could speak again. "Minutes old?" Lance's strong grip on her was the only thing steadying her right now. She had the sensation that the universe was about to tip, to spill her right into the sea, but maybe it was the gentle roll of the waves making her feel that way.

Shauna held her hand out. "This is going to come as a shock, Bailey. Grayson and I are your siblings. You were born to our mother during an earthquake that killed her. I thought you'd both died in the quake, but I found out two months ago you both survived. Grayson was adopted, but you . . ." She swallowed hard. "Your mother was the paramedic who delivered you."

Shauna dropped her hand and bit her lip. "There's no easy way to say this, Bailey. She took you. The paramedic, Olivia Fleming, took you. Stole you right out of the rubble."

*Took you. Stole you.*

Bailey gasped. Her vision blurred. Was she going to throw up? "You're wrong," she whispered through numb lips.

But it was the truth. She saw it in Shauna's black hair and green eyes, in the shape of her face and the length of her fingers. She saw it in the little bow in her upper lip and the tiny dimple by her lips when she moved her mouth a certain way. She saw the widow's peak in Shauna's hairline—just like the one Bailey saw in the mirror every morning.

They were carbon copies in appearance even though Bailey was taller.

Her knees gave out, and she would have fallen to the deck if Lance's strong hand wasn't holding her up. He hadn't said anything, but the compassion in his eyes told her he saw it too.

Shauna was telling the truth. Her mother, the woman she'd loved so much, had lied about her entire life.

*Took her.*

"I-I have to sit down."

Lance led her to a chair, got her seated, then knelt beside her. "Can you grab her some water?"

Shauna quickly brought her a bottle of water, then stood back to give her air. "I'm sorry this has rocked you, Bailey. Just know that I love you. I held you for a little while and loved you immediately."

Bailey looked up at her through a haze. "How old were you?"

"I was eight when you were born. There's so much more to tell you, but it can wait. Just know we're here, Grayson and me. We'll do whatever we can to make this easier on you. I wouldn't hurt you for the world." Her voice trembled.

Bailey saw the great love in her eyes and sighed. She didn't know what it all meant yet, but maybe she wasn't alone after all.

## *Chapter 29*

Night had fallen quickly, shrouding his garden in shadows. The trees and shrubs blocked most of the wind, and King strolled through the walkways without a jacket. This was his favorite part of the day, just as twilight fell and the moon showed its face. Out here he had peace and could usually forget the past for a bit.

Not tonight though. Why was he still so sad about Olivia? He hadn't seriously thought she would ever come back to him. He'd promised to protect her as long as she kept his secret. Once she'd told him Bailey's kidnapping as an infant would likely bring out everything, he couldn't continue to risk her testifying against him. It was as simple as that.

But tonight it didn't feel simple—it felt as tragic as the plot for Romeo and Juliet, though he wasn't about to follow Olivia in death. He had too much to live for.

He heard a sound behind him and turned as Chey opened the French doors and headed his way. "Good news I hope," King said as Chey stopped in front of him. "Are the girls all sold?"

"They are, sir. Their new owners will take possession in about four days."

"Four days is too long. Speed it up."

"I wish I could. It takes time to arrange the right boat and method of concealing them. I have a freighter heading this way to drop off its cargo. The captain has agreed to take them with him to Japan. Some of the girls will stay there, and the others will be sent on to their owners."

"How much did we get?"

Chey smiled and named a figure that made King whistle through his teeth. "That much? Excellent work, Chey."

"Thank you. I do my best."

Chey's best was always exemplary. "What about Bailey Fleming? Are you close to picking her up?"

"I've had a drone watching the house, but she's been gone most of the day. Right now she's aboard the tall ship *Lavender Lady* for a crab boil. She should be home soon."

"Take her tonight. When you have her, deliver her to my place in the mountains and let me know. I'll talk to her there. And have my attorney draw up the deed transfer. I'll get her to sign it before she's disposed of."

"I'll send out a couple of people tonight, and they can take her by boat." Chey cleared his throat. "Do you want her killed or sold? I think she could bring in a large price."

King wasn't one to turn down a profit. "Arrange to sell her then."

"I'll do it immediately."

"I'll go ahead and tell my wife I'm spending the night at my hunting lodge. I'll drive up and be waiting."

"I'll send some men out right away."

With Chey gone King continued to walk in his garden for a few minutes to calm himself. The door opened, and his wife stepped onto the brick path.

"There you are. Dinner is nearly ready."

Her smile seemed genuine, and there might even be a come-hither expression in her eyes. He couldn't remember the last time he'd seen that.

With a surreptitious glance at the time, he smiled. "I need to attend to an issue up at the hunting lodge, but I have time for dinner with you. You look beautiful tonight." He almost regretted having to leave.

Displeasure glimmered in her eyes. "We're alone tonight, and I'd hoped we could sit down with a glass of wine and enjoy the evening."

"It's only six. I can stay awhile." He looped his arm around her waist and drew her in for a kiss.

She stiffened, then relaxed and kissed him back but it was perfunctory and held no passion. What was her deal? He'd thought she wanted a romantic evening. Or did she have some other kind of "talk" in mind?

"What's going on, honey?"

She pulled away and crossed her arms over her chest. "You're not going to make this easy, are you? You never make anything easy."

His gut clenched at the way her eyes narrowed. "Make what easy?"

"I want a divorce."

A bomb explosion couldn't have caused him to flinch more. "You're joking."

She shook her head. "I'm not kidding. I've found someone else."

The thought of *his wife* in the arms of another man nearly stole his breath. He clenched his fists. "Who?"

"It doesn't matter. You're never here anyway. All you care about is the business. When was the last time you even noticed my hair or what I was wearing? I've lost twenty pounds, and you haven't even noticed. I put highlights in my hair last week, and you didn't say a word."

"This is about losing weight and getting your hair done?" He raised his voice.

"Of course not. It's just a symptom of how you've ignored me for years. I want the house, of course."

*And half of everything.* His wife would hire a high-powered attorney to poke into every single bit of his business. His thoughts raced. He couldn't allow that. While he thought he had most everything hidden too well to be found, there was no telling what a determined divorce lawyer could dig up. And his business was her family business. All his income would be stripped away.

"Have you filed yet?" He modulated his tone.

"Not yet, but I have an appointment on Friday. I wanted to give you fair warning. I hate it when women lock the man out of his own house without so much as a word."

"I appreciate that. To say I'm breathless over this would be an understatement. I'd be willing to go to counseling."

"But I'm not." Her smile was sad. "You forget I know how much you despise counselors. It would just be a way to talk me out of this. And I'm in love. Really in love. You can't change my mind." She spun around and vanished back inside.

He would have to arrange an accident for her. A fatal one. He couldn't kill her lover. She'd immediately suspect he'd done it, even if it looked like an accident. And she had to be stopped before she filed, because law enforcement would examine it more in-depth if they were separated.

He hated the pain this would cause the family, but it couldn't be helped.

⁂

Bailey was still shaking, and it wasn't just from the breeze that had kicked up. They'd moved the feast below deck. The aroma of the crab boil—corn, potatoes, crab, bay seasoning, lemon, and garlic—filled the space, but she couldn't think about food right now.

Shauna's green eyes never left her, and Bailey didn't know what to think, what to say.

She sat quietly on a chair at the big wooden table by the galley. She was cold, so cold. The trembling had started the minute she'd learned her mother had stolen her, and it only intensified.

Lance pressed a cup of coffee into her hands. "Have something to drink." His dark eyes pinned Shauna in place. "You're sure of your facts?"

Grayson put his hand on Shauna's shoulder. "Aren't you? Take a look at Shauna and compare the two of them." His voice rose and he glared at Lance, who shrugged.

"When I met Shauna the other day, I knew she reminded me of someone, but I was too intent on my mission to take the time to figure it out. The resemblance is astonishing."

Bailey took a few sips of coffee, and the shaking eased a bit. "Why do you say Mom stole me? How could something like that happen?"

"You were born in the debris of a grocery store after an earthquake," Shauna said. "We were trapped there, and our mom went into labor. I scrambled through the pieces of cinder block and debris to try to find help. Your mom quickly came with me to assist Mom. You were born pretty fast, and I held you while she tried to save Mom, but it was no use. She d-died." The muscles in Shauna's throat convulsed as she swallowed hard.

"Then what happened?" Bailey rubbed her hand over her face. "It's so hard to understand all this. Maybe that's why Mom moved so often. She was afraid of being discovered with me."

"I don't know about that, but everything was in chaos, and the rescuers finally broke through. I was hustled off to the hospital, and I never saw you or Grayson again until this year. I didn't even know to look. I was told you'd both died, but Zach found out Grayson went into the foster-care system and was adopted. He was two. There was never any mention of you. It was as if you'd never been born."

Bailey pleated a paper napkin in her fingers. "How'd you find me?"

Zach slipped his arm around his wife's waist as if he sensed how distressed she was. "We were actually just trying to find the paramedic who delivered you. We thought she might have some information to help us. Shauna remembered the name of the department she worked for, so I found a picture of the group of paramedics that year."

Shauna nodded. "I was able to pick your mom out of the photo, and we had her name."

"My sister, my adopted sister, is a writer and a great researcher," Grayson said. "She found out where your mom was living, and Shauna called her. Olivia hung up on her. That really got us wondering."

"I think I remember that," Bailey said. "The call came kind of late, and Mom said it was a telemarketer, but she was shaking after the call. I heard her calling someone in the middle of the night too." Her mother had refused to talk about it the next day.

Grayson took up the story again. "We found a current picture of your mom—and you. From the second we saw you, we knew she'd taken you. The age was right, and you looked exactly like Shauna."

Bailey couldn't deny the resemblance. It was like looking at herself in a few years. "So you were never able to question Mom?"

Shauna shook her head. "She claimed she wasn't the paramedic and had never been here."

Did she reveal what she knew so far? Bailey glanced at Lance, who gave her a quick nod. "My grandmother is still here. She lives down the road from my cabin."

Shauna leaned forward. "So you came here not knowing anything about this? Why?"

Bailey launched into the story of her mother's death, her so-called marriage to Kyle, and the deed. "After the guy tried to kill me, too, I knew I had to get away and hide. Since I had the deed anyway, the cabin seemed a good place to hole up."

Shauna addressed Lance. "And you're protecting her?"

"I'm FBI. I'm investigating a human-trafficking ring here. And I'm trying to keep her safe, yes."

Shauna clasped her hands together and stepped nearer to Bailey. "And this trafficking ring is connected somehow to Bailey?"

"Unfortunately, yes. We've found three victims on her property so far."

Shauna winced. "Is this Kyle person involved too?"

"Most likely. We're still investigating."

Shauna's concern started a thaw in Bailey's frozen emotions. For too long she'd felt so alone. "There's Lily also. She might know more than we realize, but she has dementia, probably Alzheimer's."

"You're not staying at the cabin alone, are you?" Grayson's voice boomed out, and he frowned.

"As soon as I can get her house clean enough to inhabit, I'm going to stay with Lily. Lance plans to stay in one of the guest rooms too. The FBI is trying to keep an eye on the property."

Shauna squatted in front of Bailey's chair. "You can stay with us, Bailey. I'm frightened for you. We have room."

Zach stepped closer and set his hand on his wife's shoulder. "I'll second that suggestion."

Bailey shook her head. "I can't leave Lily alone. Lance will take care of us." She glanced his way, and he smiled back at her.

"I'll help," Grayson said.

Lance gave a nod his direction. "I'll accept the offer."

Bailey stared at Shauna and Grayson. "I really have siblings? I can't quite believe it."

Shauna took her hand. "We'll have lots of time to get to know each other better. All the time in the world. You have a nephew too." Color touched her cheeks, and she put a hand over Zach's on her shoulder. "And we're going to have a new baby."

Ellie whooped. "A baby! I hadn't heard."

"We just found out." Shauna rose and went toward the crab pot. "I think it's time we ate. It's been quite a day."

Bailey's family was expanding by the minute, but Shauna hadn't mentioned their father. Who was he and where was he?

# *Chapter 30*

The aroma of garlic, tomato paste, and cheese filled the warm kitchen. In any other situation it would have given a homey feel to the scene, but there was nothing normal about the situation.

Ava had a sinking feeling this was the last stop before she and the rest of the girls were loaded aboard a ship and sent overseas—something that didn't bear thinking about. The compound sat on a promontory overlooking the water, and from the bank of windows in the back room, she saw steps leading down to the water. Oh to be able to run down those steps and swim to the island in the distance.

She pressed her forehead against the cool glass and ran through her options. She used to be a strong swimmer, and she thought she could make it if she could just get out of this house. The waves didn't look that big, and there was no storm brewing. But her despair made the attempt already seem impossible. It had been years since she'd been in the water.

The warehouse itself was cold and austere with concrete walls and floors. Their rooms were like prison cells, but even they were preferable to what awaited them.

The thought of being forced to dance in a strange country made her shudder. If she ever got away from her captors, she'd be unlikely to find help. Six other girls were with her and Jessica, two in each bedroom. They were all tense, but Ava wasn't sure if they would help her escape. They might think they'd be moved before she could get back, and it was a distinct possibility. More likely she'd be killed trying to escape. Or caught and punished.

She wetted her lips and looked around at the other girls as they chowed down on the pizza their captors had brought. A man was stationed outside at the front and one at the back. She probably could outrun both of them. She couldn't ask any of the girls for help though, not with Maly sitting there with her pursed lips and evil eyes like some kind of deadly spider.

And that's exactly what Maly was—a spider who preyed on the pain of others.

She swallowed the last bite of her pepperoni pizza, then washed it down with Pepsi. It was already cold by the time they'd gotten here with it, and it probably wasn't very good when it was hot. It was no Rocco's, that was for sure. She skirted past Maly and headed for the bedroom.

"Where you going?" Maly called after her.

She held up her hands. "To wash up and go to the bathroom."

"Not gone long."

Did Maly suspect something from her manner? Ava grunted and moved on down the hall. She didn't dare act too pleasant or conciliatory or her captor would be sure to know something was up. If there was one thing Ava was known for, it was her spark, that last little bit of rebellion they'd never quite squelched. Even training her hands and feet to flex as far as necessary for the Apsara dancing had taken great determination and practice.

She shut the door and locked it behind her, then studied the window. From here she couldn't see the guard at the back, and she guessed he was closer to the back door. She stepped into the tub and fingered the lock on the window. It flipped easily without a sound, but she didn't dare open it, not unless there was some way to make a commotion to cover the noise.

Maybe later tonight she could talk Jessica into helping her. Jessica was new and fresh, so she might be brave enough to help. Maybe she was a strong swimmer too. It was worth talking about.

Ava relocked the window in case Maly checked it out, then went back to the living room. It would take patience and careful planning, but Ava might be able to pull this off now that they were in the country. She had been a top track star in high school as well as winning most swimming competitions she'd entered, but that had been so many years ago. So many years without practice.

She had to try, but she suspected she'd be food for the fishes by the time it was all over.

---

Shauna couldn't take her eyes off her sister as Bailey took in her and Zach's house and studied the pictures of Alex on the end tables. It had taken all Shauna's persuasive skills to talk Bailey into staying here tonight instead of going to the cabin by herself. Lance and Zach had left to gather the cat and a few things for Bailey for the night while the girls went home to get the room ready. Ellie had vanished into the spare room, ostensibly to ready it for Bailey, but Shauna knew her friend was trying to give her time with her new sister.

She could sense Bailey still hadn't fully accepted the truth of what her mother had done, and she couldn't blame her. Bailey's mom had buried so many secrets Shauna wasn't sure they'd ever know the full truth of what all she did and why. And they could never ask her.

She set the kettle on to heat milk for hot chocolate and plated some Rainier cherry-almond crumble she'd made earlier in the day. Bailey followed her into the kitchen and hopped onto a stool at the island bar.

She curled her fingers around the mug of hot chocolate Shauna slid her way. "Thanks. That wind got cold." She looked at the crumble. "Are those yellow cherries?"

"Rainier cherries have a lot of yellow in them along with some red. They're wonderful." Shauna warmed a square of crumble in the microwave, then put it in front of Bailey.

Bailey took a forkful of the treat and smiled. "Delicious." She put down her fork, and her smile faded. "I can't quite wrap my head around all this, Shauna. If there's no record of my birth, why are you so sure Mom kidnapped me? I mean, you were only eight. Maybe the baby died."

*Or maybe you aren't remembering correctly.* Though Bailey didn't say the words, Shauna saw the thought hovering in her eyes. Though her doubt shouldn't have stung, it did.

Shauna pulled out her phone and reversed the camera for a selfie. She stepped around to Bailey's side and snapped a picture of the two of them together, then handed the phone to Bailey with the picture on the screen. "You tell me what the truth is."

Bailey stared at the picture. "I'm not denying we look a lot alike. Don't they say everyone has a double?"

"You're the right age, and we look *exactly* alike." She'd saved one piece of information as the nuclear option, but she hadn't wanted to use it because it would show how far Olivia had gone to hide the truth. Bailey had to hear it though. "Grayson got a copy of your birth certificate from the school and then checked the official records. The birth certificate the school has is a fake."

Bailey gasped. "You mean Mom bought a fake certificate somewhere?"

"It appears so. Or she knew how to forge it herself. When Grayson followed up with the official records, he found the hospital had no record of your birth." Shauna touched her hand. "I'm sorry. I know this has to be hard for you. It was hard for me to believe what our father had done too."

"This is the first time you've mentioned your father. What did he do?"

"The earthquake was his fault. He had built a fracking well, and it triggered the earthquake twenty-four years ago. He couldn't admit it and basically went into a major depression, from which he never recovered. H-He told me you both had died, and I found out he simply didn't look for you and Grayson. He felt he couldn't care for me, so he was sure he couldn't care for two more."

Bailey went white. "Mom would never talk about my father. I thought maybe if what you were telling me was really true, then maybe I'd find out about my father after all. This is worse than I ever imagined. I don't think I even want to meet him."

Shauna looked away. "He's dead, Bailey. He died in September, killed for the technology that could start an earthquake. Zach and I barely took down the ones responsible."

Bailey didn't react but her pupils dilated, and she eyed the contents of her mug.

Shauna touched her hand. "But I'm here. Grayson is here. We want to get to know you. I already love you and have from the moment I first held you."

Bailey looked up with a stony expression. "You don't know me, Shauna, so I don't understand how you could love me. I know you mean well, but you have no idea how I feel. How can I trust *anyone* now? My mother was a liar and a thief. She stole me without compunction from my family. My so-called husband was a liar and a cheat. He went through with a marriage simply to get me into bed, but he was already married. Everyone I thought I could trust has clearly shown me I can't." Her voice broke, and she became fascinated by her mug again.

This was the first Shauna had heard about a bigamous husband. "I'm sorry, honey. I had no idea of all you've gone through. I won't push you. You can think about everything I've told you. We can get a DNA test. I have one in the office. Once you know the truth, I hope you'll let Grayson and me into your life. If you can't handle that yet, we'll be patient."

"I think I'd like to run the DNA test. Maybe once I see it in black and white, I can begin to accept everything you're saying. I don't want to believe my mom would do something like this. I admired her all my life. She saved lives and cared about other people. It's hard to reconcile something like this with the woman I thought I knew." She tucked a lock of hair behind her ear. "Maybe you can never fully know anyone."

This revelation had shaken her poor sister to the core. Shauna wished she hadn't had to destroy her faith in humanity.

"I'll get the DNA kit. It's just a mouth swab, and we'll receive the results in a few days." She left her sister alone in the kitchen and went to the office, praying as she went.

## *Chapter 31*

Lance eyed the other men with him as they stood in Cedar Cabin's tiny living room. "I'd say this was a little overkill, guys. Between the three of us, we could take down a whole gang of traffickers."

Zach grinned. "I know my wife. She needed time alone with Bailey. How do you think she's taking all this?"

Lance wanted to ask why Zach was asking him when he'd only known Bailey a few days longer than the rest of them, but he couldn't deny the two of them had a special bond. "She's pretty floored by it all. I'd guess right about now she's questioning everything she thought she knew about her life."

The thought dropped a boulder in his gut. She was probably even questioning what was starting to happen between them. Everything in her life had been a lie. Who wouldn't be shaken by this kind of news?

Grayson dropped onto the sofa and coaxed the cat to him. "Can't blame her. I know how I felt when I found out my parents adopted me, and I still haven't fully come to terms with it. At least they simply withheld the fact I was adopted. They didn't steal me right out of my mother's arms."

"To be fair, I'd guess Olivia knew Shauna's mom had died before she took Bailey."

Zach sat beside Grayson and reached over to scratch Sheba's ears. "But she knew she had a brother and sister. She still had a father. Granted, he was a lousy excuse for one, but Olivia didn't know that."

Even from here Lance could hear Sheba's purr. "Unless she did know. Maybe she knew the family somehow. There's so much we don't know about Olivia. As soon as I find those traffickers and my sister, I thought I'd dig more into Olivia's past." The stepbrothers' alibis checked out, but he hadn't gotten any further than that.

He went to Bailey's bedroom and stepped inside. It had already taken on her scent, a light floral note mixed with vanilla. The aroma took him right back to how she'd felt in his arms, how her lips had tasted. He flexed his jaw and pushed away the memory to attend to business.

The room was spotless, and the bed didn't have so much as a wrinkle. There was a small satchel in the closet and he opened it, then tossed in a pair of jeans and a red top she'd look great in. The top dresser drawer held underwear, and he scooped up some without looking too closely.

He stepped across the hall and grabbed her toothbrush and toiletries. He brought the perfume bottle to his nose and took a quick sniff of the clean scent. Just smelling it brought warmth surging to his neck. He was like some love-struck teenager.

He shook his head, then took the items to the bedroom and dumped them in a suitcase. Anything else? He scanned the room and stopped when he saw her journal and Bible. He grabbed them, too, and put them in the case. She needed some strength from the Lord to deal with this.

A flicker of light out the bedroom window caught his attention. He frowned and stepped to the glass. The light was moving and seemed like it was down by the dock. Leaving the suitcase, he ran out of the bedroom to the back door.

"Light outside, could be a boat," he told the other men.

They leaped up and followed him out the back door and down into the yard. Even from here he heard the faint chug of an outboard motor. His phone had a flashlight app, but he couldn't give away their position to the occupants of the boat. He picked his way through the downed trees and thick brush toward the pier as quietly as he could with the other two men on his heels.

He paused at a large tree twenty feet from the edge of the water. The waves lapped at the pilings, and the wind brought the scent of salt and kelp to his nose. The moon glittered on the whitecaps and illuminated the small boat motoring closer to the dock. Two men occupied it.

Lance motioned for Grayson and Zach to stay down, and the three of them crouched behind several large trees. He unsnapped his holster and put his hand on his gun.

These two could be innocent of anything except a moonlight ride, but it was suspicious they were here at this spot. He prayed he'd learn something that would lead him to Ava. One comment might be all he needed.

The man in the bow of the boat leaped onto the dock and secured the rope, then steadied the craft for the other man to disembark. Even with the moon it was too dark to do more than make out their shapes. One was taller with wide shoulders, and he wore a cap that put even more shadow on his face. The other figure was smaller and slighter. It could even be a woman. Maybe they were here for some kind of tryst.

He strained to hear, and the words that drifted to his ears chilled him more than the wind.

The slimmer figure spoke and the female voice confirmed his suspicion. "I'll go knock on the door, and you wait at the back door. See if you can get in quietly while I keep her distracted at the front door. Got it?"

"Got it. What if she's armed?"

The woman gave an inelegant snort. "She's not the type to carry a gun. You get in and stick her with the drug. We'll carry her to the boat, and we're in and out before anyone notices."

"What if she's got company?"

"It's ten o'clock. Look, you want to do this or not? I can tell the boss I need a partner with guts."

The man straightened. "I'm ready to do it, but I thought we should talk about what to do if it doesn't go smoothly."

"If someone's there, we wait until they leave."

"I'm ready." The man took something out of his pocket that glimmered in the moonlight.

A lock pick? A gun? Lance couldn't tell, but he withdrew his gun and waited as they went past him toward the cabin. Once they were out of earshot, he directed Grayson to grab the woman while he and Zach took down the man. Then he'd take them in for questioning. They were clearly here to take Bailey.

He'd stop them and find his sister.

❧

Bailey went into the bathroom and did the mouth swab for the DNA test, but in her heart she knew everything Shauna and Grayson had told her was true. It explained so much about how often her mom had moved around, and she remembered how upset her mother had been after the late call a few weeks ago.

She stared at herself in the mirror. Her green eyes looked enormous in her pale face, and she hated her purple hair now. It was as much a lie as the rest of her life.

How did she come to grips with all this? Her entire life was a lie. Every person she loved and trusted had lied to her. Was there no truth anywhere? No honorable people? The thought of getting close to these new siblings was laden with a minefield as well. They'd betray her just like everyone else. And Lance. How ridiculous that she'd thought she might find a relationship with him or any man. All the pleasant dreams she'd hoped might come true were like fog rolling in over the strait that dissipated in the light of day.

Finding out Kyle had been faithless was bad, but this was so much worse. This struck at the core of who she was. How did she even accept this? Maybe she should just leave, get Lily settled in a nursing home, then go off by herself somewhere and find a job. Try to keep to herself and not let anyone get close.

It sounded both horrible and enticing.

She couldn't do that until Lance caught the men who were after her, and she wanted to see him find his sister. She sighed and opened the door. With the DNA kit in hand, she walked toward the crackle of the fireplace in the living room. Shauna added logs to the fire that blazed with color and warmth.

She put the poker away and turned to smile at her. "All done?"

Bailey nodded and handed her the plastic bag with the kit inside. "I think we both know how this is going to turn out. Do you know someone who could change my hair color back to normal? I can't stand one more lie in my life at the moment."

Shauna's expression softened. "I'm so sorry, Bailey. I know how you feel, you know. Our dad lied to me for years too. I hate lies." She approached Bailey and touched her shoulder. "I'm here for you, always."

Bailey wanted to respond with warmth—she really did—but the wounds were too fresh and raw. She stepped back. "I think I'll go for a walk."

She rushed for the exit and stepped out into a misting rain that touched her face like soft, wet feathers. There was no wind though, and she walked down the steps to the waves rolling to the shore. The sea spray mingled with the rain and touched her lips with a salty kiss that tasted of her unshed tears. She sat on a wet rock two feet from the water and stared at the dark sea.

Once upon a time she'd been a teenager enthralled with the Twilight series. She'd thought love was eternal and could overcome anything. She'd never dreamed that maybe real love didn't exist in the world. That it was all a mirage, a way of twisting the world into something that seemed appealing, when in reality nothing was good here.

An image of Shauna and Zach and of Ellie and Grayson standing hand in hand sprang to mind. Maybe she was being too cynical. True love did seem to exist for some, just not for her.

Everyone wore masks. That's what she'd learned in the last few months. A handsome face existed to hide the darkness inside. But was that always the truth? Did she ever dare trust anyone again?

Her phone rang, and she swiped the screen on. "Hello, Lily, is everything okay?"

"There was a man outside my window. And lights in the woods. I'm scared." Lily's voice quavered, and she began to cry.

"I'll be right there. Lock the door." Bailey ended the call and ran up the steps toward the back door.

She burst into the house and grabbed her purse to dig out her keys. "Lily called and there's an intruder. I need to go now."

"Ellie and I will go with you. I'll call the guys while we're on our way." Shauna rushed to the coat closet and grabbed their jackets. "Ellie, come here, we need to go!"

Ellie hurried down the stairs and grabbed her coat as soon as she heard what was happening. Bailey shrugged hers on as they raced for the door and out to her car.

As she peeled out of the drive, Shauna was already on the phone with Zach. "He's not answering. I left a message though. I hope the guys already saw whoever is prowling around."

Bailey tossed her phone onto Shauna's lap. "Try Lance. He should be in my Recent Calls list."

Shauna scrolled through the screen. "Found him." She held the phone to her ear for a bit, then shook her head and ended the call. "Not answering either."

Bailey's heart beat double time. For all her rejection of any relationship with Lance, her feelings were already involved. She pressed harder on the accelerator. He might be in danger along with Zach and Grayson. They could be heading into an ambush.

"You realize whoever is there might be after you," Shauna said. "I'm not sure heading straight into the hornet's nest is a good idea."

"You might be right, but we can't let the guys walk into an ambush without warning."

She cornered onto her road, and the car fishtailed in the muddy track. She let up on the accelerator a bit, but it was too late. The car veered toward the ditch. Knowing how to drive on slick roads, she turned into the slide and tried to straighten out the vehicle, but the ditch swallowed the front tires before she had time to correct it completely.

She banged her palms on the steering wheel. "Great, just great."

Trying to drive out of the ditch just dragged the car deeper into the muddy trench. She unbuckled her seat belt. "We'll have to walk the rest of the way. It's only about half a mile."

Half a mile in the rain with no way to escape with Lily. This sounded like the height of stupidity. She tried to raise Lance on the phone again but got his voice mail.

They had no choice. She couldn't leave Lily alone, afraid, and possibly in danger. Withdrawing the bear spray from her purse, she clutched it in her hand. "Let's go."

# *Chapter 32*

The misty rain would mask the noise of them moving through the woods. Lance crept toward the back of the cabin where a light glowed through the window, but it was hard to see with the thick clouds obscuring the moon and stars. Zach was right behind him. Shadows shifted, and he caught a glimpse of Grayson, hair plastered with rain, heading toward the front of the cabin. He'd called Daniel for backup and he should be arriving anytime as well.

He motioned for Zach to circle around to the right of the back door. The male intruder had to be on the back deck by now, but Lance didn't see or hear him. His phone had vibrated several times in his pocket, but any calls would have to wait until they took these two into custody.

The rain began to fall harder, pattering onto dead leaves and splashing into mud puddles. He peered through the curtain of mist, trying to see his quarry. There. Peeking in the back-door window. The man fiddled with the knob and then disappeared into the cabin before Lance could shout for him to freeze.

He and Zach rushed for the stairs, and Lance reached the

back door first. He couldn't see the man through the window, which made entering more dangerous. "Go around to the front and see if Grayson has the woman in custody," he whispered to Zach. "I don't want to be in a position where I might shoot Grayson."

Zach nodded and disappeared into the curtain of rain. The door still stood ajar a few inches, and Lance peered through the crack as a figure passed between the door and the table lamp by the sofa. There he was. By now he'd surely have realized that Bailey wasn't home. The place was tiny, so he must have explored the bedroom and bathroom and found them empty.

Lance stepped to the right of the door and listened to see if the man would come back this way or open the front door and rejoin the woman instead. Sure enough, he heard the *snick* of a lock, then the door swooshed open.

"Cass?" The man spoke softly. "You there?"

A woman's sudden shriek shattered the night. "Let go of me! I'll kill you!"

"Settle down, lady." Zach sounded angry.

"Freeze!" Grayson charged into the house with his gun out.

Lance kicked the back door open the rest of the way and leaped into the doorway as the man turned and barreled his way. He planted his feet in shooting stance, extended his arms, and aimed his gun at the intruder. "Drop your weapon!"

The man, in his thirties with an unshaved jaw, stopped and stared at the gun. He started to bring up his gun, but Grayson tackled him from behind. The two crashed onto the floor and rolled around, knocking the table lamp to the ground.

The room plunged into darkness, and Lance dug out his phone to activate the flashlight app. He kept his gun at the ready, but Grayson had no trouble controlling the intruder. The big guy could take down a bull moose in full charge.

Grayson yanked the guy to his feet and wrestled his arms behind him. "Got anything to tie him up with?" He sounded as casual as if he'd been out for an evening stroll, and he wasn't even breathing hard.

Lance stepped to the light switch and flipped on the overhead lights. He yanked out a drawer and found an extension cord. "This will work." He lashed the man's hands together. "What about the woman?" he asked Grayson.

"I'm sure Zach has her. She's a handful, but he had her pinned the last I saw. See if you can find another cord."

Lance had spotted another one in the drawer. He retrieved it and rushed to the front yard where he found Zach atop a woman. She was on her stomach with Zach's knee in her back. Her arms were pulled behind her. Her head was angled Lance's way, and if looks could kill, Zach would be six feet under. Lance knelt and trussed her hands up, then Zach removed his knee. Lance yanked the woman to her feet. Her brown eyes glinted like daggers.

He flashed his badge. "FBI. What's your name and who do you work for? Why were you trying to kidnap Bailey?"

She spat at him, but it landed on the arm of his jacket. When she clamped her lips shut and glared at him, he shrugged. "We'll see what you have to say at headquarters."

"The FBI is interested in simple home invasions now?" Her lip curled and she shook her head. "We thought we might find a little food. We're hungry."

"Don't tell them nothing!" The man inside the house struggled as Grayson brought him outside.

Lance tightened his grip on her arm. "I already heard you and your partner talking. This was a kidnapping attempt, not a simple home invasion. You could make it easier on yourself and tell me where you stashed the girls."

"What girls?" She batted her eyes and smiled at him, but there was flint in her expression.

"The girls you've stolen for your brothels." It was all he could do not to wrap his hands around her neck and throttle the life from her. It was bad enough when men abused women, but to do something like this to their own gender, knowing the toll it would take on their psyches, was beyond forgiveness.

Her eyes flickered. "I don't know what you're talking about."

She clamped her lips shut again. It was clear she had nothing more to say.

Slogging through the mud and rain wasn't the most fun Bailey had ever had. The goo clung to her jeans and coated her shoes, slowing her steps. Shauna and Ellie kept up with her as they hurried as fast as they could down the road that had turned into a quagmire.

As they neared Lily's cabin, Bailey squinted through the rain and saw the cabin door standing open. Her pulse kicked. "Someone's gotten inside." She pulled out her phone and tried to call Lance again. Still no answer.

"Should I call the sheriff?" Shauna asked.

"Yeah, I think you'd better. But I'm not waiting. Lily might be in danger."

Ellie put her hands on her hips. "And if she is, what are you going to do about it? We have no weapons."

"I have this." Bailey held up her bear spray. "I can disable someone with one squirt."

Ellie shrugged. "If you get close enough, sure. But if the intruder has a gun, he'll shoot you before you get that close."

Bailey bit her lip. "I can't just stand here."

"Hang on, let me call the sheriff." Shauna called 911 and told the dispatcher there seemed to be an intruder in Lily's house. She ended the call. "She wanted me to hold on the line, but I didn't want to do that. They're sending a car."

"Let's at least get close enough to see inside the house." Bailey gripped her can of bear spray more tightly and held it out in front of her as she advanced toward the house.

Shauna touched her arm. "Don't go to the front door. Let's look in a window."

"I'll go around back," Ellie said.

Bailey nodded and moved toward the picture window. She and Shauna crouched in the sprawling, wet shrubs, and she peeked up over the bottom edge of the window to peer inside the living room. Her heart nearly stopped when she saw two guys in ski masks standing over Lily who sat cowering on the sofa.

One of them grabbed the old woman by her arm and lifted her up. "Where is she?"

When he shook Lily, Bailey nearly cried out, but Shauna grabbed her arm and held her finger to her mouth for quiet. Bailey's eyes burned. Both men had guns, so she knew Shauna was right, but it felt wrong to crouch here when Lily was being hurt. What kind of man hurt a sweet old lady like that?

"Well, well, what do we have here?" A gruff voice spoke behind them.

Bailey toppled into the mud as the man yanked Shauna out

of the flower bed first. The bear spray flew from Bailey's fingers, and she scrabbled for it in the mud. Her fingers closed around it, and as he grabbed her arm to hoist her out, too, she brought it around and squirted him full in the face.

He screeched as the spray hit his eyes. When he let go of her, Bailey scrambled up and leaped out of the flower bed toward Shauna.

She grabbed Shauna's arm. "Go, go, go!"

Together they ran for the woods. Someone shouted behind them, and a bullet flung a bark fragment by Bailey's head. A dark shadow in front of them moved, and a man with a gun stepped out from behind an oak with the barrel pointed at Ellie's head.

"Stop where you are, both of you, or your friend goes down."

Bailey stopped short, and her fingers tightened on the bear spray. "What do you want?"

"First off, I want you to drop that can."

She heard the click as he took off the gun's safety. "Okay, okay." Her fingers didn't want to let loose of the can, but she forced herself to drop it into the weeds and watched regretfully as it rolled out of sight.

Shauna took a step toward it, but the man waved his gun. "Don't move."

Did she tell the guy the sheriff was coming any moment, or would that make him kill them now and run? She wasn't sure what to do. "What do you want?"

"You're what we want. You've been hard to catch, but everyone's luck runs out sooner or later." He motioned with the gun. "Let's go back to the cabin. I'm sure my partner will have a few choice words to say to you."

Shauna and Bailey looked at each other. Bailey wanted to

make a run for it into the shadows, but she had no doubt the guy would shoot Ellie in the head. Shauna would be next. He might not shoot Bailey herself, but he'd made it clear Shauna and Ellie were expendable. She didn't want her sister dead before she even got to know her.

She reached out with cold fingers to grasp Shauna's hand, and the two of them trudged back toward the cabin behind Ellie, who stumbled slowly beside the man. They reached the front of the cabin, where the man she'd sprayed swore as he splashed his face with a bucket of water. She didn't see any sign of Lily from here, and she prayed the elderly lady wasn't harmed.

How many guys had they sent after her? And why had they come here? Did they know Lily was her grandmother? Wait, not her grandmother. Her kidnapper's mother would be a more accurate label.

The injured man shook the water out of his face, then spun toward her with a scowl and clenched fists. "Where's that bear spray? Let's see how you like it."

"It's lost," their captor said. "Get over it. The boss wouldn't want her hurt until he talks to her."

Shauna's fingers tightened on hers, and they stopped in the yard under the pouring rain. Thunder rumbled overhead too. The man who'd captured them shoved her in the back with his gun barrel. "Inside. I need to see what the boss wants us to do with the extras. Then I want to get out of here."

Bailey shuffled with Shauna toward the open door and prayed the sheriff's car would get here in time.

## *Chapter 33*

Was that a yell? Lance shifted toward the woods and listened. He could have sworn he'd heard a man yell in pain or anger. "Did you hear that?" he asked Grayson, who was thrusting their prisoners into the back of Lance's SUV.

"I didn't hear anything," Zach said.

"I think I'd better check it out."

"I'll stay with these two yahoos and see if I can get anything out of them." Grayson angled a baleful stare through the window, and the woman smiled back with a hint of a sneer. "Man, I'll be glad to see these two charged."

"I'd just like to get some information out of them. See what you can do." Lance set off at a jog down the path that was more mud than road now. Zach came with him.

Mud caked on his boots slowed his pace, and his wet jeans clung to his thighs. Thunder followed a flicker of lightning, and he flinched at the sound. "Close," he said, smelling ozone in the air.

"You sure you heard a scream?"

"I'm sure." He stopped at a dilapidated rail fence and looked through the rain toward Lily's cabin. A light was on, but he didn't see anyone.

He glanced at Zach and saw him looking at his phone. "Let's go."

Zach held up his hand. "Hold on, I got a text from Shauna and it isn't good. She, Ellie, and Bailey are on their way to Lily's. Bailey got a call from the old lady about an intruder."

Lance frowned and stared at the cabin. "I don't see Bailey's car. When was this?"

"Half an hour ago. They should be here by now."

Lance remembered his own calls, and he pulled out his phone and listened to the message Bailey had left. "Bailey called me to say they were heading this way. It was a guy I heard yell though, not a woman."

"Let's go." Zach's voice held a thread of steely resolve.

"Stay down," Lance said. "We don't know what's happening here."

The two men made their way toward Lily's house. They had to pass through the Diskin property and the thick trees surrounding it, and he chafed at the delay.

Lance finally saw the lights of Lily's house through the trees. There was movement through the window as they neared, and the air stalled in his lungs when he saw Bailey, Ellie, and Shauna sitting on either side of Lily on the sofa. The older woman was crying, and Bailey had her arm around her.

He held his finger to his lips and motioned for Zach to stay put while he went around to the back of the cabin. If only they had two guns. He pulled out his gun again and crept around the side of the house. The deck back here was in rough shape with floorboards rotted in places and bowed in other spots. He mounted the broken steps and crept toward the back door.

He tried the doorknob. Unlocked. The intruders had probably come in this way. He eased open the door and stepped into the utility room, which smelled of detergent, bleach, and fabric softener. The dryer squeaked as it tumbled clothes, which might help mask any noise the floor might make as he crept toward the kitchen. He slipped across the room to the kitchen door and listened. There was a distant sound of voices, but he couldn't make out any words.

He eased into the kitchen and flattened himself against the refrigerator. The voices were louder here, and he recognized Lily's quavery voice.

"But I don't want to go anywhere. I have my pajamas on, and it's raining."

"Shut up, you old bat, or I'll give you something to complain about." The man's gruff voice held an edge of meanness that telegraphed that he'd like nothing better than to backhand her.

Lance gripped his gun and sidled out from the refrigerator until he could look through the opening into the living room. Bailey's purple hair lay plastered to her head, and she was muddy from head to toe. Everything in him wanted to run to her side. He forced his gaze to the other women. Shauna and Ellie were in the same shape, which explained why there was no car outside. They'd walked here for some reason.

The bigger man, one with a blond beard, slid his phone into his pocket. "Boss says bring them all. The little lady here might be persuaded to cooperate to spare them."

"Look, just tell me what you want, and I'll do it right now," Bailey said. "No reason to haul them in too. I'm going to cooperate with whatever your boss wants."

"I have my orders, lady. It doesn't pay to buck the boss's orders."

The other man, younger and slighter built with a clean-shaven face, sported bright-red eyes. "You sprayed me with bear spray like a dog. I hope he makes you suffer."

Lance didn't like the man's manner. He was probably the one who'd threatened Lily. He read him as someone who liked to inflict pain on others. Lance couldn't let these two walk out of here with the women or they'd never find them again. He gripped his gun and started forward, but a sound behind made him swing around.

A hard blow crashed onto his wrist, and his hand went numb. His gun clattered to the floor.

Another guy, as big as a sumo wrestler, tackled him and took him to the ground. He put his big hands around Lance's neck and squeezed. Lance tore at the sausage-like fingers and managed to get his knee up. He kicked the guy in the groin, and the grip on his neck slackened enough for him to scramble away and get to his hands and knees.

Before he got to his feet, the guy roared and drove him headfirst into the refrigerator. Darkness descended, and Lance blacked out.

*Cold, so cold.* Lance lifted his head. How long had he been out? A groan escaped him as the pain ratcheted up his head. The cabin was empty. No women, no Zach. Where were they? He managed to get to his feet and stumble toward the door, then staggered through it to the outside.

Zach lay sprawled in a pool of blood in the flower bed. Still dizzy, Lance lurched forward and fell facedown into the dirt beside Zach.

❧

King stood behind a two-way mirror and watched the four women in the room. He'd had them brought to his hunting lodge in the mountains, and the rain in the valley was snow up here. A lot of snow was forecast, so he needed to get this taken care of so he could handle his straying wife. The room where the women huddled was lavishly furnished with leather furniture. Various mounted animal heads stared down at them, something sure to set them on edge. The fully preserved lion he'd gotten on an illegal safari hunt stood near the door as if waiting to eat them if they tried to escape.

He badly wanted to talk to Bailey himself, but this seemed the wiser course of action right now. He smiled as Bailey paced back and forth in front of the love seat where Lily, Ellie, and Shauna sat. The older woman wept steadily, tears tracking down her wrinkled cheeks. That should soften Bailey up for what needed to be done.

He let his gaze linger on Shauna. Too bad she'd gotten involved in this.

He turned up the speaker to listen in when Bailey stopped in front of Shauna. "I'm sorry I got you into this. I don't know what's going to happen."

"It's not your fault, Bailey. Hang on to your faith. Our guys will find us."

Behind the mirror he rolled his eyes. Their men would have no idea where they were or who had taken them. They were in his hands now.

"I hope you're right. We didn't even get a chance to receive the results of the DNA test."

"You know we're sisters. Look at our eyes, our hair." Shauna rose and embraced her. "The Bible says fear not. Let's not let fear blind us to everything else. Whatever happens, God has us."

He stepped back from the mirror. They were talking about God at a time like this? He clenched his fists as his blood pressure went up a tick. They should be shaking and crying in there. This time alone was supposed to make them receptive to Chey's persuasion.

And Bailey now knew her true parentage. Olivia would be rolling over in her grave about now. It also confirmed he'd been right—this sibling search would have led to his undoing if he'd let it go. When Olivia had called him after Shauna's call, he'd known it would end this way. The first time the FBI showed up asking questions about kidnapping, she would have spilled it all.

Bailey tipped her chin up. "You're right. Whatever happens, God has this. And us." She embraced Shauna. "If we don't get a chance to know each other better, I think you're a pretty spectacular sister. You never gave up on finding me."

"Never."

The women stood with their arms around each other for several long moments. When the door opened behind them, they both squared their shoulders and turned to Chey. Strange how much courage they had in the face of such danger. He couldn't help feeling a smidgeon of admiration.

Chey shut the door behind him and crossed the room to sit in a huge leather armchair. "Sit." His voice was stern and commanding. He wore an impeccable suit and expensive shoes, just as he'd been told. He needed to look the part of the kingpin.

Bailey and Shauna glanced at each other, then Shauna settled beside Lily and Ellie, and Bailey perched on the arm of the love seat on the old woman's other side.

Bailey held out her hand. "Look, I'll do whatever you want. There was no need to bring them here."

"Silence." Chey's voice rumbled like thunder. "I'll speak, you'll listen, and we'll end this tonight."

Bailey's face blanched and she nodded. She reached over and took Lily's hand. The old woman just appeared confused and continued to cry, a soft monotonous sound that was beginning to drive him crazy. Chey probably wouldn't take it long either.

Chey reached into the inside pocket of his jacket and pulled out a crisp, folded sheet of paper. "First, you're going to sign this deed transfer right now." He stood and handed it to Bailey along with a pen.

She glanced at his face and unfolded the paper. "I'm happy to sign it, but it looks like it's going back to Kyle. I'm not sure why you even want it back unless it's to keep the FBI from finding the bodies. They've already found three."

*Three?* King's throat constricted and dread curled in his stomach.

"They've identified the girls in the shed, and they're working on the body in the garden, the one that's been dead a long time."

King exhaled and whirled from the window. A volley of

expletives burst from his mouth. He'd known this was coming if he didn't act fast. Why did that woman have to break all this open? Part of this was Shauna's fault. She just couldn't let it go.

What was he going to do? He feverishly ran through his options. Much of his money was in a Swiss bank account. He could escape to a foreign country that had no extradition treaty. He had a house in Cambodia and another in the Maldives. Either would do if he could arrange transportation. He'd have to move quickly.

All three of the younger women would bring a pretty penny in China. Once all the girls were sold and the money transferred, he'd make sure Chey took the fall while he got out. Things might be coming to an end here, but he'd be free to pursue his business in his new homeland with plenty of money. And the good thing was his wife couldn't touch him. She could have the house and deal with the shame of the media attention.

Just what she deserved.

# *Chapter 34*

Everything in her wanted to tremble, but Bailey couldn't give in to fear. She stood with her hands clasped. Where were they? They'd been blindfolded on the way to this place, but she knew they'd traveled over unpaved roads. They could be anywhere in the Olympic Mountains or down some deserted byway nearer to Lavender Tides.

Lily had finally quit crying, and she sat wringing her hands in her lap. Ellie paced by the window. Shauna seemed to be the only calm one, only betraying her agitation by twisting a strand of her long black hair in her fingers. They had to get away somehow. Bailey had signed the deed without hesitation. What difference did the cabin make to her now when all she wanted was to make sure they survived this?

She didn't have a lot of hope the man would let them go. He'd left with the deed half an hour ago and hadn't been back. There'd been something in his dark eyes that made her shrivel inside. A dismissal of who she was as if she didn't matter. And she probably didn't to him. They were all expendable. Bailey didn't understand why he'd wanted that cabin signed over either. The only time he seemed rattled was when she mentioned the bones found in the garden.

A large mirror caught her gaze, and something seemed off about it. She walked over to examine it and felt around the edges. It seemed to be part of the wall itself. Her suspicion was confirmed when she tried to pull it out from the wall to look behind it and it wouldn't budge. She'd read something about this, and she pressed a fingernail to the mirror's glass.

Shauna joined her. "What are you doing?"

"I think this is a two-way mirror. Someone was probably watching us through here." A shudder went up her back. Who had been back there and why? "Does that mean the guy we talked to isn't the leader? Did you notice how he hurried out when I told him the FBI had found that body in the garden?"

"I noticed that too. Maybe that's why he wanted the deed signed over, to get in there and move those bones." Shauna studied the mirror. "I wonder if we could break this and get into the room behind it. Maybe we could escape that way."

"It's worth a try. I don't think they're going to willingly let us out of here." Bailey picked up the desk lamp. The brass fixture weighed several pounds. "This is fairly heavy. It might work. Stand back."

Shauna went over to calm Lily while Bailey raised the lamp over her head and brought it crashing down on the mirror. The surface cracked but held together, and the sound made her wince. She'd have to hurry before someone came.

With the second blow the cracks in the mirrored surface spread out from the top to bottom of the frame, but the pieces didn't fall. Maybe one more strike would do it. Bailey took a better grip on the base of the lamp with both hands and brought it down.

This time pieces of the mirror tumbled to the floor, and she could see into the space behind the mirror. Using the lamp, she broke out the rest of the jagged pieces until there was enough space to crawl through.

She held out her hand to the other women. "Let's go. They may have heard the breaking glass."

Shauna hustled Lily to the space. "Ellie, you go first so you can help haul Lily through while I boost her."

Bailey nodded. "My thoughts exactly."

Ellie crawled through the opening into the darkened room. "I'm in. Looks like it's about six by ten. There's a door." She held out her hand to take Lily's. "Come on, sweetie."

Lily shook her head and began to cry again. "It's dark in there."

"We aren't staying long." Shauna helped Lily lift her leg into the space. "Take Ellie's hand. Bailey and I are right behind you."

She urged Lily through the space, then crawled after her. Bailey found Shauna pulling Lily to the door. The space held several video screens and computer equipment as well.

Shauna sniffed. "That male cologne is familiar." She twisted the knob, then eased open the door and peered out. "It leads to a hallway. I can see the front door from here. We'd better hurry. Someone has to have heard us breaking that mirror."

"For sure." Bailey took Lily's arm and moved toward the door with her. "Hurry, Lily. We have to be very quiet."

Lily didn't resist as Bailey guided her behind Shauna and Ellie. The wind howled and the shutters rattled against the windows. "It's kind of loud out here. Maybe no one heard us."

"Maybe." Shauna went to a table in the entry. "I was hoping to find keys. I'm not sure where we go from here, but we can't stay and wait for them to decide what to do with us. We need to find some keys and a vehicle. See what you can find."

Bailey left Lily in the middle of the entry and surveyed the area. They appeared to be in a log cabin, a large one. The log walls still smelled of pine, so it was probably fairly new. Across the space the elaborately carved front door was flanked by two fancy wall sconces. The outside lights revealed a near white-out with snow already at least six inches deep and still coming down. It blew nearly horizontal in the howling wind.

She and Shauna exchanged dismayed glances. "Now what? We don't have winter gear or even warm coats."

"We might still be okay if we can find an SUV with keys." Ellie cupped her hands to the glass and peered outside. "There's a Suburban or something by the garage. Let's see if we can find keys."

"You mean these keys?" a male voice asked.

Bailey turned toward the man when Shauna shouted out his name.

❧

Lance opened his eyes to the smell of some awful stench. "What the heck is that?" He waved away the vial under his nose and sat up to the squeak of nurse's shoes on vinyl floors and the rattle of carts in the hall.

Hospital. He was in the hospital.

He sat up and looked around. "Zach?"

"He's okay," the male nurse said. "In the room next door. His head wound bled quite a lot, but it wasn't anything life threatening. He's asking about you too."

Lance eyed him. The guy didn't look old enough to be out of high school, let alone taking care of patients. Blond guys tended to appear younger. "Were several women brought in too?"

The nurse shook his head. "Mr. Bannister is asking about his wife too. There's an FBI agent outside eager to talk with you. I'll send him in."

Lance swung his legs over the side of the bed as Daniel came into the room. "No sign of the women?"

There were dark circles under Daniel's gray eyes, and he shook his head. "Lily's cabin was empty, and the doors were both open. We found tracks leading to the water, so we think the men took them out that way. We found Bailey's car in a ditch half a mile from Lily's too. They walked the rest of the way."

*Gone.* His mouth went dry. Bailey couldn't be gone like Ava. He had to find her.

He looked around for his shoes. "How long was I out?"

Daniel glanced at his watch. "About an hour. You were brought in by ambulance a few minutes ago. Grayson stayed with the perps at Cedar Cabin until the deputies arrived, but he's out in the waiting room now."

"What about the two we caught at Bailey's cabin? You get anything out of them?"

"Not yet. They've lawyered up."

Lance clenched his fists and slid to his feet. His head swam and he grabbed the edge of the mattress to steady himself. "We've got to find them."

A figure loomed in the doorway, and Zach stepped into the room. Stitches held together the edges of a two-inch wound on his forehead.

The nurse followed on his heels. "Mr. Bannister, you have to lie still. Please come back to your room."

Zach shrugged off the nurse's hand. "I'm leaving. My wife is out there somewhere, and I'm going to find her." He stared at Lance with a pleading expression. "Any word on the women?"

Lance shook his head. "Not yet."

The anguish on Zach's face echoed in Lance's chest too. They both knew these were high stakes. Bailey had sneaked into his heart when he wasn't looking. If anything happened to her, he'd never be the same.

"Shauna's pregnant." Zach pulled on his jacket. "I have to find her."

Lance set his hand on Zach's shoulder. "The FBI is putting all their resources on this. We'll find them."

He felt like puking at the confidence he'd forced into his voice. No amount of resources had found his sister. What if these guys were planning to traffic Bailey, Ellie, and Shauna as well? They were beautiful women. He couldn't figure out why they'd taken Lily though.

"Let's get out of here." He nodded to the nurse. "Thanks for your help, but we're leaving."

The male nurse held up his hand. "I have paperwork for you to sign."

"We don't have time." Lance brushed past the nurse, and Zach and Daniel followed him to the waiting room where he told Grayson about the men he'd seen with the captured women.

Grayson clenched and unclenched his fists. "I should have been out there looking for them. I didn't realize they'd been captured." He strode ahead of them to the ER exit.

It shocked Lance to see the dark night outside the glass doors and windows. The disorientation from the head injury had made him expect to see daylight.

The door to the waiting room flew open, and Mac, her face pale and streaked with tears, rushed into the room. "Where's Ellie?"

Grayson opened his arms, and she rushed into his embrace. He stroked her hair. "We'll find her, Mac. We're about to get back out there and search."

She lifted her head and stared up at him. "What if she's dead? It's more than I can bear."

Lance clenched his fists. The thought of Bailey lying dead somewhere was a spear to his heart. He barely heard Grayson comforting Ellie's sister as his head filled with noise and fear. He pushed it away as best as he could. They had to find then.

Mac swiped her eyes with the back of her hand. "I have to tell Jason." She rushed out as quickly as she'd come.

Lance pulled out his phone. "Kyle Bearcroft knows more than he told Bailey. We need to talk to him. Let me see if I can find a number for him." He called headquarters and waited. After a few minutes on hold, he had something better than a number.

"We got lucky. He's got a boat out in the sound, and he's been staying there a couple of days. The FBI had a couple of agents watching him, and they followed him here to the hospital. The boom swung around and cut his forehead. He's getting stitches."

"Good work," Daniel said.

Lance approached the desk and pulled out his badge. "FBI. What room is Kyle Bearcroft in?"

The young woman with bleached-blonde hair glanced at

the badge. "He just left." Her gaze went over Lance's shoulder to a door swishing shut.

Lance wheeled around and saw Kyle with another man walking toward the parking lot. The streetlights spotlighted him.

"Thanks." He set off at a run with Daniel, Grayson, and Zach keeping pace. The wind and rain buffeted him, and he had to struggle to maintain his balance. This dizziness was seriously bugging him. It had dropped twenty degrees since he'd been brought in here, and the night seemed especially black with the heavy cloud cover still blocking any light from the heavens.

"Bearcroft!" he called.

The singer stopped, then frowned when he saw the men charging toward him. "No interviews, guys." He touched a bandage on his forehead. "I have to get some rest."

Lance flipped out his badge. "FBI. We have a few questions."

Bearcroft zipped his coat up around his neck. "In this weather? Let's do this another time."

"Let's do this at headquarters if you're too fragile to talk now."

The other man, a guy in his forties sporting a suit and tie, stepped between Lance and Kyle. "Mr. Bearcroft has been injured. Your questions can wait."

"They can't. Four women's lives are at stake right this minute. He either answers our questions or we'll haul him to the field office for a little less friendly conversation," Lance said.

The man sighed. "I think you'd better talk to them, Kyle. We'll make it short."

The cold wind stung Lance's face, and he saw Bearcroft's ears were bright red and his nose was running. "My SUV is right there. We can talk in it."

## *Chapter 35*

Jason's house was dark, and though he was probably asleep, Mac pressed the doorbell, then pounded on the door. "Jason! It's Mac. I have to talk to you." She rang it again and shouted out his name.

It seemed forever until the dead bolt clicked and the door swung open. Jason, dressed in jersey shorts and a T-shirt, stood blinking. His eyes were sleepy below his tousled brown hair. "Mac? What's going on?"

She brushed past him into the foyer. "It's Ellie."

He shut the door and faced her. "What's wrong with Ellie?"

She burst into tears and flung herself against his chest. He rocked on his heels and managed to stay on his feet, but he held himself stiffly with his arms hanging down until she wailed out the story of her sister's kidnapping. Only then did he embrace her, and she burrowed as tightly as she could against his stalwart form.

He rubbed her back and murmured something she couldn't hear past the wild pounding in her ears. "I feel so hopeless, like she's dead. She can't be dead, Jason, she just can't!"

His grip tightened on her. "I'm sure they'll find her. The FBI will know what to do. And you know how much Grayson loves her. He won't stop until he finds her. Bailey and Shauna were taken too?"

She lifted her head and nodded. "Zach and Lance were both injured."

When he dropped his arms, she stepped back and flipped on the hall light. "Let's go to the living room. I'll make coffee. I don't think I can sleep."

"Me neither. No matter what's happened between us, Ellie will always be my sister." He shuffled into the living room while Mac went to the kitchen.

The house was still neat. Bailey's training must be working. Mac found a tub of guacamole and a bag of baby carrots in the fridge, so she set them on a plate with the cups, then blew her nose and washed her face while she waited for the coffee to brew.

She poured the coffee and carried the tray into the living room. Jason had started the gas log, and the remote was still in his hands. He sat staring toward the fire but turned his head at her approach.

The tray clanged when she set it on the coffee table. She carried a cup toward him. "Careful, it's hot."

His lips twisted as he reached for it. "Yes, Mom."

Rage rattled her, and she slammed down the cup, sloshing coffee in the process. Grabbing him by the shoulders, she shook him until his dark hair flopped onto his forehead. "You idiot! Doesn't it mean anything to you that when I'm worried or hurting I come straight for your arms? Doesn't it matter to you at all that I'm sorry? I was stupid, okay? I threw away the best thing I had in life. I love you."

Drained, she released her grip on his shoulders and stepped

back, then burst into tears. "I can't do this." She ran for the door. He might have called out her name, but she couldn't hear past the sobs tearing their way out of her throat.

He didn't love her. She'd ruined everything.

❧

Bearcroft sat in the middle of the SUV's backseat with Daniel on one side and Lance on the other. Grayson and Bearcroft's manager were in the front seat with the engine running and the heater on, and Zach was in a third-row seat. The vehicle rocked with every gust of wind as Lance and Daniel hammered Bearcroft with questions.

The man was cold. Even knowing women were in danger, he said nothing more than, "I don't know," for half an hour. Lance lost all patience. "Bailey is missing! I'm sure you know who has her. Do you want her blood on your hands?"

Bearcroft finally showed some emotion when his lids flickered and he looked down at his hands. "I really loved Bailey."

*Loved*. Past tense. Lance clenched his fists. "If you cared anything at all about her, you'd tell us who has her. Don't pretend you don't know. We know it's someone connected to Baker Holdings. And we know all about the fake marriage as well. You wouldn't know the truth if it bit you in the rear end."

Bearcroft spread out his fingers and shrugged. "I've never heard of that company."

"You transferred the deed of the cabin to her from Baker Holdings, so you have to know about it."

Bearcroft's manager straightened. "I think we're done here.

Mr. Bearcroft has cooperated, and he's clueless about this investigation."

Zach slammed his fist down on the armrest. "He's given us nothing!"

The manager shrugged and opened the front passenger door to step into the wind. "We're leaving. Come on, Kyle." He opened the back door on Lance's side. "Let him out."

Either he had to arrest the man or let him go. He had no time to deal with arresting the singer right now, but he could call it in and let one of the other agents leverage what they had on him. "We'll be talking more, Bearcroft."

The singer stepped past him and didn't answer. A headache raging, Lance watched them head to their vehicle. He got back in the SUV. "Sorry, Grayson, you'll need to drive. I've got a little double vision going on."

Daniel gave him a worried glance. "Maybe you'd better go back inside."

"No, I'll be fine. I'm going to call in an arrest on Kyle. Maybe he'll talk a bit when his head is on the line." He pressed a throbbing spot on his temple and tried to think. Some line of questioning was just out of his reach. What was it?

He lifted his head. "What about those bones in the garden? Do we know anything about them?"

Daniel turned up the blower on the heater. "Yeah, we've got a DNA match to a missing persons from twenty-four years ago. The crime-scene guys had recovered blood from the scene and saved it. The vic's name was Robert Colley."

"That name sounds a little familiar. Let me think about it," Zach said.

Lance snapped his fingers. "Bearcroft's real wife, Amy Boone. Has anyone talked to her?"

"Not that I know of," Daniel said. "I've got her number though. I thought maybe you'd want to call her."

Lance pulled out his phone. "Give me the number, and I'll call right now."

"It's nearly midnight," Zach said. "If she doesn't answer, leave a message and tell her it's a matter of life and death." He choked out the last few words.

Lance punched in the number, and it rang. His phone number would be tagged FBI, so maybe she'd answer it.

A groggy woman's voice answered. "Hello?"

Lance enabled the speakerphone function so the other men could hear. "Mrs. Kyle Boone? Amy Boone?"

"That's right. Is Kyle all right?" Her voice rose and grew clearer.

"Yes, he's fine. This is Lance Phoenix with the FBI in Washington State, and I'm sorry for calling so late, but we're investigating some missing women who are in imminent danger. I hoped you might help us."

"Missing women? I don't understand. I live in Idaho. I don't think there's anything I can tell you about women missing in Washington."

"Have you ever heard your husband mention Baker Holdings?"

"Baker Holdings? Well, sure. It's part of my family's business."

"Your family?"

"Yes, the Colley family. I was a Colley when we got married. What does Baker Holdings have to do with anything?"

Lance's gaze linked with Daniel's. The Colley family.

Bearcroft was in this up to his neck. "Do you know who runs the company?"

"My aunt's husband. Well, really my great-grandfather is the head, but he's old and infirm, so Uncle Harry takes care of it for him. Harry Whitewell."

Zach made a strangled sound and stared at Lance. *Know who that is?* Lance mouthed and Zach nodded.

"Your uncle Harry? Where does he live?"

"In Lavender Tides. You can't think he'd know anything about missing women. He's a judge, for heaven's sake."

A judge. Lance glanced at Zach who was nodding vigorously. "What kinds of businesses does Baker Holdings have?"

"They do lots of things. Importing and exporting all kinds of manufacturing goods. I think they specialize in a lot of goods exported to China."

*Like women.*

Lance clenched his jaw and bit back his anger so his voice would be calm. He didn't want to shut off the flow of information. She sounded like an innocent in all this. "You live on a ranch in Idaho? Do you ever get over here to Washington?"

She laughed. "Not really. I let my uncle handle any family business. My horses don't like me to be gone, and quite honestly, I-I suffer from agoraphobia. I literally can't breathe when I leave the ranch."

The perfect patsy for Kyle. Lance pressed his lips together and shook his head. "Anything else you can tell me about Baker Holdings?"

"I really think you're looking in the wrong direction. It's a perfectly legitimate company. Talk to my uncle, and you'll see."

"I intend to. Thank you for your time, Mrs. Boone." He ended the call without telling her about Bailey. She'd learn about her husband's faithlessness soon enough when this all exploded.

"Harry Whitewell is a friend of ours," Zach said. "I can't even believe this."

"You know where he lives?"

"Of course. Let's go there now."

⁂

Shauna blinked at the smiling face holding the keys. "Harry? Thank goodness you're here! You've got to call the FBI right away. The four of us were kidnapped. How did you find us?"

He wasn't speaking and didn't show any surprise.

She stared at him. "Harry?" The familiar scent of his cologne wafted toward her. That was the cologne she'd smelled in the viewing room.

His fingers curled around the keys and the knuckles in his fist whitened. "I'm sorry you got caught up in all this, Shauna. Really sorry. I've always liked you, and Taylor will be disappointed not to get her flight lessons."

Aware her mouth was dangling, Shauna closed it, then reached out and held Bailey's cold hand. "You're the one behind this. B-But you're a judge." She saw the purse she'd had in the car on his desk. "A-And your own daughter was targeted."

"I disposed of the idiot who let that happen. He's supposed to keep a better eye on the men he hires." His voice vibrated with outrage.

Bailey clutched her hand hard, and the two shuffled closer together for support. Lily huddled near Ellie, and Bailey reached out her other arm and pulled the other two in close to her side. A united front.

"A perfect cover, don't you think?" A gun emerged in the hand he'd had in his pocket. He gestured with it. "Let's go to the living room for now. This blizzard is delaying your transportation a bit, and we might as well be comfortable. Come along."

When they stayed where they were in the foyer, his smile vanished, and his hazel eyes went flinty. "I'll shoot the old lady first. No one will miss her."

Shauna tugged Bailey toward the living room, and Ellie steered Lily that direction too. While there was life, there was hope. Somehow they had to defeat this man and his minions, snag the keys to the Suburban, and get out of here. A tall order, but she'd been in tight places before. They had to stay alert for their chance.

The living room was easily thirty by fifty, a huge space with high ceilings soaring to twenty feet. Pale wood covered the ceiling, and the walls were painted a light gray. The floor looked like heart pine, and the furniture was Italian leather. Harry always liked the best of everything. Had his love of money and power led him here? Poor Gina and the kids.

She and the other women sank onto the plush sofa. Perched on the edge, Shauna looked out of the corner of her eye for a weapon. Harry was the only one here right now. If they could overpower him and take his gun, they might have a chance.

There were several heavy vases, big tomes of hardback research books on the floor-to-ceiling shelves against one wall, and end tables that might serve as a weapon. If one of them got the opportunity to seize something and swing it at his head.

Bailey's green eyes flashed, and she clenched her fists. "Why are you doing this? I signed over the deed. What more do you want?"

His gaze raked over her face and down her figure. "You're very pretty. You look just like your sister. Some buyers in China or the Middle East will be very pleased to have either of you." His gaze moved to Ellie. "And you'll fetch a high price too."

Bailey sprang to her feet. "You're the trafficker? A judge? You should be ashamed."

"It's just business." He shrugged. "A business that's gotten a little too much attention lately, I might add. I plan to sell my current stable and get out of the country." His finger wagged their direction. "If you hadn't come to town, Bailey, I wouldn't be faced with this." He stared at Shauna. "Is it true the FBI found bones in the garden?"

She held his gaze. "Yes. The medical examiner was working hard on an ID, last I heard."

His lips flattened and he scowled. "I'd hoped that was bravado, but it was too specific not to be true."

"You know how good the FBI is though—they're bound to figure it out. Did you kill him?"

"How do you know it was a male?"

"They figured out that much from a ring or something."

He glared at Shauna. "This is all your fault. If you hadn't started looking for your sister, it would have all stayed hidden."

"You killed my mother?" Bailey whispered.

He shrugged. "I didn't pull the trigger. Olivia agreed to stay quiet about what she'd seen as long as I didn't say anything about her taking you. I sweetened the pot with a little money now and again to keep her quiet, but once Shauna tracked you down, I knew it would all come out. To be honest, I'd hoped

Olivia would come back to me eventually, but she never did. Not unless I divorced my wife, and I couldn't do that."

Bailey struggled to assimilate what he'd said. He'd been behind everything, and he had to be the older man her mother was seeing in high school. He was the reason Bailey had never had a real home and had been yanked all over the country for years.

The judge stalked to the bar and poured himself a scotch, then tossed it back and sighed. While his back was turned, Shauna started to reach for a heavy paperweight on the table beside her, but Bailey was already on it. She picked up the round paperweight, hefted it in her hand like a softball, then threw it straight at the back of Harry's head.

He made no sound and pitched over onto the polished bar. The scotch and the glass in his hand shattered as they hit the floor.

Bailey darted forward and dug the keys out of his pocket. "Hurry! His men are likely to come in here anytime."

Shauna and Ellie had to lift Lily bodily from the sofa and hustle her toward the door to the foyer. There was no sound anywhere in the house, at least not at the moment. Lily was shaking, and her teeth chattered. Leaving Ellie to tend to Lily, Shauna went to the closet and pawed through the coats to snag four of them. There was a blanket on the shelf, and she took that too.

Bailey had the door open, and cold wind blew in snow before they could get their coats on. "We have to go now!"

Shauna's heart sank as they stepped outside and into a drift that came up to her calves. "We can't get anywhere in this."

Bailey spoke past clenched teeth. "This is nothing. I've

driven in snow up to the grill on my SUV. I know how to drive in it. Get in."

The doors beeped and the lights flashed as she unlocked the vehicle. She reached in and grabbed an ice scraper. "Everyone, get inside. Shauna, start the engine so the defroster is going. Seeing is crucial in this kind of weather."

Shauna obeyed, but she kept peeking through the windshield at her little sister who had suddenly become a superhero. Maybe Bailey could get them out of this.

# *Chapter 36*

A puzzled frown creased Gina's brow as she stared at Lance's badge, then at Zach as they stood in the entry of the house. Daniel as well as Grayson had joined them, and a tightly coiled tension rolled off Grayson in waves. They were all on edge.

Gina's hair was mussed, and she wore a silk wrap over pajamas. "I don't understand why the FBI would have questions about Harry, especially at this hour. Let's go to the living room."

Her slippers slapped on the marble tiles as she led them into a massive living room with ceilings that soared thirty feet high. The stone fireplace was the focal point, and the massive brickwork rose clear to the roof.

She gestured toward the leather sofas and chairs. "Have a seat. Can I get you come coffee? I'll need some to wake up." She went to the kitchen and started the pot, which must have been set up for morning.

Lance sat on the sofa. Grayson and Daniel each found an armchair, but Zach went to stand by the fireplace.

"None of us would say no to coffee." Though he'd had no sleep, Lance felt as wired as if he'd already had a pot of coffee. His headache had finally subsided, which helped.

Zach couldn't seem to sit down. He kept clenching and unclenching his fists, and Lance rose to put his hand on Zach's shoulder. "We'll find them." He infused more confidence into his words than he felt.

Every time he closed his eyes, he saw Bailey's green eyes. They all sensed the women were in imminent and grave danger.

Zach stared at Gina when she rejoined them. "We haven't started telling people yet, but Shauna is pregnant. My wife and our child are at risk here. We have to find them."

Gina raised her hand to her mouth. "Shauna is missing?"

"We're hoping you can shed some light on it," Zach said.

"The coffee will be ready in a few minutes." Gina tightened the belt on her wrap and perched on the edge of an oversized red leather chair. "Tell me what's going on."

Lance returned to his seat. "Have you ever heard of Baker Holdings?"

"Of course. It's our family business. My grandfather started it. My dad took over for a while, but his heart was never in it. He loved music and went off to Nashville. My brother, Robert, took over when Dad left town, but he disappeared three years later. Then Harry began to run the companies. We had only been married about three years, and he just started his law practice. My grandfather is still around and can do whatever he likes, but he mostly lets Harry run things."

Lance exchanged a long look with Daniel. "What happened to your brother?"

Her lids swept down. "No one knows. He simply vanished. My grandfather clammed up and wouldn't talk about it. I always suspected someone killed him though."

"Was his name Robert Colley?" Daniel asked.

"Yes."

"And your dad?" Lance asked.

"Still in Nashville. He's a music producer and helped my niece's husband get his start. Kyle Bearcroft. You might have heard of him. Dad still has no interest in the family business."

Daniel leaned forward in his chair. "Why would you suspect someone killed your brother?"

"Just the way my grandfather acted. He hired a private investigator, and he and Harry holed up in the office quite often talking about it. Every time I asked, neither of them would tell me anything though."

"Do you know what kinds of businesses Baker Holdings runs?"

She frowned and shook her head. "Not all of them. They make scotch and some other liquor. One of the businesses is a gun shop. All kinds of things. I try to stay out of it."

"Do you have any other family? Other siblings?" Zach asked.

"Just the niece I mentioned, my brother's daughter. She lives in Idaho. I haven't seen her in years."

"Amy Boone?"

Gina nodded. "She's married to Kyle Bearcroft, though Boone is his real name. He dabbles with the business some, I think, though Harry doesn't like him much." She lifted her head at a beep in the kitchen. "Let me get the coffee." She rose and went into the kitchen.

All the pieces were falling into place. Lance's gaze connected with Daniel's. If they could just get some kind of clue as to where Harry had taken the women. There were a lot of questions still to ask Gina.

She came back with a tray of coffee mugs and passed them

around to the men before taking one herself and retreating to her chair. "I should tell you that I told Harry earlier today—well, yesterday now—that I'm divorcing him. He's never home, and we haven't been close in years."

Lance took a sip of hot coffee. "How did he take that?"

"He offered to get counseling, but he was just stalling. He doesn't love me—he only loves the power being married to me brings him. I'm sure he's worried Grandfather will toss him out of the business when we're divorced, and quite honestly, it's possible. You still haven't told me what this is all about."

"The FBI has been investigating a trafficking ring operating in the area for some time. In fact, I suspect my sister is a victim of this ring. We'd been watching a cabin out on Red Cedar Road for some time because there was evidence the place was being used for trafficking. It was deeded to Baker Holdings. Then Bailey Fleming showed up with a deed to the place, and during more investigation we found the bodies of two young women. Further investigation turned up a male skeleton, probably killed about twenty-four years ago."

Gina's lips parted. "Twenty-four years ago is when my brother disappeared. Is it him?"

Daniel nodded. "The ME just identified him."

She held her hand to her mouth. "This will kill my grandfather."

"Are you familiar with the cabin that had been owned by Baker Holdings?" Lance asked.

She shook her head. "Not really."

Struck out there. "Four women went missing earlier tonight. Shauna, Bailey Fleming, Ellie Blackmore, and an elderly lady named Lily Norman."

"I know Ellie, of course, and Lily. She's the mother of one of Harry's many mistresses, Olivia Fleming." Her eyes went wide. "Wait, you said Bailey Fleming. Is she related to Olivia?"

"Her daughter. Well, it's actually complicated."

Gina's mouth turned down. "Harry's daughter?"

"No. She actually kidnapped the child." Lance didn't want to muddy the waters with a full explanation. "So you knew Olivia when she lived here?"

"Yes, for a lot of years." Her mouth twisted. "I actually worried for a while Harry would divorce me over her, but she finally left town."

Lance shifted on his feet. "We suspect Baker Holdings is a front for the trafficking organization. Your husband runs it. We think he might have the women."

Gina gasped and put her cup of coffee on the table beside her. "I can't believe he'd do something so evil."

"Do you have any idea where he is now, where he might have taken them?" Zach asked. "Please, Gina, Shauna's life and our baby's life depend on it."

"Of course I'll help you. He said he was going to his mountain hunting lodge. I can tell you how to find it. But the rain we've gotten here is snow up there. I'm not sure you can get through."

"I've got a plane with snow rails," Zach said. "I'll get us there."

❧

Every second of Bailey's life compressed to this moment behind the wheel with the snow blowing across the windshield and the wind buffeting the car like a giant shaking a tree. She gripped the cold wheel with both hands and peered through the small hole made by the defroster. The blower blew out as much warm air as it could, but the engine wasn't fully warm yet.

In the passenger seat Shauna twisted around to look behind them. "There are two guys with guns!"

As she screamed out the words, two bullets pinged into the back of the vehicle, and Lily cried out, cowering down in the backseat.

"Get onto the floor!" Bailey pressed on the accelerator as fast as she dared, and the vehicle slid in the thick snow covering the drive.

The blanket of white came halfway up the tires, so a good six inches. She'd driven in worse conditions, but not under such duress. Their lives depended on her keeping this Suburban on the road. Barely aware she was praying, she mouthed the words, "Help me, God," over and over.

The Suburban fishtailed as she maneuvered around the end of the drive and onto the road, then headed away from the lodge. "Which direction?" she asked Shauna. "I have no idea where I'm going."

"I don't either. I've never been up here, though I've flown over it. Let me see if I can find a landmark." Shauna chewed her lip and peered out the window. "It's all hidden by blowing snow. I can't even make out any houses."

They were in trouble if they were heading in the wrong direction. Bailey glanced at the compass on the dash. "We're heading south. Is that good or bad?"

"Bad, I think. South of town are the Olympic Mountains. I think we're on Mount Olympus, so we might be heading up not down. Can you tell if we're on an incline?"

The snow distorted everything. Bailey slowed and rubbed her palm across her window to look out at the landscape. "I think we're going up. I'll need to go the other way."

"But we'll run the risk of encountering those men with guns." Shauna slammed her fist on her leg. "If only we had a phone."

"I'll have to risk it. The snow will be worse higher up, and we're likely to get stuck. We don't have any gear to survive this kind of storm on our own."

Bailey slowed and searched for a place to do a one-eighty. A few vehicles had come this way, and she could only pray there were enough tracks to confuse their pursuers. The men would likely think they'd headed toward town, so this could work out in their favor.

Shauna pointed at a driveway with tracks leading in. "There! I think I see a barn. Maybe a cabin too."

Bailey slowed and turned into the tracks. She didn't dare back out onto the road, not with the limited visibility. She could drive to the cabin back here and find a turn-around spot.

"Shut off your lights," Shauna said suddenly.

Without asking questions Bailey switched off the headlights. Just before they were plunged into darkness, she'd seen a small track leading to a barn, and she veered into it and stopped. "You saw them?"

Shauna was staring out the back window. "I saw headlights. I thought it might be them. It looked like a truck, and it went on past the drive."

"Let's try to go the other way now." Bailey put the vehicle in reverse and pressed on the accelerator.

The tires started to grip, then began to spin. The Suburban

slewed sideways and headed for a huge snowdrift to the right of the drive. "No, no," Bailey muttered. "Come on."

No matter how she coaxed the vehicle or turned into the slide, the vehicle tracked toward the drift until the rear bumper was firmly buried in the snow.

Bailey slammed her palms against the steering wheel. "We're stuck. Let me see if there's a shovel in the back or maybe in the barn."

When she got out, the frigid wind took her breath away. She had no hat, no gloves, just this jacket she'd found in the closet. It was much too lightweight to stop the cold wind from coursing down her back. There was nothing in the back of the Suburban but a jack and a toolbox. No shovel.

She thrust her hands into her pockets and rushed to the barn. The door slid open when she shoved it, and she found a dry floor with tools hanging on the walls. She grabbed a shovel and carried it out to the SUV.

She found Shauna trying to move snow with her hands. "Stand back," Bailey said.

She shoveled snow out from around the tires. "Let me try it now."

Sliding under the wheel was exquisite relief from the cold. She waited for Shauna to get in, too, then gently accelerated. The tires began to grip and edged the vehicle out of the snowbank.

"You did it!" Shauna's smile vanished as she looked out. "There are headlights veering into the drive."

Without stopping to think, Bailey accelerated into the still-open barn door. She threw the vehicle into park, then jumped out and slid the door shut and stood against it, her heart hammering.

Had they been seen? She could only pray the blowing snow had hidden the outline of the vehicle sitting there with no lights.

Ellie and Shauna got out and eased the SUV door shut, then joined her. "Smart thinking," Ellie said.

"It won't be too smart if it's them and they saw us drive in here. We'll be trapped. They will surely see the tracks."

Shauna frowned. "Visibility is terrible. They might not be able to see the tracks unless they actually get out."

"At least we're out of that wind." Shauna's breath fogged in the cold air, and she went to peer out the icy window. "The truck drove to the house and turned around. It's coming back now." She ducked under the window.

Bailey listened for the slamming of a door or the sound of voices but heard only the howling wind. Her pulse throbbed in her throat until Shauna eased up to peek out again.

"I see taillights. I think they're leaving."

Bailey sagged against the door. Now what?

# *Chapter 37*

Lance hunched forward and stared out the airplane window at the blowing snow. "Can we make it?"

The rain had changed to snow quickly. "I'm used to flying in Alaska," Zach said. "This is a baby compared to some weather I've flown in. My plane is equipped with radar, and I've already plotted our course."

Snow and wind buffeted the plane, but it flew steadily toward their destination. It was too dark and the visibility was too low to see much through the windows.

Zach consulted his map. "According to my map, there's a field behind the barn at the lodge Harry owns. I'll land there and we'll walk in the rest of the way. It shouldn't be far."

Grayson pointed. "Is that it?"

Zach glanced at the screen. "Looks like it."

The falling snow had begun to lessen, but the wind still howled like a banshee. Lance tensed as Zach fought with the controls, then brought the plane down into the field.

He could only pray the snow wasn't covering a big boulder that would appear out of nowhere and smash the nose of the plane. He only managed to exhale when the skis on the plane touched down, and the plane slid to a final stop.

"Let's go." Lance fought to shove open his door against the wind. He didn't wait for the other men to join him but set out through the three-foot-high drifts toward where he thought the cabin should be.

Squinting through the darkness and blowing snow, he thought he saw a curl of smoke from the chimney. He prayed he'd find Bailey and the other women, safe and unharmed. He couldn't let himself think about any other result.

Zach went around him and reached the cabin first, but Lance and the rest of the men were right on his heels. Zach pressed the doorbell. When no one came immediately, he pounded his fist on the door. "Harry, it's Zach!"

No lights were on inside, so it was strange there was a fire sending smoke up the chimney.

The other men went around to the side of the house. "No access there," Daniel said.

Zach opened the door and poked his head in. "Harry, you here?"

Only the crackle of the fire answered him. He pushed on inside and Lance followed.

"I'll check upstairs," Lance said. "Grayson, you check the kitchen. Daniel, see if there's a basement. Zach, you can look in the living room."

The men spread out and began to search. Lance started for the stairs.

"In here!" Zach called moments later.

Lance rushed into the living room. Zach stood by a bar. Blood lay in pools on the floor and on the bar itself. There was a shattered bottle of scotch and a broken glass on the floor as well.

"The girls have been here." Zach choked out the words.

Lance whipped out a plastic bag and used it to pick up a glass paperweight. "There's hair and blood on this. I think it was thrown at someone's head."

Zach's hands curled into fists. "I hope it wasn't one of the girls."

"I doubt they'd have been here pouring themselves a shot of scotch. It was more likely one of them threw the paperweight at one of their captors. Bailey has a mean arm. She was an all-star softball player," Lance said.

Daniel called out from somewhere. "Hey, down here in the basement."

Lance put down the paperweight, and they both rushed out to find the basement steps. They were in the back of the house near the kitchen. The basement door stood open, and Zach plunged down the steps toward the light.

"Back here," Daniel called to their right.

The basement had over eight feet of headroom, and it had been nicely finished with drywall and tile floors. Lance barely noticed the pool table and Ping-Pong table as he rushed to where Daniel stood in the doorway of a small room. Grayson crowded into the space that was filled with electronics and screens.

Glass crunched under Zach's shoes as he pushed in too. "What happened here?"

Daniel stooped and surveyed the scene. "Looks like someone broke out a two-way mirror. I'll bet it was one of our resourceful women." He stepped through the door into the other room. "So they were probably being interrogated here while someone else watched. My money is on Harry listening back here. Then the girls were left alone, and one of them bashed out the window so they could escape."

Lance wanted to believe they'd gotten away, but it didn't all add up. "What about the blood upstairs? I would have guessed they would have left here and rushed outside."

Daniel shrugged. "I don't know. Let's go scout around outside and see if we find any vehicles or people to question. The rest of the team should be coming soon."

The men hurried upstairs and through the kitchen to the entry. The wind still whipped around as they stepped outside into the darkness. A couple of post lamps sent a bit of light into the swirling snow, but it was hard to see. Lance pulled a flashlight out of his pocket, and the other men did the same, but even with four flashlights, the darkness only retreated a few feet.

Grayson knelt. "Looks like a few vehicles came through here recently. The tracks have started filling in with snow."

Lance gestured to the outbuilding. "Let's see if there are any vehicles in the barn we can take to follow."

Tension strummed down Lance's spine, and he wished the dawn would come so Zach could take them by plane. He waded through the thick snow to the barn and shoved open the door. "There are a couple of snow machines in here."

"One of them is mine," Zach said. "I have to be there."

"We all do," Grayson said.

Bailey rubbed her freezing hands together. "Okay, we've got to get down the mountain to town and find help. We will probably need to make a run at getting out of this barn and through the drifts. Everyone back in the vehicle."

The sound of her own fake optimism made her want to throw up, but she couldn't let the other women know how her knees trembled at the thought of maneuvering this big Suburban down the mountain in the snow. She'd seen no guardrails, and the slightest mistake could send them off the edge of the road and into disaster.

Her gaze connected with Lily's, and the old woman's blue eyes were lucid and clear. "The judge is a very bad man. Olivia didn't want me to tell the police what I saw." She looked away and plucked at lint on her sleeve.

Bailey touched her shoulder and prayed for the clouds to stay gone. "What did he do?"

Lily looked back up. "He buried a man in the backyard. I think that's why Olivia left him."

Bailey tried to make sense of Lily's words.

"Their affair started when she was in high school. He was older and already married."

That explained why Mom didn't date. The judge was the mystery man who already had her heart. "She saw the murder, didn't she?"

Lily's eyes were clouding again, and she looked past Bailey's shoulder to the barn door. "The curse of Cain. Devil's spawn."

Bailey wanted to ask more questions but it was useless. The storm wasn't letting up either, and if they had any hope of getting out of here alive, they had to move.

She opened the SUV's back door and helped Lily inside. Ellie got in with her, and Shauna got into the front passenger seat. Bailey stepped to the barn door and yanked it open. She froze and blinked at the snow swirling across the opening. How could she even see the road?

Bailey went back to the car and got in. The heater blasted out heat. She gripped the steering wheel. *It will be all right.* Unfortunately, her bone-dry mouth told a different story. They'd never make it.

Shauna's voice broke her paralysis. "Bailey?"

Bailey wetted her lips. "I'll never be able to see the road in this. I don't think we should try to make it down the mountain until the storm dies down."

Shauna reached over and switched off the engine. "I think you're right. Let's hole up in the cabin. We can leave the vehicle here, safe and hidden. In the morning we'll try to get down the mountain. Maybe there's a phone inside as well."

Bailey nodded. "I don't see any other options."

Ellie leaned forward. "We'll have to help Lily to the cabin. Those drifts are deep."

"Wait here until I get the front door open," Bailey said. "There's no sense in wearing her out if we can't get in." She started the Suburban again. "Ellie, you take care of Lily. I'll see what I can do."

"I'm coming too," Shauna said.

Bailey knew better than to argue. She got out of the Suburban and spotted a crowbar on the wall. If she couldn't get in any other way, she could force the door or break a window with it.

Shauna rummaged through a toolbox in one corner. She held up a screwdriver. "We might be able to jimmy the lock with this."

"Take more than one size," Bailey said.

Shauna stuck several smaller sizes in the pockets of her jacket. "Let's go."

The barn door was still open, so Bailey stepped out into the snow with Shauna right behind her. The wind buffeted her at once, and she staggered and fell into a four-foot drift. The intense cold took her breath away, but she struggled out of the snowdrift with Shauna's help and bent her head into the wind. It was only in slight cessations of the blowing snow that she caught sight of the cabin's roof now and then, but it was enough to keep her oriented in the right direction.

Finally, her foot hit a step, and she fell facedown into the snow again. The softness enticed her to lay still, just for a moment. To enjoy the way the drift enveloped her and protected her from the worst of the wind. *No.* One moment would flow into the next, and she'd freeze to death out here.

Shauna grabbed her arm. "You have to get up."

Bailey forced herself to get up, to face the wind again. Her face and fingers felt numb, and it was hard to think. The cold was taking its toll. She rapped on the door first, just in case there was an occupant, but the cabin had that empty, lifeless feel.

"Can I have the smallest screwdriver?"

Shauna put it into her hand, and Bailey inserted the blade into the lock and moved it around. It felt like a hopeless task, but she persisted.

There. Was that a tiny click? She twisted the knob and shoved. The door opened, and she nearly fell inside. She felt along the wall for the switch and flipped it. Nothing. This was probably a winter cabin without heat or electricity. Probably no water either, but that was the least of their worries. She made out the vague outline of a woodstove. Maybe they could at least have some heat.

Shauna crowded in behind her and went to the fireplace. "There's a lantern and matches here."

There was a scratch and light flared into the dark space. Shauna adjusted the wick and held the lantern aloft. "And there's a supply of wood! Praise God. You get a fire started, and I'll go for the others."

Bailey closed her eyes in a brief moment of relief and thanksgiving. "Hurry. Everyone needs to be out of the storm. I'll see if I can find some blankets to wrap around Lily. Older people can die of exposure quickly."

They all could die on a night like this.

## *Chapter 38*

The skin on Lance's face felt numb even with the ski mask on as he drove the snow machine on the road up the mountain. The tire tracks had come this way, strange as it seemed. The snow was filling in the tracks at an alarming rate, and if they didn't find the women soon, it might be impossible. The snow machine was low enough to the ground that they were able to see the tracks much better than if they'd been in a vehicle.

Daniel rode behind him, and he leaned forward to shout above the wind. "This is crazy, Lance. The tracks will be gone in another five minutes, and we don't even know if we're following someone who has the women or some random person."

Lance shifted his head and shouted back, "I know, but this is the only lead we've got."

Grayson and Zach were on the other machine beside them in the road, and he knew the other men were just as anxious.

*Hang on, Bailey, I'm coming.* All he could do was pray and talk to her in his head as he focused on staying on the road.

The whine of the engines vied for dominance with the howl of the wind. The other snow machine revved up to take the lead, and Lance let Zach move into the front position. He didn't know this road at all, but he hoped Zach did. The snow machines began to labor up the incline, and he had to squint to make out the tracks in the headlamps. They rounded a curve and came to a crossroads.

The engine on Zach's snowmobile powered down, and Lance stopped as well. He and Zach got off to examine the tracks. There were faint tire impressions in both directions.

Zach studied them carefully, then sank to his knees in the deep snow. "I can't tell which way they went!" His anguished voice was almost a wail.

"Stay calm, Zach. Remember, we're not even sure these tracks have anything to do with the women. How about we split up? You guys go west while Daniel and I continue up the mountain. Let's meet back here in an hour."

Zach sprang up and nodded. "Let's do that. We have to find them."

Lance understood the man's desperation. He'd lived it daily for the past five years searching for Ava, but words of comfort wouldn't move past his tongue. Platitudes wouldn't help in this moment. There was a very real possibility things would *not* be okay no matter how much they desired it.

Zach remounted his machine and gave a quick wave as the engine revved and carried him and Grayson to the west. Lance got back on his snowmobile. "We'll go this way."

His head throbbed from squinting to see in the snow, and he couldn't feel his face or his hands any longer. They came to another crossroad, and when he stopped this time, no tracks were visible. Only the blowing snow in their headlights. It would take hard work and a miracle to get back down safely themselves.

He slammed his palms on the handle grips. "Where could they be? We haven't seen another vehicle at all."

"Maybe they took refuge in a house somewhere. The snow was blowing too hard for us to see any cabins, but there are probably some along here. I think we have to go back, Lance."

He sat on the snow machine and tried to tell himself they had to go back, but it felt wrong. What if they were just ahead, around the next bend in the road? But how long did they push forward with no tracks? Could a vehicle even make it through this much snow? He wasn't sure he could maneuver his Acadia in this kind of weather.

He yanked off a glove and pulled out his phone, but his fingers were so numb it took two tries to get Zach's contact information. He placed the call, and it rang four times before going to voice mail. "Zach, we're turning back. The snow is bad up here. I don't think they could even drive through this. Call me back and let me know if you've found anything." He ended the call and pulled his glove back on.

"Give me your phone and I'll answer it if Zach calls back," Daniel said.

Lance handed it over and turned the snow machine in the other direction. Though this decision was wise, it still didn't feel right when he wanted to find them with everything in him. He prayed they had found shelter somewhere. The thought of them out in this weather didn't bear thinking about.

They rode back the way they'd come. The snow had nearly obliterated their tracks already. He dimly heard Daniel speaking, so he must be on the phone. Lance slowed the machine as Daniel put the phone back in his pocket.

"Zach's turning back too. The road is impassible except for

a snowmobile. He's pretty devastated. He plans to go back to the lodge and see what he can find by plane."

"Maybe the storm will clear by the time we get back and he can see something."

It was a vain hope. He'd seen these kinds of storms, and this one showed no signs of letting up for hours yet. It would probably be morning before the wind died, and maybe not even then.

He lowered his chin to his chest. God had them in his arms, just like he had Ava. His sister was alive when Lance had thought all hope was gone. That was the only thing he could cling to right now.

❦

The sky had quit dumping white stuff, but it continued to blow and pile into higher drifts. Bailey threw another log on the fire. The other women slept huddled together under one blanket close to the stove. She and the other two women had taken shifts keeping watch over Lily all night.

Lily had gotten sick around midnight, and she looked bad. Her color was high, and she was burning up with fever. They couldn't wait for the plows to clear the roads. This far up the mountain that could be several days, and Lily needed attention now. Bailey knew how quickly fever and illness could take someone Lily's age.

Shauna stirred and opened her eyes. "What time is it?"

"A little after seven. Sun's coming up and it doesn't look good. There are huge drifts out there. I don't think we can even get out of the drive."

She'd snooped through the cabinets and found a few cans of soup and dry goods. If they rationed it, they might not starve for a day or two, but it wouldn't be fun. Some bottled water was stored in a closet, but they could also melt snow on the stove. The bigger question was how to get out of here. There was a phone but it wasn't working.

Shauna crawled out from under the blanket and stood. "I wonder if there are any snowmobiles in the barn or the shed outside."

"Not in the barn. I searched it pretty well last night. I haven't checked the shed yet, but I'll go look. This place appears to be a summer cabin, so I doubt we'll find anything useful."

"Even snowshoes would be helpful. Lily's not good. One of us could get to a house with a phone and call Zach to come get us by air." Shauna's eyes went wide, and she put her hand to her mouth. "Excuse me."

She rushed for the back door, and the wind carried the sound of retching into the cabin. Bailey went after her and grabbed a paper towel from the kitchen counter. She handed it to Shauna. "Morning sickness?"

Shauna dabbed her mouth with the paper towel. "I think so. I'd been feeling a little nauseated for the past few days, but this is the first time I've thrown up. Of all times for it to start. I've got to figure out a way to get us out of here."

"I've been thinking about it. I'm going to walk to the road and take a look at the conditions. If I think I can get through on foot to find help, I'll go on while the rest of you stay here. Lily needs medical attention."

"I don't want you to go alone, Bailey. I'll come with you."

"You're pregnant. Even the effort of walking in deep snow

might be harmful to the baby, plus you could fall. I'm used to snow. I can handle this." At least she hoped she could.

Shauna's eyebrows drew together, and she pursed her lips. "I don't like it, but I have to admit you're probably right."

"I know I am. I don't want anything to happen to my new little niece or nephew." Bailey headed for the tiny bedroom. "I need to find the warmest coat I can as well as gloves or boots. Anything winter weather related. See what you can find too."

A few minutes later they had a pile of lightweight jackets, a ball cap, cotton gardening gloves, and rubber rain boots. Bailey had checked the shed and found a pair of snowshoes that might help too. She braced her hands on her hips and examined what she had to work with. "I'd hoped for more."

"And what about using a towel as a ski mask? I can cut holes for your eyes and we can tie it around your neck with something. I saw kitchen shears in one of the drawers." Shauna went to the kitchen to rummage in the cutlery drawer and held up a pair of red shears. "Got 'em. And you need to wear Lily's parka. It's the warmest thing we have. You can layer a lighter weight jacket under it."

Bailey looked at the coats the other women were wearing. Lily had on the warmest one, a true parka. She hated to wake the elderly lady when she was so sick, but Bailey needed the coat. "Okay."

Shauna measured the towel on Bailey and cut out holes for her eyes. "I found twine in the drawer too. I think we can make this work. You need to eat, too, maybe some chicken noodle soup." She pulled a pan out of the cabinet and opened a can of soup. "I'll heat it on the stove."

"I need to get going. I can drink it cold."

"It will warm in no time, and we still need to get Lily's coat. I'll heat water, too, and look for coffee or tea." Shauna banged the pan down on the stove and clanged the spoon against the side of the pan. "This should wake her." She made more noise, and Lily's eyes fluttered open.

Ellie sat up and rubbed her eyes. "It's morning."

"Yes." Bailey told her what they'd planned.

"Let me go with you."

"There's only enough warm clothing for one of us to go, and I'm used to snow. You stay here and help Lily. Get as much fluid down her as you can."

Ellie glanced at Lily who snuggled close to her side. "I guess I don't have a choice."

While Bailey swallowed as much of the soup as she could manage, Ellie got the coat off Lily and another jacket on her, then settled her back under the blanket.

"I found some instant coffee and a thermos. Take this with you." Shauna handed Bailey a small thermos. "Let me get the towel on you."

A few minutes later and Bailey was decked out in a makeshift ski mask, layers of coats, rubber boots, and cotton gloves. She tucked the thermos inside her jacket and headed for the door.

"I'll be back with help as soon as I can." Bailey stepped out into the wind and strapped on the snowshoes.

The snowshoes kept her on top of the snowbanks, and she slogged down the drive to the road. The drifts were just as high here, but she gritted her teeth and headed down the mountain.

# *Chapter 39*

Lance's hands hurt as they began to warm up and so did his face. The men had parked the snow machines near the tree-line, then made their way back to the plane. They'd had to dig it out of the banks of snow trapping it in the clearing, but they were inside and ready to take off now.

Zach's face was grim as he ended the radio call with the sheriff. "He's going to talk to the county and try to get plows up this way as soon as they can, but it's going to take time. I want to get in the air and see if we can see anything."

"I talked to our supervisor too. He'll do what he can to get us some help, but operations are paralyzed by the blizzard," Daniel said.

The sense of urgency and fear grew as Zach started the engine and got the plane in the air. The wind buffeted it, rocking it from side to side until they were airborne.

"I'll fly as low as I can, but that will make for a bumpy ride," Zach said.

Lance nodded as he brought binoculars to his eyes and began a visual sweep of the white landscape below. Grayson had some, too, and they flew in silence with everyone's attention on the search. Time ticked by but nothing moved below them. No cars or trucks braved the thick snow, and he saw a few curls of smoke as the plane swooped over rooftops and snow-covered fields.

"I'll have to head back to Lavender Tides to refuel." Zach's voice was tight and choked.

None of them wanted to leave the search—Zach least of all—but they wouldn't do the women any good if they crashed the plane into the mountains or a field.

Lance's thoughts tumbled and intertwined as he tried to think of who might know where the judge had gone. If they found him, they'd be a lot closer to discovering the women's location. For all he knew they'd been on a wild-goose chase ever since they left the judge's house.

Lost in thought, he roused only when Zach set the plane down on the runway at Hurricane Roost Airport. It was a different world once they got away from the snow. The grass was green from the recent rain, and the blue of the ocean held no trace of snow or frost.

Zach was out of the plane in a flash, and the rest of the men followed. The first thing Lance needed to do was make Zach understand that going back up the mountain to search might not be the best course of action.

Zach was shouting for help from his workers to help get the plane refueled. Lance motioned for him to come over, and Zach frowned but strode his way.

"I need to get us refueled and back in the air." His voice was clipped.

Lance put his hand on Zach's shoulder. "Zach, stop and think. We don't know that those tracks we were following had anything to do with the girls. We don't know where the judge took them. Now, we could go back up there and continue to search, but the wiser choice would be to follow any leads we can dig up to the judge's whereabouts. He's the only one who knows where they are. There's a vast area in the mountains to search, and we don't have any idea if we're even close to their location."

Zach absorbed the words in silence, but his blue eyes turned bleak. "What if they're stranded in the snow up there?"

"What if they're not and we're spinning our wheels looking in the wrong place? The FBI is pulling up everything we know about the judge as we speak, but you know the guy personally. Can you think of anything, anything at all, that might tell us where he might run in a situation like this?"

Zach shook his head. "Shauna used to babysit for his kids, and now his daughter watches Alex sometimes. We aren't bosom buddies or anything."

"Would the daughter know anything? We only talked to Gina, not their daughter. How old is she?"

"Sixteen. She might know something." Zach pulled out his phone. "I could call Gina and ask to speak to Taylor."

"Go ahead while I call the office and see if they have any leads."

Zach nodded. "If we don't have anything else to go on, I'm going back up the mountain to continue to look."

"Fair enough."

Lance turned away and called the field office. They had a list of properties the judge owned, but most of them weren't in the area. It was likely the judge had access to other properties not in his own name. He told the agent to check Baker Holdings as well.

When he ended the call, the plane had been refueled and Zach stood by the door with a thunderous frown. "Taylor didn't know of any other places her dad might have gone?"

Zach shook his head. "I can see by your expression that you don't have anything either. I'm going back up there."

Lance couldn't blame him, and he stepped back as Zach got into the plane.

❧

Bailey's chest burned, and her breath whistled in and out of her mouth behind the towel, which hadn't done much to stop the brutal wind from biting her skin. Her legs ached, and she had to stop to massage out a cramp every few minutes. How far had she come? Maybe five miles though it was hard to tell. She'd never used snowshoes before, and they weren't as easy as she'd hoped.

Another cramp struck her, this time in the left leg, and she groaned as she knelt and rubbed it. Her throat was parched, but the coffee was long gone. When the cramp released, she yanked off a glove and scooped up a handful of snow. Carefully lifting the towel without dislodging it, she gulped a mouthful of snow. It was heaven on her hot tongue. She let the moisture trickle down her dry throat, then stood. She took out the thermos and scooped snow into it, leaving off the cap for now so it could melt.

The movement loosened the towel on her face, and the makeshift ski mask slid down and into the snow. "Oh no!" The bite of the wind intensified as Bailey grabbed it and tried to figure out how to get it back on. She took off her ski cap, and the shock of the wind in her hair made her gasp.

When she heard the whine of an engine, she turned around

expecting a snow machine, but a huge truck with a snowplow rumbled toward her. A jolt of energy shot up her spine. Help was here, which was almost too good to believe.

She waved her arms. "Stop! Please, I need help."

The truck slowed and stopped a few feet from her. Two men were inside. The passenger door opened, and a man in his twenties got out. He had a heavy black beard and wore a ski cap and parka.

His white teeth flashed in a smile. "You've led us on a nice chase, Bailey, yet here you are. A pretty little surprise with the purple hair."

Her breath caught in her throat and she took a step back. This wasn't a county truck but a private plow. She spun around to flee, but his long arm shot out and he grabbed her by the forearm. The thermos in her hand tumbled to the snow to land beside her makeshift ski mask.

"The boss will be so happy I might even get a raise. Where are the other women?"

"Safe." She lifted her chin and glared up into his gleeful face.

His smile dimmed and his brown eyes narrowed. "Where are they?"

"I'd rather die than tell you." She prayed the wind had blown enough snow over her tracks to keep her friends safe. The man had mentioned his boss. Did that mean the judge still lived?

The man's face twisted into a snarl. "I'm sure the boss can arrange that." He shoved her toward the big cab. "Get in."

He pushed her inside into the middle of the bench seat, then climbed in behind her and slammed the door shut.

"What do you want to do?" The driver was older than the other man, probably in his forties with long, grizzled sideburns.

The guy on Bailey's right pressed his lips together and fell silent for a moment. He finally shrugged. "Let's get this one to the boss. She was his priority, and he has the resources to make her talk."

"You don't want to follow her tracks back?"

"I told you what we were doing. A mile from here and snow will have filled in the tracks. Turn this thing around and let's get out of this snow. I'm sick of being cold."

The driver said nothing and backed the truck up until he could turn around in the area that had already been plowed. The truck rumbled faster down the mountain in the plowed lane, and Bailey huddled between the two of them and tried to figure out what to do.

The blast of warmth from the heater was heavenly, and she pulled off the wet cotton gloves to rub her hands together. Her skin drank in the heat like a thirsty sponge, and she edged her feet farther under the blower. She had to figure out a way to send help for the other women. They only had enough wood for a couple of days. They wouldn't know what had happened to her either.

The truck rolled past farms and houses where the residents were beginning to dig out from the snow, and she recognized a couple of places. They weren't far from the judge's lodge they'd fled from. Were the men taking her back there? Maybe she could get to a phone and call Lance.

But the truck didn't even slow at the drive to the lodge. She curled her hands into fists. "Where are you taking me?"

"To the judge. He has plans for you."

"His place is back there."

"He has lots of places."

She fell silent. How did she get them to stop? The big truck ate up the miles, and they'd be off the mountain in no time. There was a gas station not too far from here according to a sign she'd seen. "Listen, I need to go to the bathroom. Could we stop at the gas station up ahead?"

The man sent an incredulous glance her way. "You think we're stupid, girl? If you have to pee, we can stop and you can do your business by the side of the road."

She sank back against the seat and tucked her chin into her jacket. "I can wait awhile."

What was she going to do? She had to get help to the others.

## *Chapter 40*

Shauna's head throbbed from lack of sleep and stress. Bailey had been gone nearly five hours, and she was beginning to fear something had happened to her sister. She'd been as sparing with the wood as she could, but it would only last a couple of days. They'd be facing surviving somehow with no heat in this cabin without insulation.

Lily had been confused and agitated ever since Bailey had left—probably because of the high fever. Ellie sported dark circles under her eyes from trying to keep the older woman calm. She'd found a game of checkers in a drawer and had coaxed Lily into playing, but the elderly woman simply moved the pieces around randomly and didn't seem to understand what she was doing.

Shauna paced back and forth across the living room and finally went to stand at the window to look out onto the snow-covered porch. "The wind is dying down. I can see the barn from here now."

Ellie rose and rubbed her neck. "Maybe we should take another look at things in the barn. I could get a shovel and we could take turns digging out the driveway. The Suburban is still out there. If the plow comes through, we could drive out of here and search for Bailey." She came to stand by Shauna at the window.

"You're worried about Bailey, too, aren't you? I doubt the plow will be through today."

"She's been gone too long. If she found help, our guys would have found a way to reach us."

Shauna nodded. "Zach has skis for one of his planes. He'd be in the open field before I could blink."

Her stomach still roiled, and she felt off. If she were home, she'd crawl into bed and let Zach bring her warm cocoa and toast with strawberry jam. Instead, she was charged with making sure they all got out of here alive.

Surely the snowplow would be through within a day or two. This far out, it might not be today, but she had to believe they might arrive before the wood ran out.

"You're right—let's try to shovel out the drive while we still have a bit of food left. If we wait, we might be too weak to do it."

Ellie pulled on a jacket. "I'll take the first shift."

"Put on another jacket over that one. Layer up." They had no hats, no gloves, no boots. Just jackets and determination.

Ellie pulled on another jacket, and opened the door. The wind gusted inside and hit the stove, making it flare. Lily cried out and backed away from the fire, and Shauna went to soothe her.

Ellie closed the door behind her, and once Shauna had Lily calmed down, she went to peer out the window again. Ellie had found a regular shovel, but it was better than nothing at all. She watched her friend attack the drive into the barn first. The

Suburban would have to get out of there first. The drifts were three feet high, even higher in some spots. Even in four-wheel drive, the vehicle wouldn't be able to make it through without the drive being cleared.

She watched the time and when a half hour had passed, she opened the door and called for Ellie to come in and warm up while she took a turn. Ellie trudged back inside. Her nose and cheeks were red from the wind, and her knuckles stood out with bright red as well.

"The wind is brutal. I got the area at the barn shoveled, but we've got at least thirty feet to go to reach the road. It's going to take hours."

"We'll rest when we need to." Shauna's stomach was still uneasy, but she took the jackets Ellie shrugged off and zipped them up.

She stepped out and tried to walk in the holes Ellie had already made. The cold made her chest hurt, and every exposed inch of skin stung from the wind too. She'd be lucky to stay out here half an hour like Ellie did. She grabbed the shovel and attacked the closest drift. The shovel was shaped wrong, and some of the snow fell off before she could toss it aside. Gritting her teeth, she pressed on until she'd cleared an area about three by five feet.

She paused a moment to wipe the perspiration from her forehead with the back of her arm. A familiar sound made her turn and squint into the sun. A small plane banked over the mountain and hovered low to the ground as if searching. Her heart leaped and she dropped the shovel to jump up and down and scream, though the pilot would never hear over the sound of the engine. From here she couldn't tell if it was Zach's plane, but every part of her being hoped her husband was out looking for them.

"Zach!" She waved her hands again, then grabbed the shovel and held it aloft as well. Did he see her?

The plane's wings wagged back and forth, and it began a slow turn to the open field to the east of the cabin. It was landing!

"Ellie!" She stumbled for the front door and threw it open. "I think it's Zach's plane. It's landing!"

Without waiting for a reply, she shut the door behind her and slogged through the thick snow toward the field. She'd only made it fifteen feet by the time the plane slowed and stopped on its skis. Two figures emerged, and her husband's deep voice called her name.

"Shauna! Stay there. We'll come to you with a sled."

Grayson was with him and pulled a sled behind him. A few minutes more and she was in Zach's arms, not caring about the wind snaking down her neck. His embrace was like heaven.

She pulled back and looked up into Zach's blue eyes. "Thank God Bailey got through to you."

His smile dimmed. "We haven't heard from Bailey. She's not here?"

Shauna's exuberance fell away. "She left this morning to try to get help."

Where was her baby sister? Lying frozen along the road somewhere?

❧

Gulls cawed overhead, and Mac zipped the Windbreaker up to her chin. Even with the sun shining, she was so cold. She stood on the deck of her ship and stared out toward the ferry chugging across the strait. Being on her boat always brought her comfort, but not today. Was her sister dead? There'd been no word through the long, lonely night down in her cabin. The soothing sway of the waves hadn't brought her its usual solace.

She'd give anything to hear Ellie's cheerful voice and see her contagious smile. And to top it all off, Mac'd made a total fool of herself with Jason. What had possessed her to admit she still loved him? She slapped a hand to her forehead and groaned. If she could only go back a few hours.

But that didn't matter, not really. All that mattered was Ellie right now. Her phone rang and she grabbed it off the deck. Grayson. She closed her eyes and summoned a deep breath, preparing for the worst. "Grayson? Did you find her?"

"We found her and Shauna! They're all right."

She smiled at the elation in his voice. "What about Bailey?"

"She went for help. We have a search team out looking for her now. But Ellie is fine. We're bringing her home."

A sob rose in her throat. "Thank God. Thank God, thank God." She didn't think she'd ever stop thanking him for saving her sister. Only by God's grace was Ellie all right. "Let me know when you find Bailey. And hug my sister for me."

"Will do!"

She switched off her screen and closed her eyes. Tears trailed down her face, and she sniffled as she let the rocking ship envelop her in peace.

A scraping sound rose above the gentle noise of the boat's creaking, and she opened her eyes, then angled toward the shore. A hand slapped at the top of the ladder. "Who's there?"

She ran to the ladder and stared down. "Jason?" She looked past him to the bobbing boat below.

Mayor Weaver waved from the dingy tied up at the boat's hull. "Call if you need me to come get him."

Jason finished clambering up the rope ladder and swung his legs over the railing. He lifted his face to the sun. "I haven't been outside in the sunshine for a while. It feels good."

She took a step closer to him. "What are you doing here?"

He stretched and grinned her way. "You didn't come back when I called."

"I didn't hear you." Her heart thumped so loudly, she thought he might hear the commotion.

"Any word on Ellie?"

"Grayson just called. They found her and Shauna, but Bailey hiked out for help. They're still looking for her."

"Shew, I'm so thankful." He shuffled a little closer.

She told him about Harry's involvement, and he shook his head. "Hard to believe the judge could be part of this."

"You've spent a lot of time with him. Fishing and hunting."

He nodded, then a thoughtful frown crouched between his eyes. "You might tell Lance about a property Harry owns. He was really weird about making sure I didn't tell anyone about it."

She grabbed her phone again. "Where is it? I'll tell Grayson just in case it's important." She shot off a text with the location, then stared back at Jason. "You still didn't say why you're here."

He reached toward her, but his fingers barely grazed her shoulder, so she took another step closer. His other hand gripped her forearm and pulled her toward him.

"I should have come sooner," he said. "I wasn't sure you really meant what you said, but then I remembered something

Bailey told me. 'For God is not a God of confusion but of peace.' I realized I was wallowing in everything but peace. It didn't let me see anything good left in my life. My anger and confusion didn't even let me realize all my rage and anger were because I still loved you, not because I hated you. After you left, it took me a little while to sort through all my feelings."

She placed her palm atop his hand on her arm. "You still love me?" She could barely choke out the words.

"Yeah, crazy, huh? I'm a brute for punishment I guess." He cupped her face with his other hand and his smile vanished. "I'll admit pride played a role. I wasn't going to tell you until I could see, but I called Tom anyway and asked him to bring me out. On the way here, I saw a little flash of light. It might not mean anything, but I'm taking it as a good sign."

She stepped closer into his embrace and slid her arms up around his neck. The scent of his aftershave enveloped her. "Shut up and kiss me."

She closed her eyes as he obliged. His arms were the safe haven she'd been looking for all her life.

# *Chapter 41*

By the time Bailey saw the water, the driver had turned down the heat, and the man in the passenger seat had lowered his window an inch or two. She had shed her hat and one of the jackets she wore. They'd driven down the mountain, through a large tract of forest without any houses until the road narrowed even more into a drive to a building back near the water. The long, nondescript building appeared to be a warehouse.

The snowplow rolled to a stop, and the driver switched off the engine and got out, leaving her with the man on the passenger side. Both men had been careful not to mention names. The driver went into a large garage off to the side of the warehouse.

The other man, who seemed to be in charge, reminded her of Leonard from *The Big Bang Theory* only with a beard. He got out and motioned to her to climb down.

She slid out and stared at the building. "What is this place?"

Several armed guards spared her a glance before looking past her with indifference. Maybe they'd seen captured women before. There were high fences topped with strands of barbed wire lining the perimeter, almost like a prison. And maybe that's what this was—a prison where trafficked women were held captive. It would be difficult to break free.

He grabbed her arm and shoved her toward the gray metal door. "You'll find out." He unlocked the door and opened it, then pushed her ahead of him inside. The place felt cavernous with its high ceilings and open spaces. The floor was stained concrete, and the few high windows were small and didn't let in much light.

The Leonard look-alike flipped a switch and industrial lights flooded the space, revealing how old and dingy the place was. Still holding her arm, he marched her across the main room to a small hallway. Doors equipped with big locks appeared along both walls every five feet or so and added to the prison feel. She caught a glimpse of a barren concrete shower room through the only open doorway.

"The boss wants you stowed until he's ready to talk to you." Her captor opened the door at the end of the hall on the right, thrust Bailey inside, and slammed the door shut.

The lock clicked as she turned back toward the door. Though she knew it was hopeless, she grabbed the knob and yanked on it.

"Those locks are impossible to crack," a voice said behind her.

A young woman sat on one of two narrow cots in the small room. She had the kind of Asian beauty that would make anyone stare in appreciation. Petite and fine-boned, she sat calmly on the bare mattress with her hands folded in her lap. Her black hair touched her shoulders in a jagged cut that looked like she'd taken shears to it herself. She wore jeans and a red T-shirt. A blonde was on the other bed, but she stared out the window and said nothing.

Bailey approached the black-headed woman. "It sounds like you've tried."

"I've been trying to escape for years. Tonight it's do or die time though. They're shipping all of us overseas." Her small chin tipped up as she narrowed her eyes. "I'm not going."

Was that to be her fate too? Bailey went to the window and watched two men with guns conversing. She looked at the girl again. "You have a plan?"

"I always have a plan. Tonight's will either end in freedom or death. There is no other option."

"What's your name? I'm Bailey Fleming. I think I'm likely marked for the second option since the judge won't want me to tell everyone what he's doing."

"You know him?" The girl rose from the cot, and her dark eyes flashed. "I thought he was always too careful to get caught. This is good news. Are people looking for you?"

"I'm sure there are. The FBI is even on the case."

"My brother's looking too. He's with the FBI." Her voice was wistful.

Bailey gasped. "Are you Ava?"

Her dark eyes went wide. "I-I am. You know Lance?" Tears shimmered in her eyes.

Bailey felt as though she could float right off the floor. Lance's sister was right here in front of her. "I do. He's been searching tirelessly for you. He's saved my life already, and I'm sure he'll figure out where we are."

Ava's mouth turned down and she shook her head. "The judge is full of resources. I'm not so sure Lance can locate this place. We need to get out of here before the boat arrives to take everyone away."

"What can we do?"

"There's a bathroom across the hall with several windows.

I've checked them, and several of the bars outside them are loose. I suspect other women have worked on them trying to escape. We have to finish removing them, then sneak out the window. I'm a strong swimmer, and I will swim to the island across the way and fetch help."

The plan felt too uncertain to Bailey. "What if we can't remove the bars?"

"We have to. Remember what I said—there are only two options."

"I think we need a backup. We don't have any tools for working on the bars. There are two of us. Maybe we can snatch a gun away from one of the guards."

Ava went to the window and looked out. "The judge might want to talk to you first. You might be our best hope."

Sheba curled in Lance's lap in the passenger seat of Daniel's SUV like a big, warm rug. He'd stopped by to feed the cat, but Sheba was so glad to see him he brought her with him. She was the closest thing he had to Bailey right now, and seeing the cat had brought all his worry to the surface. They'd gotten a call from Grayson an hour ago saying they'd found everyone but Bailey.

The FBI was looking for Harry Whitewell and several of his top men. The FBI pored over every property he owned but had come up empty. And no one knew where Bailey was.

A thousand scenarios ran through his head, most of them bad. No trace of her had been found other than her abandoned snowshoes, a thermos, and a towel near the spot where a snowplow had turned around. Every snowplow operator employed by the county had been asked about her, but no one had seen her.

She could be lying frozen in a snowdrift, but he had an urgent feeling that she was in imminent danger—and not from the weather.

He wanted her in his arms where he could stare into those beautiful green eyes. He wanted to hear her laugh and to see her play with Sheba. He wanted to watch her care for Lily and everyone else who was lucky enough to be in her life.

His phone rang again, another call from Grayson, and he answered it on the first ring. "You found her?"

"No, sorry. Ellie talked to Mac and Jason is beginning to get his sight back. That's great news, but it's not why I'm calling. Jason is good friends with the judge. When he heard what had happened, he told her about a property where he's gone fishing with Whitewell. He only went one time, but the judge asked him never to tell anyone about it. That piqued my interest. She texted me directions to the place, and we're on our way back now. Our ETA is about forty minutes. Zach has arranged for one of his chopper pilots to fly you there immediately. It will be faster than driving. We'll join you as quickly as we can."

A fishing spot wasn't exactly his idea of a hideout. "Did Jason see anything suspicious out there?"

"The buildings looked commercial, but he said the place was guarded like Fort Knox with fencing topped by barbed wire. He even thought he saw the glint of a rifle in a guard tower."

Lance's hand stilled from petting the cat, and he sat up. "That sounds interesting."

"Doesn't it though. Where are you now?"

"About five minutes from the airport. We're heading there

right now." He thanked Grayson and hung up to tell Daniel what he'd discovered. "I think we should call the supervisor and ask for backup. This might be it."

Daniel executed a U-turn and headed for the airport. "It might be a little premature, Lance. A fishing spot with a warehouse doesn't sound like a place to keep trafficked women. Especially since it's so remote. Their johns would find it difficult to get out there. Let's at least check the place out first."

Daniel's reasoning made sense. Lance's personal involvement in this case could easily cloud his judgment. "Okay, let's get out there and see it."

Daniel nodded. "There's the airport up ahead. We going by plane or chopper?"

"Chopper."

Daniel pulled into the parking lot, and a trim blonde dressed in a flight suit flagged them down. Daniel parked and Lance got out with Sheba in his arms.

She jerked her head toward the chopper. "Valerie Baer. Zach told me it was urgent. The bird is fueled and ready to go. I took a look at our destination, and it's heavily wooded. There's a small clearing about half a mile from the place where I can set down, but you'll need to walk the rest of the way. If this is your quarry, I can't guarantee they won't see us land."

"We'll take that chance." Lance followed her to the helicopter with Daniel.

"What's with the cat?" she asked.

"A friend's cat. She doesn't like being left alone." Aware of how stupid it sounded, he grinned. "This isn't your average cat."

"I can see that." She opened the doors. "Get in."

Lance let Daniel climb in first, then handed the cat to him

and swung up into the chopper. Sheba leaped onto his lap and lay down as soon as he was seated, and her purr started immediately. She didn't seem to be bothered by the noise of the engine as Valerie started it.

In a few minutes the chopper was swooping over treetops and houses. They flew over the strait and headed for a spit of forest to the east. As they neared their destination, Valerie pointed out the clearing. By the time she landed the chopper, he'd convinced himself this was a wild-goose chase.

"If we're not back in an hour, go back and call this number." He passed Valerie a card with the field office's phone number on it.

She pocketed it. "You taking the cat with you or you want me to keep it?"

"You can keep her if you don't mind." He passed Sheba to Valerie, but the cat let out a hiss and leaped out of her arms, then dashed into the woods. "Great, just great."

"Go on and check out the building. I'll coax the feline out with some smoked salmon I brought."

Bailey would be devastated if anything happened to her cat, but all cats loved fish, didn't they? "Okay, do your best. Come on, Daniel."

The two men set off with the GPS on Lance's phone guiding them along a faint path along the river. The building was just ahead.

Lance squinted toward a tree. "I think I saw something move." The movement came again. "It's Sheba. She followed us."

The cat bounded to them, and he picked her up. "Nothing like doing some reconnaissance with a cat."

He'd just caught a glimpse of the fence topped by barbed

wire when something whined past his head. "Get down!" Lance dove for the fallen leaves as Daniel landed next to him. The cat yowled and shot off into the brush.

He drew his gun from his holster. "You okay?"

Daniel had his gun out too. "Yeah, not hit. The shot came from that big tree."

"Drop your weapons, both of you."

He jerked his gun around to find four men aiming at them.

"Don't try it," a big Asian guy said. "Ease your fingers off that Glock and stand up."

His gut had been right about this place. Lance had no choice, so he obeyed.

## *Chapter 42*

Bailey paced the tiny room, then paused to look out the window when the gate clanged. She caught her breath as familiar figures came into view. Lance and Daniel.

She reached out a hand to Ava. "They've captured Lance and his partner, Daniel."

Ava rushed to the other window. "I can't believe it—it *is* Lance!" She fell silent as they watched four men march the FBI agents through the gates and toward the building.

"I knew he'd figure out where we were, but where are the rest of the agents? I don't think he'd come here without backup." Bailey looked past him to the trees but saw nothing but bare branches and leaves blowing in the wind.

The group stopped in the front yard, and the judge's men forced the FBI agents to their knees. One of the men held a gun to Lance's head. Was he going to shoot them right in front of her? Her hands squeezed into fists. She couldn't let that happen.

"No!" Bailey beat on the window.

Lance's gaze met hers. He held the connection for several moments, and she read the regret in his eyes. No backup was coming. She knew in her bones that the two men were on their own.

"They're going to kill them," Ava whispered. "I can tell by their stance."

Maybe if they distracted the men, Lance and Daniel could escape. Bailey searched for something to use to break the glass. She yanked out the top drawer of a small dresser and slammed it into the window. The glass shattered, and the guards looked her way.

At the distraction Lance reached up and twisted the gun from his captor's hand. He was on his feet in an instant and held the gun to the man's head. "Throw down your weapons."

The men glanced at each other, then another one of the men snaked out an arm and grabbed Daniel. He put a gun to his head. "Looks like we have a standoff. It's still four against two. If you shoot you'll both be dead in two seconds."

What could she do to distract them again? Bailey looked around wildly, but when she saw nothing that could help, she turned back to the window. *Please, God.* There had to be a way to save them.

She whirled as a key scraped in the metal lock. Harry stepped inside and his grim hazel eyes pinned her in place.

The smile lifting his lips held no reassurance. "You've caused me quite the problems, Bailey. Until today I suffered a bit of regret at the thought of the plans I have for you. You've made the sale I have in mind quite easy now. A rich sheik is transferring half a million dollars for you as we speak."

Bailey took a step back. *Sold?* "No!"

The blur of motion passed in front of Bailey. Her fists out like claws, Ava leaped at Harry and dug her nails into his face.

He yelped, and blood flowed down his face as she continued

to tear at his skin until he grabbed both her shoulders and attempted to pry her away. Ava wrapped both legs around his waist and screamed as she raked his face again with her nails.

Ava wouldn't be able to overpower him by herself. Bailey flung herself atop Harry's back and wrapped both arms around his neck in an effort to choke him. He flailed around, staggered back, and slammed her against the wall.

The breath left her lungs, and her head spun from the blow. She couldn't hold on to him and fell back against the wall.

He managed to fling Ava to the floor, but before he could attack either of them, Jessica awoke from her stupor with a shout and leaped on his back. She grabbed a hank of his thick hair and yanked.

Harry howled and smacked her against the wall, too, but she clung like a limpet to a rock.

Bailey shook away her stupor and looked around for a weapon. Nothing. He'd dropped the key to the door, and she snatched it up and unlocked it. The sound of the struggle would bring him help if they didn't move fast. She motioned to Ava, who darted past her into the hallway.

In the next instant Harry, his face red, toppled to the floor, and Jessica rolled off of him. Footsteps thundered toward them. They were trapped.

Lance caught a glimpse of movement in a tree behind them, and Sheba came into view. The cat's tail was already thrashing behind her, and her fur was up. She crouched on a branch above the men who hadn't noticed her yet.

The cat flattened her ears back and launched into the air. Her claws struck Daniel's captor in the neck, and he screamed, flailing blindly to try to knock Sheba away.

Daniel twisted out of his grip and disarmed him, then grabbed the ringleader around the neck and put the gun to his head. "Checkmate."

The cat released the first man and stalked toward the second. Wide-eyed, the other men backed away and threw their weapons to the ground. Lance picked them up and stuffed them in his belt, then scooped up Sheba, who had finally stopped and was licking her paws.

Blood trickled from the neck of her victim, and he glared at the cat as he swiped at his skin. "What is that thing?"

Lance shoved the man he had captured toward the building. "Open the door. Now."

The approaching footsteps galvanized Bailey into action. "Jessica, here!" She stepped out into the hall as Jessica rushed for the door.

Harry turned his head and his eyes promised retribution as he struggled to regain his feet. Seconds before he ran for the door, she slammed it and turned the key in the lock.

Ava beckoned from the other end of the hall. "This way!"

Jessica ran toward Ava and the two disappeared around the corner of the hall. Bailey started after them as the footsteps thundered up the stairs toward her, but before she'd gone two feet, Lance called her name.

"Bailey!"

"Here, I'm here!"

She was in his arms in seconds.

"I was afraid you were dead," he murmured against her hair.

His embrace was fierce and felt like coming home. She burrowed into his chest and inhaled the scent of his cologne. He held her tight and pressed a kiss against her hair. She didn't want this moment to end, but there was an even happier reunion awaiting him.

She released him and stepped back. "There's someone else here you want to see. Come with me."

She took him by the hand and led him down the hall and around the corner to another staircase. Her pulse thundered in her ears as she led him down into another room. An outside door stood open, and she caught a glimpse of the other two women standing under a tree.

"There she is."

He lifted a brow, and his forehead furrowed until his gaze went over her shoulder. He stiffened and his eyes widened. "Ava?" He stepped out into the yard.

"Lance!" Ava barreled into his arms. "I knew you'd find me."

Tears wet Bailey's cheeks as she watched brother and sister embrace. This had been a long time coming, and it was a true miracle. She and Lance had plenty to talk about, but they had all the time in the world to explore their feelings for each other. He needed this time for Ava, and she needed him. After all she'd been through, it would take God's healing touch to make Ava whole again.

Bailey's gaze went to the blonde who hadn't moved in spite of the open door. Healing for all the women.

The past two weeks had flown by in a whirlwind for Bailey. While Harry Whitewell's indictment had Lavender Tides buzzing with shock, she'd taken care of getting power of attorney over her grandmother and had officially moved into Lily's cabin. She'd taken steps to clean up her diet in hopes of helping to slow the progression of the dementia. With the official diagnosis of Alzheimer's, the doctor put Lily on meds and had prescribed cold laser treatments on her brain as well. Bailey thought she was seeing signs of improvement in her grandmother's behavior.

A cold wind rattled the windows and whistled through the eaves as Bailey prepped the Thanksgiving turkey for the meal later in the day. Pumpkin pie sat cooling on the counter as she bagged the bird and slid it into the electric roaster. Two cherry pies were finishing baking in the oven. When the doorbell rang, she wiped her hands on her apron, then hustled to answer the door before the noise woke Lily, who slept in the recliner with her mouth open.

Her pulse skipped when she saw Lance and Ava through the window. Bailey threw open the door. "Oh, good, you're early. I was hoping you'd come sooner than four." She stepped out of the way. The scent of fallen leaves and sunshine followed in their wake, and she shut the door behind them.

Lance sniffed. "Smells good. Pumpkin pie?"

She nodded. "And cherry." She hugged Ava. "You look great."

The shadows in Ava's eyes were still there, but a glimmer of joy snuck in when she looked at her brother. She appeared to have gained a couple of pounds, too, and her face wasn't so gaunt. Jeans and a sweatshirt hugged her slim curves, and she'd gotten a trim to neaten up the ragged edges of her black hair.

Ava held on to her for a long moment, then released her.

"Thank you. I'm so glad to be home, though Mom won't quit hovering. I'm glad to be staying with Lance where I get some peace. They'll be here at four. I threatened them with dire consequences if they came early. I'm just happy they put away their boxing gloves for now."

Bailey smiled. "You mean Lance is *not* hovering? I find that hard to believe."

He dropped his arm around Bailey's shoulder. "I try to do it while she's sleeping. She doesn't know it, but I've added several locks and alarms to the doors and windows."

Ava punched him gently in his belly. "Liar. There are no new locks. You're just as bad as Mom, but you don't make me feel like a zoo specimen."

Bailey chuckled and led them to the kitchen. "I just made coffee, and I made some vegetable soup yesterday if you want something before the big dinner."

"I wouldn't say no to soup," Ava said. "I could eat a horse these days, and dinner is still four hours away. You mind if I go outside? I've been cooped up so long, I get antsy inside. I can't get enough of the blue sky and fresh air."

"Of course. I'll bring your soup out when it's warm."

Ava opened the back door and stepped out onto the deck.

Bailey stepped into Lance's arms for a kiss and brief embrace. "Until I came here, I wasn't sure there were truly good men in the world. Then I met you."

He rested his chin on the top of her head. "What about Zach and Grayson? There are lots of good men in the world. You just had the bad luck to meet some skunks."

"Them too," she agreed.

"I love you, you know," he said into her hair.

Though he said the words often, she never tired of hearing them. "I love you too." She pulled away and met his eager lips with passion of her own.

They didn't have all the details figured out, but they would. Marriage, a life together with children—that would all come in due time. She was content to wait until God put all the pieces into place. She was finally home and would never have to wander again.

# *Epilogue*

SIX MONTHS LATER

The aroma of flowers permeated the air: roses, gardenias, and honeysuckle. The white jasmine over the wedding bower had the strongest fragrance, and Shauna inhaled the intoxicating scent as she placed the last blossom. Grayson and Ellie would say their vows today, and Bailey would marry her handsome FBI agent next month. Jason and Mac had already remarried.

Zach came up behind her and slipped his arms around her waist. "How's our son?" His hands slid down to her swollen belly.

"He's been kicking me. Little pistol is going to be a handful."

"I think we can handle it." Zach spun her around to face him and smiled down into her face. "Life's changed a bit, hasn't it, Flygirl?"

"I was just thanking God as I finished up. A year ago I could barely put food on the table, and every day was a struggle to get past the grief. I didn't see how anything could ever be good again, yet here we are. I'm married to my wonderful husband, and my brother and sister are alive and with me. I never dreamed there could be so many blessings to rise out of the ashes."

Zach pulled her close, as close as he could with her belly between them. "My heart is full too. Life is never static. God's given us so many good things, and I'm grateful beyond words."

His freshly shaven chin felt heavenly, and she inhaled the scent of his aftershave. "Life won't always be perfect."

"That's okay. If there were no downs, we wouldn't know to enjoy the ups. No matter what happens we know God has us. And that's enough for me."

"And for me," she said. "Well, it's enough if I get some chocolate ice cream at this wedding. The baby is clamoring for some."

Zach's blue eyes crinkled in a smile. "I have a whole carton reserved just for you."

"What a guy." She linked arms with him, and they turned to watch the wedding party begin to assemble.

Her gaze lingered on Bailey and Grayson, and she waved at them. Her heart nearly burst when they linked arms and walked her way. She had found her siblings, and Shauna would never let them go again.

## *A Note from the Author*

Dear Reader,

Lies slip off our tongues so easily. We convince ourselves that little white lies aren't so bad and we forget falsehood leads to bigger and bigger sins—sins that keep us from being real with each other. Bailey found herself the victim of so many lies that she found it hard to know what was real and what was false. God is the one true foundation we can cling to when everything else is shifting around us. Bailey managed to keep that in mind through all the lies bombarding her.

I hope you close this book with a happy sigh at the ending. Life doesn't always turn out perfect like it does in a novel—in this life. But our real life in heaven is perfect, and God is in charge of our happily ever after no matter how impossible it seems sometimes. ☺

I love hearing from you! Email me anytime at colleen@colleencoble.com.

Colleen Coble

# *Acknowledgments*

I'm so blessed to belong to the terrific HarperCollins Christian Publishing dream team! It's been sixteen years, friends! Can you believe we've been together that long? You are like family to me. I learn something new with every book, which makes writing so much fun for me!

Our fiction publisher and editor, Amanda Bostic, is as dear to me as a daughter. She really gets suspense and has been my friend from the moment I met her all those years ago. Fabulous cover guru Kristen Ingebretson works hard to create the perfect cover—and does. And, of course, I can't forget the other friends in my amazing fiction family: Becky Monds, Kristen Golden, Allison Carter, Jodi Hughes, Paul Fisher, Matt Bray, Kimberly Carlton, Kayleigh Hines, Laura Wheeler, Jocelyn Bailey. You are all such a big part of my life. I wish I could name all the great folks at HCCP who work on selling my books through different venues. I'm truly blessed!

Julee Schwarzburg is a dream editor to work with. She totally gets romantic suspense, and our partnership is pure joy. She brought some terrific ideas to the table with this book—as always!

My agent, Karen Solem, has helped shape my career in many ways, and that includes kicking an idea to the curb when necessary. We are about to celebrate twenty years together! And my critique partner of over twenty years, Denise Hunter, is the best sounding board ever. Thanks, friends!

I'm so grateful for my husband, Dave, who carts me around from city to city, washes towels, and chases down dinner without complaint. My kids—Dave and Kara (and now Donna and Mark)—love and support me in every way possible, and my little granddaughter, Alexa, makes every day a joy. She's talking like a grown-up now, and having her spend the night is more fun than I can tell you. Our little grandson, Elijah, is twenty months old now, and we just added a new baby brother, Silas, to the family. Exciting times!

Most important, I give my thanks to God, who has opened such amazing doors for me and makes the journey a golden one.

## *Discussion Questions*

1. Kyle was willing to do anything to get what he wanted from Bailey. Have you ever known someone that ruthless?
2. Bailey wanted to remain pure for her husband, which seems a rare trait these days. Why do you think purity is ridiculed today?
3. Lance's obsession with finding his sister went on for years. Many people would have given up. What drives someone to continue when hope seems lost?
4. Bailey valued honesty above all else. Why can it be so hard to be real with people?
5. We hear about trafficking all the time in the news. What would you do if you suspected a woman was being trafficked?
6. Bailey's trust had been shattered by her mother's lies. Most of us have been lied to and hurt. What steps do you go through to forgive and still trust people?
7. It's easy to put on a false mask even with friends. How do we stay real with each other?
8. Ava had a long road to recovery after being rescued. How would you cope with real life after such an ordeal?

A young lighthouse keeper must navigate the dangerous waters of revolution and one man's obsession with her to find safe harbor with the sea captain she loves.

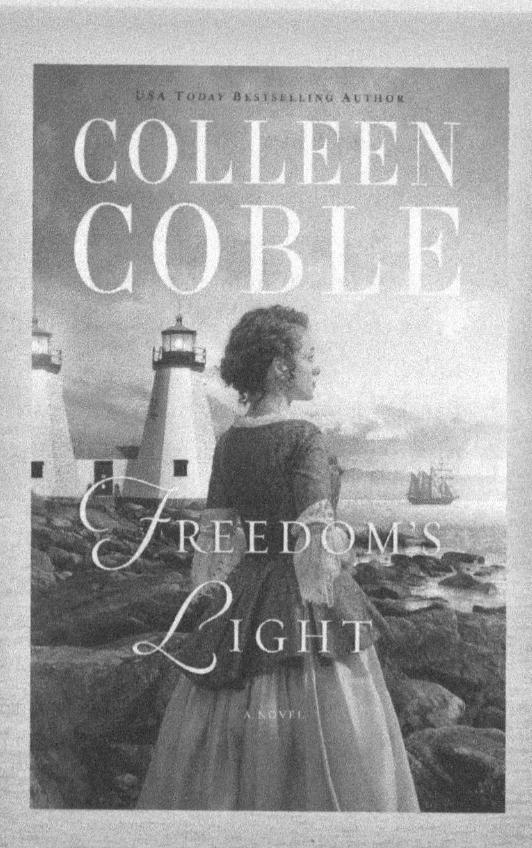


**Available in print, e-book, and downloadable audio**

# Read more from COLLEEN COBLE!

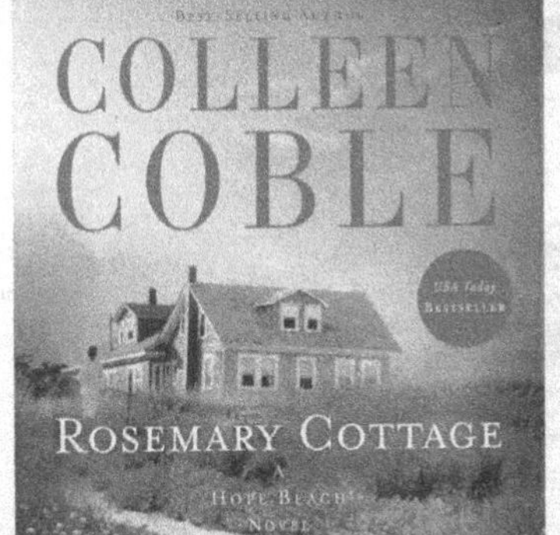


COLLEEN
COBLE

SEAGRASS PIER

Available in print, e-book, and audio

THE
# ROCK HARBOR
*series*

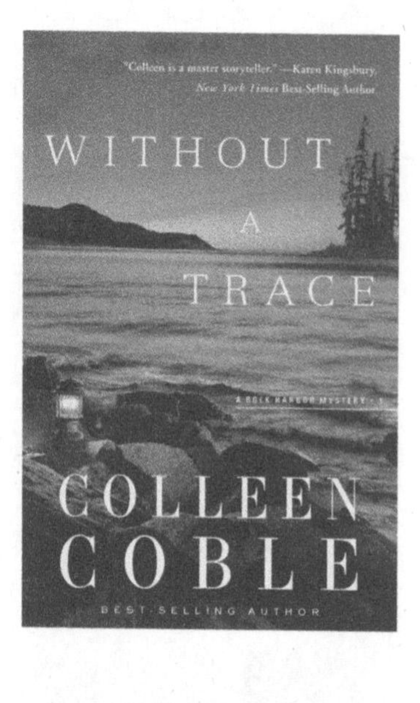

"Coble is a great writer . . . She knows what readers want and she does not disappoint."
—*Romantic Times*
CRY
IN THE
NIGHT
A ROCK HARBOR MYSTERY · 4
COLLEEN
COBLE
BEST-SELLING AUTHOR

Available in print, audio, and e-book

# THE SUNSET COVE *series*

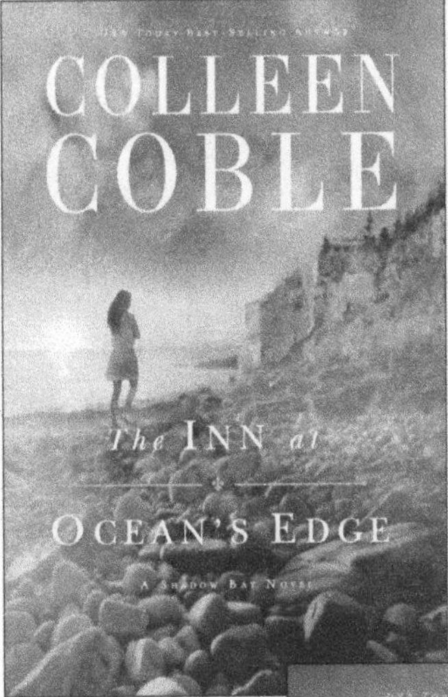


AVAILABLE IN PRINT,
E-BOOK, AND AUDIO



AVAILABLE IN PRINT,
E-BOOK, AND AUDIO

AVAILABLE IN PRINT, E-BOOK,
AND AUDIO SEPTEMBER 2016

## RETURN FOR MORE ADVENTURES IN

# LAVENDER TIDES!

Available in print, e-book,
and downloadable audio

## *About the Author*

Colleen Coble is a *USA TODAY* bestselling author and RITA finalist best known for her romantic suspense novels, including *Tidewater Inn*, *Rosemary Cottage*, and the Mercy Falls, Lonestar, Rock Harbor, and Sunset Cove series.

Visit her website at www.colleencoble.com
Twitter: @colleencoble
Facebook: colleencoblebooks